I0718973

Tea, No Sugar

Morgan Klein

SRL PUBLISHING

SRL Publishing Ltd
London

www.srlpublishing.co.uk

First published worldwide by SRL Publishing in 2025

SRL PUBLISHING

THINKING DIFFERENTLY, DELIVERING CHANGE

ISBN: 978-1915073-46-4

1 3 5 7 9 10 8 6 4 2

A CIP catalogue record for this book is available from the British Library

SRL Publishing is a climate positive publisher offsetting more carbon emissions than it emits.

S.K.H.C. We made it.

One

Ali's throat constricted and his vision narrowed to each white, pock-marked chip along the doorframe.

'I'm sorry, Mr Morgan.' The secretary, a woman with strands of grey threaded across her hair, placed a hand on his arm.

Ali jerked it away. He steadied himself against the wall, the tiles edged in grime dampening his hand. The last thing he wanted was to be touched.

Ali wanted to talk to Trevor, but the kids in the classroom behind him wouldn't wait. Trevor always knew what to say; he'd fold Ali into a hug, and the world would melt away.

High above the row of lockers, light streamed into the whitewashed corridor.

Ali had expected his father to die. They'd all seen it coming, but the news still caught him off guard. Bitter memories mixed with bile in his throat, threatening to boil over if he didn't speak, didn't keep moving. *Move forward; there's no use in getting hung up on today*, his father would have said while reaching for another beer.

'Thanks.' An automatic response. 'I'll finish this class.

Can you arrange cover for the rest of today?' Ali's voice came out hollow and distant. The secretary squinted at her phone in response. 'Where's Janet?'

Ali's mum might have finished for the day because she only came in part-time now. She didn't have the energy to be around people all day anymore. Not after the way his father had ground her down.

'Your mum took the call. She's in the staffroom but wanted me to let you know.'

Typical Janet. She'd hate the scene it would cause, and smoothing things over as quickly as possible was more her style. He wasn't sure if her tears would be real or fake today. Ali knew she remembered a time before his father's drinking started.

He'd only witnessed her tears once before during the summer holidays after his A-levels. On the day she caught Ali with his pants around his ankles as he sat on the edge of the bed, and her tears had fallen thick and fast before Ali shoved George from between his legs and slammed the door in her face. His parents' arguments escalated after that. And by the time Ali left for university, the three of them—Ali, Janet, and Grant Morgan—became three islands, each made of the same sand but separated by stormy seas.

'Thank you. I should be getting back.'

'Anything you'd like me to pass along to your mum? I'm going back that way.'

'Tell her...' *Congratulations* is what he wanted to say. She'd finally won. Grant drank himself to death because Ali had pushed him to his limit, pushed him over the edge. He coughed.

'Tell her I'm sorry.' In response, the secretary nodded and, with a weak smile, spun on her feet and left with her heels clattering down the tiled hallway.

A hushed classroom greeted Ali on the other side of the door. Unusual for this early in the afternoon when students were likely wired from snacks at lunch and lack of rest. High school students could be a handful at times, but they clearly sensed something was wrong today. Despite their outward appearance of tough, scowling, sneering teenagers, they were a good bunch. They'd given him hell in September, but nearing the Christmas break, they'd developed some trust.

'You alright, Mr Morgan?'

'Yeah. You look rough, sir.'

Ali ran his hands over his hair. He wanted a drink, but that would have to wait. Right now, he had to get through the rest of this class. One day at a time. The students sank back to their work, heads bowed over their English coursework folders. Even the regular troublemakers on the back row had unplugged their earphones and looked to be actually working.

Ali circled the classroom on autopilot, looking over shoulders and pointing out errors in the students' work.

His father was dead. The father he knew in his teens, the one who appeared after the drinking began. The one who Ali had failed and let down. A warmer one existed further back in his memory. A father who taught him to ride a bike, who brushed off his knees when he fell. A father—

'Sir. Can you look at this?'

Startled, Ali lowered himself into a chair beside Paul. The gnarled, ink-splattered pages of Paul's work spread out across the desk. They were aiming for a passing mark, but Paul's ADD symptoms meant sustained focus produced paragraphs of widely varied lengths and mismatched grammar strewn across the page.

Ali blinked, and Paul's expectant gaze met his. The words on the page crisscrossed and the letters bled into each other. But Paul had rewritten this page multiple times, and it now resembled something they could work with. 'This is nice, Paul. Here—pull back on the description of that house and take us inside with the character.'

Paul nodded alongside him. He had a wonderful imagination but often couldn't get the words on the page to match up with what was in his head.

'Thanks, sir. I've been trying to do what you said. Live inside the characters. And I think it's working.'

'I can see that.'

'It's way better, sir.' Abby, seated on the opposite desk, giggled, and a glow crept into her cheeks. 'And it actually makes sense now. I felt something.'

'I bet you did—'

'That's enough. Thank you, Marcus.' Ali side-eyed the boy elbowing his friend, cracking jokes like they didn't have a care in the world.

As Ali stood to address the class, his gaze fell on the back of heads moving in unison with pens skating across paper. If they messed up this year, it could change their lives forever. Ali's father had always focused on Ali's faults. Ali's attempts at art or stories were met with a sneer or thrown out straight away if his father had been drinking. The crumpled edges of the paper peeked from the kitchen bin in the morning next to green wine bottles and beer cans.

'You should be really happy with how that's turned out, Paul.' The boy grinned in response to the praise. 'Really excellent. I'm pleased for you. Ten minutes left, everyone.'

The rest of the class passed in a blur. After packing his bag, Ali checked his phone again; they'd arranged to meet in their usual spot. Not hidden, but out of the way.

Trevor stood facing him in the shadow of the lockers at the end of the hallway. Ali wanted to place his hand on the blue knitted arm of Trevor's sleeve. He didn't dare. Not during school hours.

'I don't think it's sunk in yet.'

'It'll take a while.' Trevor smiled, his gaze hovering over Ali's shoulder before returning to meet Ali's own. He nodded to a pair of students who noisily walked past. The two girls nudged each other and giggled.

'I'll take a walk. Clear my head.'

'How's your mum?'

'She went home already. I'll ring her later.'

Trevor nodded in reply. Ali didn't have anyone else to call. Not many people gave a shit about Grant Morgan at this point. Ali chewed his lip.

He glanced behind him and, seeing the empty

corridor, planted a quick kiss on Trevor's cheek. He'd expected waves of emotion or some great unveiling of truth when his father eventually passed. All that hung over him was a heavy loneliness.

Trevor's eyes filled with concern and creased at the edges.

'Don't get wasted, okay?'

Standing on the road outside of the school, with the sunshine warming his neck and a breeze touching his cheeks, Ali floated through his grief like a man in a place where nothing had existed for a long time.

He'd walk home slowly. No point in rushing now. The grey pavement rolled under his feet. This was what people did when someone died—they soaked it in. Lived it. He'd read that somewhere.

On Easton Road, the pub door swung open before Ali had decided to go in. The scent of ale and the bitter tang of wet dog pressed together with leather polish and bleach. He'd only have one drink. His dad would have taken a drink. And another one, and Grant wouldn't have stopped until he was spread out on the floor.

So early in the week, the pub was dim and quiet at this time. The tan carpet indented from the barstool. Ali's knees pushed up against the wooden bar and he smiled at the barman. He'd have a gin, thanks.

Sharp on his tongue, that first sip, always the sweetest. His dad was a whisky guy. Gravel-voiced and yellow-stained fingers from the Bensons. He'd been a carpenter most of his life. A white-van man, down at the pub at lunch for one with his pie. Then a couple more beers after work.

This was the kind of pub Grant would go to. Ali had jobbed with the crew for a couple of summers during high school. All those men, coarse words, builder's cracks, an underlying sexual energy he'd picked up on. His father hadn't asked him to work with them again. Not after he'd been caught with George and his boxer shorts around his knees.

A guy in a hi-vis vest at the bar leaned across to the barman. He caught Ali's look and winked.

Sober, Ali barely looked at another guy. But with alcohol in his system, he ramped up inside and his feelings for Trevor took on a glassy quality. It wasn't that he forgot about him, yet Ali's selfishness and sexual urgency grew and filled the space in his head. Anyway, they had both been with a couple of other guys. Trev's gym was a hot bed of horny men, and it just meant getting your rocks off. Meaningless, really.

After a couple of drinks, it didn't matter who Ali fucked. The booze drowned the shame, and all he craved was release.

Hi-vis guy toyed with his straw and glanced over his shoulder again before turning away when Ali showed little interest. Men could be fickle and wanted to drink and fuck. Fuck and drink.

No, he didn't want that tonight.

He'd told Trev he'd be home for dinner.

Ali didn't have a drinking problem. His father had just died. They'd expected it because it was impossible not to look into Grant's watery eyes, and see those veined cheeks, and know something was close to bursting. Grant had looked pickled from the inside when Ali had last seen him. Propped up in bed, his wheezy breaths interspersed with a hacking cough and mucus spit drooling down the side of the plastic bottle he kept by the bed.

Seeing his father that way had inspired Ali not to repeat the same mistakes. He wouldn't live his life that way. Allowing the drink to come between himself and the world wasn't for him. He wasn't like that and wouldn't do the same.

One for the road. Ali's gin and tonic glistened on the bar, beads of condensation pooling on the brass fixture and dark stained wood. He eyed the back of the barman. His black shirt stretched nicely across his shoulders and tapered down into dark jeans at the back.

The edges of the smooth bar rippled warm across Ali's fingertips. It was cold outside now; the bar doors opened and closed, letting in gusts of brisk December air. The chill blunted against Ali's skin, the warmth of the alcohol seeping in alongside the roar of the open fire at the other end of the bar. He rumbled the ice cubes in the glass. Another one would send him over the edge. That much Ali knew—the rickety bridge between enough and too much. His foot tapped to the music coming over the speakers. He could dance. He was so close to dancing, but not yet. He would need another drink or two. Then he'd be on his feet. And the night was still young.

Trevor hated dancing. They'd been out last weekend.

Their anniversary—they didn't call it that, but Ali had kept count of the days since they'd met. Figures and numbers always made him feel safe. And he'd counted the days. One by one. Counting towards his father's death, or away from the moment he met Trevor. A flicker of winter against his ankle when the pub door swung open.

He wanted to commit to Trevor. To throw all these other guys and bad mistakes into the past where they belonged. They could make a go of it.

Trevor expected him home. Another drink would smooth the edges, anything to escape his own thoughts. Ali knew how to cover over his own cracks and sand away the rough edges of the world. Navel-fucking-gazing, his dad would say.

Get a fucking grip. Ali swirled the ice cubes and tipped the glass. The lime fell with the remaining slumped ice cubes, and he took them in his mouth. His tongue touched the sharpened corners, but they melted away along the edge. Like most things in this shitty life, they stood up for a brief moment but quickly fell away when any pressure was applied.

The barman took his glass and cocked his head to one side. Another one, then he would go. The door banged open—winter outside. It was nearly Christmas, and his dad had just died. Trevor was waiting for him at home. His warm home, where he had everything he needed. He didn't need to sit in this bar and drown himself like this.

Trevor waited at home for him. That was what he

needed because he'd known for a while that his father's drink problem bled into his own life. He wasn't going to let it happen again.

Home. That's where he should be.

Two

The car seat cupped Trevor's butt in a grey Eastville car park, hiding from the shitty UK weather. He'd always loved small spaces. They were like being wrapped up in a hug, protecting him from whatever was out there making him miserable. Rain, or drizzle as they called it in the UK, dribbled down the windscreen. Tears pricked at the edges of his eyes, and he wiped them away furiously. Trevor blew into his hands; his grey fingerless gloves unravelled around his knuckles. He chewed on the thread, wanting to tug at it, expecting it to fall apart. His stomach grumbled and the thought of food, for the first time since lunch, crossed his mind.

Ali would want something to eat when he got home. Trevor's biggest fear was Ali turning into his father. A dead drunk. Ali's father scared Trevor—even though he'd never met him, and now he wouldn't ever get the chance. Grant sounded brutal from what Ali had said about his time growing up. His name like stone, a great lump of fucking rock.

An emotional weight had been hanging over Ali. Trevor sensed it. Sophie told him once that he was an empath because he could sense a vulnerable animal in a dense forest. That, his friend said, was why he'd picked Ali. A project, but it wasn't anything like that—they leaned on each other, and Trevor gained more from the relationship than he lost. They were each other's first real relationship; that's what kept them together. But tears were falling because it scared the shit out of Trevor to let it go if Ali went too far again. They'd been through some tough times, sure, but he wouldn't go back to being the scared closeted guy he was before. He'd seen how damaging that could be. His childhood friend, Dee, his upturned smile blurred across the glass. Walking away then hadn't changed anything. He'd been running scared, and he wouldn't be ashamed anymore.

A seagull waddled across the grey asphalt.

Trevor shook his head. Kicking over his past again wasn't doing him any good, and what was the use of living in the past. The overhead mirror needed cleaning, so he wiped his thumb over the grime. Ali didn't need this stress around Christmas. Not again. They couldn't have a repeat of last year. Ali wouldn't do it again. He'd promised.

Trevor dug around in the glove compartment for his loyalty card. The giant building he was parked in front of was the best Asian supermarket in Bristol. For Trevor, it was a taste of home; he came at least once a week. Nothing beat his mum's pork dumplings and ginger soup, so why was he stalling? Sitting in the car like a mug. What was he waiting for?

Christmas meant one thing to Trevor. It meant New

Year was just around the corner. The holidays didn't often bother him, but it didn't stop him from missing home. His parents would be gathering with friends and multiple relatives while UK schools started back in cold, miserable January. He looked up at the sky over the Lucky Gate supermarket. He should go in, but he needed a minute to himself. His black jacket skimmed his knees; his hands rested on the cold leather of the steering wheel.

Christmas last year was nasty. The bent Christmas tree, the multicoloured string of lights shattered on the wooden floor.

Get it the fuck together.

Trevor shivered at the biting air outside and scuffed his foot on the grey tarmac before ducking against the wind and moving towards the shop.

Roaming the aisles, Trevor glanced at the dried Harbin sausage, rice papers, and golden crackers stacked high, and missed home even more.

He wanted to cook for Ali. Food had been his comfort growing up—when his mum whipped up dumplings in the kitchen. Pushing alongside his sister, he'd shove Mel out of the way and crowd around their mother's legs, trying to grab the steamed parcels before they were packed up for customers.

In those early days, he and Ali had cooked together, standing side by side in the narrow kitchen. They should get back to that. They needed to make time for each other.

He'd get Ali relaxed with some good food. And make him talk. They didn't do that enough—talk before things turned nasty, and Ali said something he couldn't take back.

Most of the items were easy to find, but he spent an extra minute hunting for the Sichuan peppercorns which gave the soup added depth.

Two women sat at the checkout with their backs to each other. One filed her nails, listening to the other talking behind her. They could have been sisters with their equally tight hot-pink T-shirts and shoulder-length black hair.

Trevor approached and set his basket on the edge of the counter. It nearly tipped over, but one woman caught it in time.

'Careful, handsome,' she teased. 'Your wife would be angry if you came back with a bent eggplant.'

The second woman snorted and handed over coins to her customer. They were joking around, but Trevor's cheeks burned. At his age, back home, he'd be married with a kid on the way. Well, if he was normal and had followed his parents' wishes.

He glanced up to check the total and met the cashier's gaze. He handed her the loyalty card, and she swiped it without taking her gaze from his face.

'A handsome man like you, but no ring. You must be engaged, mister.'

Being used to the direct casual conversations between people his age didn't do anything to quieten Trevor's discomfort. He tugged his shirtsleeve a bit lower over his hand.

'Not yet.'

She looked him up and down when she handed back his card but didn't say anything further. To be outed in a public place had been Trevor's greatest fear growing up. Not so much for his own embarrassment—people his generation cared less about which way people swung—but for his parents. They were different.

He piled the items into the bag. It should be enough for someone whose father had passed away. Someone who didn't really like their dad in the first place.

What would Ali do if Trevor's own dad had died? He didn't know—but he'd probably want to drink. Trevor didn't get that. In China, people drank to celebrate, but here drinking on a Tuesday for no apparent reason was normal. Whatever. "*What's normal, anyway?*" Ali's words rang in his ears. Ali had held Trevor's hand more than once when he'd had a few glasses of wine too many and everything had fallen apart.

Trevor was such a lightweight. Booze made him introspective and heavy. And he'd mull over his life and his own issues with being gay. They'd melt into each other on the sofa. Just the two of them—before any of this other shit happened.

He'd grown into his sexuality in the UK. It was much more open-minded and liberal than back home, where he didn't feel threatened but he didn't feel especially celebrated. Being gay was unacceptable from his parents' point of view.

He glanced back as he exited, and the two women had resumed their animated conversation. Just some banter for them but, for Trevor, shame edged into his heart.

Ali had come along like an apparition when Trevor needed a guide, someone to show him the ropes during his first weeks in the UK. There was no gay scene back home. Ali was everything. His heart, his protector, his saviour.

The seagull pecked at a cigarette packet next to his car. Trevor swung the carrier bag in its direction, and it took off, disappearing into the dim evening light.

The house was quiet, but he'd expected that. Trevor's keys sat lonely on the kitchen island. A small space, but it was theirs for now. Ali's place really—everything was in his name. Trevor had been meaning to get added to the lease, but they'd never got around to it.

He cooked. The kitchen boiler grumbled as he rinsed off the vegetables under the lukewarm water. Familiar scents rose to fill his nostrils. Star anise, Sichuan peppercorns, and bay leaves. Dried tofu fried with oyster sauce was another of Ali's favourites. Trevor glanced at the clock—he should be home by now. Unless he'd stopped off on the way. Hopefully, he hadn't gone to the bar for too long. Drunk Ali, combined with the news about his dad, was not what Trevor fancied tonight.

Trevor waited. A couple of decorations hung in their living room. They'd picked up some cheap ones last year and reused them because Ali hated waste. They'd never been much into the Christmas spirit, but last week Trevor had unboxed the tree and some tinsel they'd picked out last year. They'd strolled arm in arm and picked a tree from the supermarket. "*A tree for life. Our lives,*" Ali had said.

This would be the third Christmas they had known each other. The wind outside whipped around the edges of the house. When Trevor first arrived in the UK, it had freaked him out. China had wind, sure, but the way it howled around the estate unnerved him.

Ali hadn't returned by eight. The clock hands touched the highest point and began their descent to the next hour. Trevor ate alone at the table. Ali might have been with his mum, so there was no use panicking because he'd be back… at some point.

It wasn't like Ali would use this opportunity to end things with Trevor. Would he? Things had been good recently. Trevor tapped his knuckle on the table. He hated being alone, especially in winter.

Each shadow of a car moving down the street or the silhouette of a branch outside, creating black patterns against the white blinds, made him shudder.

Headlights washed over the back of the sofa and filled the room. Trevor jumped up. Thank god. Knowing Ali had come back in a taxi filled him with a sense of peace. Ali calmed him, most of the time, and he relied on Ali to make things better for him. Ali was the piece of his heart that was missing, being the complete opposite to him. The yin to his yang. Trevor needed Ali to keep him safe. Trevor wanted that Ali tonight.

'Hey, baby.' Ali didn't sound drunk. That was good, although the glint in his eye and a shimmering across his gaze extending to the looseness of his jaw meant he'd had more than a couple.

Trevor pulled Ali close. He helped him peel off his jacket. Gin, or some other bitter spirit, tinged Ali's breath.

'There was a fit guy at the bar. He probably wanted me,' Ali giggled.

Trevor rolled his eyes. Ali thought he got smoother and sexier when he drank, but in reality, he became sloppy, and the burnished scarlet creeping to his cheeks was unappealing.

Ali rolled a cigarette. Another one of the things Ali justified. It helped him relax. Hooking up with other guys helped him relax, too. They didn't believe in monogamy per se, but they wanted trust. And they'd agreed whatever happened outside wouldn't come back to their flat. Trevor convinced himself it was okay—he didn't want to restrict Ali and force hetero-norm standards on him.

Hell, he'd even hooked up with a couple of guys himself. After a workout, with sweaty bodies and open showers, it was easy to slip in and get some quick relief. It didn't mean he felt any differently towards Ali. What they had went deeper than sex.

They settled into a comfortable silence on the sofa. Trevor sensed Ali studying him. The familiar prickling of heat on the back of his neck.

Their gazes met. Trevor's hand found Ali's stretched over the back of the sofa.

'Feels weird he died days after our anniversary. Don't you think so?' Ali said. The tiredness in his voice was evident.

Where was he going with this? It sounded like the

start of one of his rambles. How much had he drunk?

'You don't need to feel bad about anything.' Trevor's words sounded hollow. Both of them hid. They'd hide together, like they had for more years than was healthy.

But it was better now.

'I'm not sure I feel anything yet.' Ali's resigned tone. 'But I do feel it's partly my fault. He might have stopped drinking if I… if we hadn't—'

'Don't, Ali. That's not going to help.' Trevor lowered his voice. 'And it's not true.'

A lorry thundered past on the road. Something Trevor never got used to. Buildings in the UK vibrated in a way Chinese ones didn't. Unsettling, just like the wind.

In the months leading up to Grant's death, Ali had wobbled. It had been a drink after work and then a couple more. Watching Ali grow tense and angry about his father had been one of the hardest parts of their relationship. Trevor almost walked away last Christmas, but that was the past and it should stay there.

Ali's jaw clenched, and he turned to flick through the channels on the TV.

Ali had been wasted last weekend. Like he'd sensed his father's death. All loved up one moment—but he had a glint in his eye, and a mean streak. Trevor knew to keep things cool when Ali's eyes darkened.

Trevor took Ali's hand. Cold. Trevor rested his head on Ali's bicep. The tension across his shoulders was obvious.

'You don't believe that, do you?' Trevor couldn't bear for him to think that way. To think he was to blame.

Nobody was to blame. His dad was a drunk—a mean one, by all accounts.

Ali's eyes shuttered and he mumbled something.

'Say that again?' Trevor leaned closer and ran a hand over Ali's brow. Hot. Covered in a thin sheen of sweat. *Don't get sick, Ali. Stay strong, please.*

'I fucked up.' Ali's garbled worlds rattled from his lips and made Trevor wince even though the sofa absorbed most of the sound.

The fight had gone out of Ali as he leaned into Trevor's shoulder. His breathing slowed and became even. He sounded exasperated, sending out air through his lips.

Ali had shut him out again. The drink opened a window into Ali's psyche; a faint breeze would appear for a few moments, sometimes an hour. And Trevor would see the guy underneath—a fun-loving guy. The guy he thought was Ali. That Ali did his own thing, was unpredictable, was not to be relied upon.

A sigh erupted from Trevor's lips.

How did they get here? They were as bad as each other.

He'd tied his life to Ali. The visa kept him working in Bristol and without it, he'd be forced to return to China. Everything he had and everything he owned lay within these walls. They didn't have much, but what they did have was theirs. Ali, the good Ali, the one who cooked dinner when they'd first met, the Ali who would carry him laughing to the bedroom, the Ali who kissed his eyelids as he lay strewn across the bed after the best sex he'd ever had.

Where was that Ali?

This one, with his cold hands, and colder heart… Trevor wouldn't walk out on a guy who'd lost his father. He needed to finish his placement and complete at least another year—his visa depended on it. Everything tied together under this roof. There was no Plan B.

He'd wait. Trevor understood more than most people how it felt to be trapped in your own head, trying to escape your family but unable to do it. A burden he'd carried and would always carry. He couldn't turn his back on Ali, but he hated fighting.

This was better than nothing, better than the alternative. Better than being alone.

Trevor rolled over and lowered his feet to the floor. The carpet fibres sat dense between his toes. He pushed down, and each compression caused grooves to embed into the grey woollen material.

They had everything they needed. A bit of warmth from the cold outside. Last Christmas was a mistake— anyone could mess up. He'd made Ali angry; he shouldn't have pushed him.

Ali would relax a bit now his dad had passed.

It would get better. Trevor's father—a John Lennon fan—would turn up the volume on a Beatles song and over dinner quote him: things would be alright in the end, and if it wasn't alright, then it wasn't the end.

Three

Ali stubbed out the cigarette with trembling fingers, pulled the piece of chewing gum from his mouth, and pushed it into the dashboard ashtray. Snapping it shut, he glanced into the wing mirror at the dark circles around his eyes. Thursday night parties were a bad idea. With his dad dead, he'd been out for three nights in a row. Not that he had many, but different friends wanted to buy him drinks. He knew the haze wouldn't last, and he'd have to get his head straight soon.

Trevor had been slamming things around in the kitchen this morning because Ali had arrived home after midnight, although he hadn't planned to. An image of their front door banging crawled into his memory.

He'd woken Trevor up by hammering on the door. The night had started as a few drinks with a couple of mates, but they ended up in Play nightclub. Things got hazy after that. He felt shit from the previous night, and the one before, and the only thing that made sense was to have a drink.

But it was nearly the weekend. And after three years together, Trevor had seen him in worse states. He'd have to make it up to Trevor, like take him away for a weekend. They needed to focus on them for a while. His chest tightened at the memory of his lowest point last year—the Christmas tree and the shattered lights.

Ali exhaled. Once Trevor said yes, he'd knock the drinking on the head anyway; it was about time to settle down. Ali glanced through the windscreen. The school gate was a blur, maybe twenty metres away from him. He could do this. It was only two classes today, then the god-awful parents' meeting after lunch. Ali ignored his growling stomach and stepped onto the wet tarmac before striding towards the main school building, a sour taste lingering in his mouth.

Luckily, there wasn't a soul in the B-block hallway, and he made it safely to his classroom. He leaned back in the chair and examined both hands for any damage, but luckily there was none, *this* time.

He wanted to chat with Trevor about their Christmas plans before double English with the infamous Class Nines. His stomach growled again. Maybe he could pass by Trevor's classroom on the way to the canteen. Trevor would tell him he looked like shit.

Angry Trevor wouldn't last long. Today, especially with this pounding headache, Ali needed his partner to be gentle.

He'd make it up to Trevor and take him somewhere nice to eat for their anniversary dinner. Hopefully, Trevor would forgive him. He wasn't one to hold grudges. It had only been drinks with a couple of friends, and anyway, it wasn't Ali's fault Trevor hated going to bars. He smiled at the thought of their warm bodies against each other later, and something stirred in his lower stomach.

Ali pulled the ring from his pocket to study it again and traced his finger over the gold band with a small ruby. It shone between his thumb and forefinger. Trevor would forgive him after this. And a surprise for their actual anniversary, the timing was perfect.

A door slammed somewhere at the end of the corridor, and Ali sat up in his chair. A thudding sound followed—the metal lockers taking a pounding. An irate student, probably. The sound echoed down the corridor, each dull thud becoming louder as whoever they were approached.

Christ, the weekly hallway monitor job meant it was now Ali's problem. A deep sigh escaped him, and he scrunched up his face at the familiar tang of alcohol that filled both nostrils. Tucking the ring back into place, he scrambled about, looking for another piece of chewing gum before heaving himself off the chair and out into the corridor. Trevor would see he was ready. He'd messed up and the drinking was stupid, but he was in control; he could stop whenever he wanted to. This year would be better. Better than last year.

Michael Addler stood a couple of metres away, his black hair scraped back and too-tight trousers clinging to his hips. The student didn't look like much, but he had garnered a reputation among his peers and staff as a nasty troublemaker in the short time he'd been at Haylestone.

He slunk towards Ali, pounding each locker with his fist. That bomber jacket made him look like a skinhead in the making, and he looked older than his seventeen years.

Not today. Not with the parents' meeting after lunch. With a mother like Mrs Addler, it was best to be careful when handling her son. She likely had hundreds of questions and complaints for the teachers. Everyone else, besides her perfect son, was to blame for his failing grades and bad attitude. Michael Addler, dropped in from a referral unit during September, had caused nothing but trouble from day one.

Already sick of hearing Michael's name on the lips of every teacher in the weekly "panic" meetings, Ali stepped towards him.

'Hey. How about not giving those lockers such a hard time?'

Why did Michael always have that sneer on his lips?

'Faggot.' Michael slammed his hand against the nearest locker.

A burning sensation spread across Ali's forehead and around his ears.

Michael rubbed his nose on his sleeve and grinned at Ali. His gaze darted from one end of the corridor to the other, and he chomped his gum with an open mouth.

'Isn't this a Catholic school? Are you even allowed to be here?'

Michael dropped the words like a hammer.

'Pardon me?'

Ali's arms remained folded as he studied Michael.

'I could get you fired after what you did. You know that, right?'

This was ridiculous.

A soundless laugh escaped Ali's mouth. The only time Ali and Trevor had walked through the school car park together was last Monday in the rain, his arm wrapped around Trevor's shoulder under an umbrella.

'I don't know what you're talking about, Michael.' Ali's neutral teacher voice didn't waver.

'I've been following you and your boyfriend.' Michael cracked his knuckles. 'Sinner hunting.'

Ali uncrossed his arms and took another step towards the boy.

'There won't be any need for hunting anyone. Let's get you to Mr Ladner's office.'

Michael shook his head. The headmaster's name didn't appear to put him off.

'I think you know what I'm talking about, Mr Morgan.' He reached into his blazer pocket and waved his phone towards Ali. 'Did you forget? Luckily, I've got pictures.'

Ali watched Michael's thumb scroll between a couple of blurry photos. Trevor's black-and-white chequered shirt on the screen. His own hands wrapped around his partner's waist, clasped together at the small of Trevor's back.

Those pictures weren't taken in school, though.

His face burned.

'You understand, Michael, that whoever you have been stalking here has the right to go to the police? You understand that, don't you?'

Michael withdrew the phone but continued to stare at the pictures. The grin on his face was almost as wide as his eyes.

'Fifty quid. And you and your little Asian friend are safe for another playdate.'

'Those pictures don't show anything.'

Michael arched an eyebrow.

'You don't think?'

'That could be any two men in those pictures. You could have got them off some website. Any kid could—'

'You have forgotten,' he snorted. 'Check out the shoes.' Michael thrust the phone closer to Ali. His thumb and finger moved expertly to zoom in on the picture.

Fuck. Those were Trevor's shoes. The distinctive red wolf on the back of the heel. The Septwolves brand he had brought over from China.

'Don't know many people who wear Chinese shoes in this part of London. Do you, Mr Morgan?'

Michael tapped the toe of his black Nike trainers against the base of the locker.

'Looks like DV8 club to me.'

'Why are you even going out to nightclubs, Micha—'

'DV8 lets anyone in. You'd remember that… if you hadn't been so wasted.'

Ali clenched his fist as his throat tightened.

His mind raced back to the dim club, to Trevor, the Saturday before. With their anniversary coming up, Trevor had rolled his eyes and agreed to go out for once. He could put up with the sweaty bodies and pounding music for one night, he'd said. If it made Ali happy.

Ali had decided that night at the club to buy a ring. He had Trevor wrapped in his arms, vodka shots pounding through them both. His heart had lurched, and he wanted to spend the rest of his life with Trevor.

'He's a bit younger than you, isn't he?' Michael continued, his voice a low rasp.

Ali's mouth filled with saliva. This kid wanted to ruin everything they'd worked hard to build. Ali had promised Trevor he didn't need to live in fear now that he was in the UK. They just needed to be careful because of the school. Ali furrowed his brow. Had they been too casual?

'Gimme that phone.'

Ali lunged, but Michael ducked. The phone slid into Michael's blazer pocket, and he crouched like he was ready to throw a punch at Ali. Michael's eyes narrowed and his nostrils flared. It didn't look like the first time he'd been in a fight.

Ali grabbed the front of Michael's shirt and shoved him up against the lockers. The fabric bunched in his fist, and Michael gasped.

With his free hand, Ali went for Michael's pocket. He needed to get that phone. Smash it into hundreds of pieces. Or delete whatever crap Michael had saved on there.

Michael squirmed out of his reach, but Ali brought his knee forward to skewer his leg.

'Get the fuck off me!' Michael growled, his body jerking back and forth, but Ali's grip didn't loosen.

'What is going on here?'

The headmaster's voice cut through the scuffling sounds of Michael kicking back against the metal doors. Ali turned at the sound. His breath rattled.

'Mr Morgan. Is there a problem?' Ladner jabbed a stubby finger in Michael's direction, his mouth set in a thin, narrow line.

Ali's mouth opened and closed to find the right words. Between each tooth, sourness erupted onto his tongue. Ladner's bottle-green chinos hurt Ali's eyes, and the black belt pinned too tightly against his bulging gut.

He released the material bunched in his fist, leaving Michael muttering expletives under his breath.

Ali's gaze moved behind Ladner to where students' faces pushed up against the glass in the biology classroom. Ali's mother, Janet, attempted to direct them back to their chairs. A low rumbling filled the silence as wooden stools were slid back into place under desks.

Michael shoved past Ali. His elbow neatly made contact with a rib, causing Ali to clutch at his side. Little shit.

He retched as the pressure across his forehead, mixed with the bright lights of the corridor, caused his stomach to flip. He wiped his left hand over his lower lip where the stickiness of his breath sat.

'He attacked me.' Michael adjusted his shirt and tugged his tie back into place. 'And he stinks.'

Ali couldn't summon the words to respond. He blinked again, a sharp pain running from behind his ear and across his temple. The sounds of birds came into focus through the window leading out onto the playground.

Mr Ladner tutted and shook his head.

'Michael.' His tone changed as he smiled at the

student. 'Please go and take a seat outside my office. I'll be along shortly to sort this all out.'

Michael's mouth worked overdrive on a piece of gum.

'Whatever.' Michael retreated down the hallway, but before he turned the corner by the stairwell, he slammed his fist once more into an unlocked door, causing the locker to bounce open. The noise brought Ali back to the present.

Ali wiped at his eye.

'It got out of hand. He had a phone and I attempted to take it—'

'Are you drunk, Mr Morgan?' Ladner wrinkled his nose. He lowered his voice as his eyes tracked back and forth between Ali and the dented locker behind him.

A bead of sweat broke through on Ali's hairline as a warming sensation crept across his lower back. *Fuck.*

Four

In the staffroom, Trevor set his pen down and pushed away the paper. He winced at the headache blooming behind his eyes.

Ali had banged on the door at around three that morning. After calming him down and washing the blood from Ali's hand, he'd only slept for a couple of hours. Ali could be really fucking selfish sometimes. He appreciated that Ali was struggling with his father's death, but he didn't need to take the whole world down with him. There had to be some reason why Ali wouldn't stop drinking. Anyway, they'd have to talk about that later tonight. He picked up the pen and tried to regain focus on the task in front of him.

A door slammed out in the corridor. A rhythmic metallic slamming drew slowly closer, like a student was approaching the classroom, punching every locker door on the way.

The aggressive nature of British students still surprised him, especially in high school. Three years in the UK, and he still found the behaviour shocking.

He muttered the mantra about making it to

Christmas and moved a stack of files to the side so he could see the full scope of the multicoloured weekly planner.

Footsteps echoed up to and passed the door.

Ali would deal with whoever it was if he'd made it into school. He was on the mid-morning duty today, and he usually dragged himself in on time despite a night's mess.

Trevor leaned back in the chair. *Stop getting distracted.*

Luckily, as a trainee teacher, he only had a few classes a week, but a ton of paperwork to get through. It seemed like teachers spent more time making paper trails than actually teaching. *Who reads all this stuff, anyway?* After this placement was documented and signed off, he could spend a little time and effort on planning. Ali had almost a decade of teaching under his belt; he couldn't imagine doing anything else, he'd said. The kids loved him.

Trevor scanned the documents again. He needed Ali to look over these plans before he typed and submitted them to Janet. It was weird to have his boyfriend's mum as his mentor, but Ali had insisted. "She can get to know you before we tell her," he'd said. "Before we blow up her world." Trevor still had doubts. Was Ali stalling and not telling her because he wasn't sure about them? Ali said it would be easier once they told her.

When he met Ali, Trevor had thought Ali was out and proud. However, like Trevor, Ali kept his sexuality hidden away most of the time. A little secret they kept to themselves. Perhaps that was why they bonded so easily. Two men sharing a common shame.

Trevor sighed.

Janet was obsessively picky. Not like his own mother. She wouldn't be fussed with all this paperwork. "Just get on and do it," she'd say.

He missed his mum and wanted to see her, to show her England. She hadn't known how unhappy he was before he left. To her, happiness was meeting a nice girl, settling down and doing the family proud by making babies. And that was never going to work, not with a woman anyway.

Voices from the biology room next door drew Trevor back to the present. He chewed on his pen.

He looked up as the sound of footsteps approached the staffroom and someone yanked open the door.

Ali stood in the open doorway, his face ashen. His cheeks flushed despite the paleness of his skin. He looked rough as hell.

Mr Ladner loomed behind him, clearly pissed off about something.

'I'll just grab my water bottle.' Ali stepped into the classroom and moved to the back area piled with junk.

Trevor trailed behind him, throwing a glance at the headmaster who remained glowering in the doorway.

'Is everything okay?' Trevor said in a low voice. He instinctively reached out towards Ali.

Ali sidestepped him and rummaged through some jackets bundled on top of each other.

'I've got to go and talk to Ladner.' His gritted teeth didn't disguise the alcohol funk surrounding him. Fuck, Ali must have been reported for being late or smelling of alcohol. What a fucking disaster.

'What about?' Trevor wanted to grab hold of Ali.

Ali's gaze darted from Trevor's face and down to the floor. 'Michael Addler.'

'Who?' The name rang a bell, but Trevor didn't know the high school kids very well.

Ali clenched his fist and took a deep breath. Trevor didn't like seeing him like this.

'Some kid. I'll talk to you later. If you hear anything from anyone, it's not true, okay?'

'What do you mean? What's not true?'

'Later. I love you. Remember that.'

'Ali…?'

He grabbed a bottle that Trevor knew wasn't his and moved back towards the door.

Ali's clenched jaw did little to hide the fear Trevor saw in his trembling hands.

'Got it,' Ali called out to Ladner, who turned towards them.

Trevor remained in the doorway for a moment watching Ali retreat down the corridor. Ladner glanced into the classrooms as he passed before both turned at the end row of lockers and headed down the stairs. Trevor gathered his coloured notes spread out on the table. *What the hell is going on?*

Ali had been out most nights that week, but it was just the holiday mood in the UK. They all seemed to get overexcited and tanked up around Christmas, probably because it was dark when they left for work and dark when they got home. Ali's father's death had removed any excuses for Ali not to go out and "have a good time." This week hadn't been a good time at all. They were going to make plans, make this year different to last year.

Japan, skiing, and flights tumbled in his mind with his ideas for the Christmas holiday. With schoolwork out of the way, they could relax and celebrate together. They needed a better Christmas this year. Trevor hated how Ali's eyes changed each time he drank; it was like an evil shadow possessed him and took over.

Just now, Ali looked awful. They'd talked before about his drinking, how Ali would quit, and how he didn't need help, he'd said. Just some fun once in a while. Trevor had been hearing that for years. Believing it would work kept Trevor going. Justified his decision to leave his family behind because he knew, deep down, that he was running from something. Ali, despite his faults, was better than living like that.

Trevor's chest tightened at the thought of the conversation they needed to have if things didn't change. It had gone too far. His own uncle had drunk, and drunk, until he knocked his auntie out cold and pushed her down some stairs at home. He wouldn't stand for that, and Ali would never get to that point. Everyone fucked up. Everyone had something they were trying to work through—this was Ali's, and Trevor would stand by him.

He was partly to blame. If Ali wanted to talk sometimes, Trevor didn't know what to say. He wasn't used to sharing his feelings or saying how he really felt. Growing up, he'd kept things to himself. Only Ali had spent time getting to know who he really was.

Ali was probably frustrated. He wanted to talk and have fun to relieve himself of his shitty day, and his shitty father, but Trevor couldn't let go—wasn't able to let loose like Ali wanted. He wanted to make Ali happy, make him proud, like his family never would be. He just wanted to be good enough. Good enough that Ali didn't need to drink and didn't want to fuck around. To have Ali to himself.

Tears pricked at the corners of his eyes. He clenched his jaw and sighed deeply, barely able to keep his tears from falling.

Sophie called Trevor an enabler. She'd not seen Ali at his worst, but she saw Trevor the day after Christmas last year, when he'd rocked and sobbed in her arms. She'd said it was her duty as his best friend to tell him the truth. He'd call Sophie later today, not that she understood why Trevor stuck with Ali.

'Fuck it.' He'd give Ali a couple more months. Maybe until the summer, but that was it. It would be over.

The room came back into focus. Who was Michael Addler? The name sounded familiar. He only had classes with the year seven students, but Mr Ladner proposed adding some extra Chinese lessons from January if all his paperwork was in order.

Trevor sniffed and wiped his nose when the familiar scent of gin filled his nostrils. Ali wasn't even here, yet still stinking the place up. Trevor clenched both fists, attempting to get his thoughts in order and away from Ali's issues, once again. He had a demo class next period and needed to focus.

Trevor gathered up the papers from the table and shoved everything else into his satchel. He clicked off the light and leaned on the doorframe where Ali had stood just a moment earlier.

Trevor needed to get it together.

The walk to the classroom was short, and after smiling to the assembled teachers outside the room, he ushered in the waiting parents and greeted the class. Once he'd switched into teacher mode, there wasn't time to think about Ali anymore. This felt like his safe space, away from the madness.

Trevor raised his hands in surrender to a student holding a cardboard sabre sword that he swished back and forth, aimed at Trevor's gut. The remaining students circled closer or leaned in, alongside the three teachers observing the lesson, to get a better look at the duel. Learning didn't get much more active than this.

'And that… is how you disarm an emperor.' Trevor plucked the foil-wrapped sword and flipped it around so he was holding the handle. 'Thank you very much, Harry, please take a seat.' The students burst into applause and slid back to their seats.

The year sevens, ever eager to please a teacher in front of their parents, showed off their basic Chinese skills until the final bell rang.

As students with their bags stuffed with books and papers filed outside to waiting parents, Jessica, one of his students, lingered with her mother, who stood beaming in the doorway.

'Do you have it?' Jessica glanced between her mum and Trevor as he collected scraps of paper from under chairs and a few stray coloured pens that had rolled under the desk during the demonstration class.

He straightened up to see the girl take something from her mum. 'Yes, Jessica.'

The mother collected a navy coat from the peg by the door and held a book bag in one hand.

Jessica kept her eyes down, raven pigtails bouncing as she moved forward, and handed the piece of paper to Trevor. He took it carefully from her.

It was a paper butterfly, folded multiple times from a single sheet of paper. The girl had coloured some pink and blue spots onto the red background.

'Thank you, Jessica. Did you make this? It's beautiful.' Trevor crouched down as he examined it. She blushed and raised her eyes to meet his.

'You can open it, Mr Trevor.'

'Now?' He smiled, emphasising the suspense, causing Jessica to giggle. She nodded.

Trevor unfolded the wings of the butterfly. The body lifted up and concertinaed out, exposing some neat handwriting and a heart.

'Wo ai ni de ke.' *I Love Your Class.*

Trevor felt his cheeks stiffen and his eye twitched at the corner.

'Thank you, Jessica. This is very sweet of you. And I love having *you* in my class.'

Jessica twirled around, her white socks neatly flowered around her ankles, and her grey school skirt spun out as she returned to her mother's side.

'Jessica, you go to the entrance. I just want to have a quick word. Don't go outside, though.'

'Okay. See you next week.' She waved and skittered off down the hall towards the door.

Jessica's mother stepped into the classroom.

'I'm Lynn. I just wanted to say thank you. To you. I suggested she make a butterfly because since coming to your class, well, she's really come out of herself.'

'Oh. She's a lovely girl. That's very sweet of you both.'

'I really mean it.' Lynn placed her hand on Trevor's arm. 'She didn't feel like she fitted in very well. She's new here.'

'So am I, actually,' Trevor smiled. 'Perhaps we both noticed we needed a friendly face.'

'We hope you stay here after your training is over. I truly mean it.'

'I hope so, too.' Trevor's mind flashed to the corridor earlier. He forced a smile. It would all blow over, whatever it was. These types of things always did.

'I'd better be going. Catch up with that little rascal,' Lynn grinned.

'Take care now.'

Trevor gathered up the remaining materials from the class and checked his phone. No text from Ali. Maybe he'd gone home after meeting with Ladner, or he was still tied up defending school policies about homework and uniforms to parents who always, without question, knew better. Trevor sighed before separating the forms he wanted Ali to check, though it was unlikely that would happen today.

A minute passed, the clock ticking audibly above his head. He'd never noticed it before. This room was never silent.

Five

'This way, Ali.'

The hallway outside Ladner's office filled with the sinking glow of the afternoon sun. A golden hue set off by clouds cast a dark shadow on the doors they passed.

Ali shivered; something had changed, and he didn't believe it was just the seasons.

On the executive floor, his feet sank into the thick carpet and Ladner coughed gently behind him. A mixture of muttering and murmuring came from around the corner ahead.

Michael and Mrs Addler arrived a moment later. When Mrs Addler saw Ali, her shoulders tensed under the pale blue material of her jacket. She swept her dark hair back with one hand and held Michael behind her like a goose guarding its flock. A flock of one pain-in-the-butt gosling.

She was on them before they were halfway down the hallway.

'Mr Ladner, you never mentioned… teachers like this.' She flapped her hand in front of her. Even with her claws seemingly embedded into every aspect of her son's schooling, there was no way she could know about him and Trevor.

In response, Ladner leaned around and opened the door, gesturing the three of them into his office.

As they filed in, Ali let the hot-tempered Mrs Addler take the lead and stepped back to avoid contact with Michael in the alcove of the doorway.

Mrs Addler continued to rage, her voice softened only by the thick ivory wallpaper and dense maroon carpet.

'You find it acceptable to physically assault a student? I thought this was a decent school. When we brought Michael here…' She dragged two of the chairs, set in a semi-circle in front of the imposing desk, away from the other one, then waved her hand for Michael to join her in the separated pair of chairs. 'When your secretary said I should come down to your office, I wouldn't have suspected it was for something like this.' Mrs Addler sat down.

Michael caught Ali's eye and the sneer returned to the boy's lip. The family resemblance between the two Addlers was unmistakable.

Ladner lowered himself into his own chair behind the desk and clasped his hands together as if in prayer.

'Mr Morgan appears to have made an erroneous judgement.' His thick baritone filled the space, and Mrs Addler stilled in her seat like a good parishioner before her preacher.

'Michael was well on his way to causing damage to school property.' Ali spoke matter-of-factly. 'He also held a concealed mobile device. So I decided to use appropriate measures to remove his phone.' Ali's voice faltered. 'For his own safety.'

'Michael. What do you have to say about Mr Morgan's assessment?' Ladner pointed his steepled hands in Michael's direction.

Michael sniffed and folded his arms. He didn't look fazed at all, like he was enjoying the torture.

'Mr Morgan seems to be leaving out some info.' Michael turned to Ladner. 'So last weekend—'

'You were out with Simon,' Mrs Addler interjected. 'You told me you were staying to finish coursework.'

'We were. Simon had his camera, and we wanted to take some pictures, so we decided to take a walk and just ended up on Bridge Street.'

'I don't see what this has got to do with—' Mrs Addler cut in.

'Mum. He probably can't even remember seeing me.' Michael nodded in Ali's direction. 'He was totally wasted.'

'Look, I was with a friend. We were out dancing. You know how it is?' Ali sat back in his chair.

Michael continued. 'He saw us out on the street. Then he took us into the club. He tried to kiss Simon and get us to go back to his house with him.'

'What? Chris, he's making this up.' Ali didn't remember seeing Michael or anyone else that night. A grey blur filled the space where the memory should have been, but he would never drag a student into a club, would he?

Ladner furrowed his brow at the mention of his given name. 'Let him finish.' His no-nonsense growl silenced Ali.

Mrs Addler glowered in her seat.

'And so today. I think he's pissed off at me. But he tried again in the corridor. He offered me money to go with him'—Michael gestured his thumb in Ali's direction—'for sex. He wants to have sex with me.'

'What?' Mrs Addler cast her gaze to a cross mounted on the wall next to the seating area and back. Ali's vision locked with Mrs Addler's over the top of her son's head. Her lips bunched together in a snarl as she rose to her feet.

'You heard.' Michael clenched his jaw.

'If I'd known your kind were here in this school…' Mrs Addler narrowed her eyes. Her finger pointed and shook towards Ali. A thin finger, a little orange from fake tan and tapered to a Barbie-pink nail. Fuck. She clearly knew Bridge Street and what those rainbow flags stood for which hung outside the bars.

'Mr Morgan?' Ladner's voice filled the space once again. He glanced back towards Mrs Addler, and Ali noticed they shared the same sneer.

Ali's voice faltered, his mind racing over the night at the club. Trevor's arms up, laughing, two guys dancing with them. Strobe lights flashed and the pounding bass punched into their guts.

'I was just telling Michael he needed to watch his behaviour in the school corridor.' Ali couldn't read Ladner's expression, but his eyes narrowed while he took in the Addlers.

Ladner's hand hovered over the phone on his desk. 'Mrs Addler. Michael. Please take a seat in the reception. I need to make a couple of phone calls. We will get to the bottom of this.'

'This *predator* in your school has clearly gotten to my son. If you ever'—her voice faltered, and she stepped towards Ali—'*ever* touch my son again. You pervert. I'll kill you myself.'

Mrs Addler turned to Michael, took him by the arm, and steered him towards the door. Ali's father always said he'd fuck things up, that he wouldn't amount to anything, and here it was—he'd finally fucked everything up.

The afternoon sun, over the tennis courts, stretched lazily to a broad sweep of poplar trees.

'They're baseless.' Ali ran his hands over his face.

'I have to say, I am very troubled by these accusations, Ali. We've never dealt with this sort of issue before.' Ladner spoke matter-of-factly, his words blunt. 'Michael is also not an easy—'

'You saw him. And her. They've both got it in for me.'

'We have to conduct a full investigation.'

'I am being targeted.'

'You have to understand, Ali'—Ladner shifted in his seat and lowered his voice—'it's standard practice.' He raised both hands, exposing his palms as if the gesture would explain away his position. 'It's really up to the board in these cases. It's out of my control.'

Ladner's mild manner was grating.

'How would you feel about being accused of something that might mean you lose your job? You've seen how these things play out. I can't lose my job. My father.' Tears choked Ali's throat. 'For fuck—'

Ladner rattled off from the piece of paper he held. These accusations were serious, and the school lawyer was on her way and would be briefing Ali before he left that evening. He should think about legal help. Words washed over Ali. It was nearly the holidays. He and Trevor were spending Christmas together and Ali couldn't fuck it up again this year. He needed to get the holiday right; he owed Trevor that much.

Later that day, the lights flicked on next to the sports field and surrounding streets. Ali remained on the twin sofa set by Mr Ladner's coffee table. A hush had descended over the school; everyone readied to leave after the final bell. Trevor would think he'd gone home. He scratched his thumb along the ridges in the wood grain, back and forth as the school lawyer reeled off protocol from a thick binder.

Gina, or Miss Hart in her official capacity, addressed the two men. She dressed all in black, golden buckles on her shoes the only splash of colour.

'Have you called your union rep, Mr Morgan? We advise you have someone present.'

'I'm not in a union. I thought they were just for those wanting a pay raise.'

'Without a teachers' trade union rep, if these allegations stretch further, they could end up being very costly. You are looking at five to ten thousand pounds for legal defence.'

'I won't be needing that.' Ali's head spun. This couldn't be happening. But it was.

Gina continued, 'There are two factors we must consider here. It really is quite clear in the documents regarding accusations of this nature. They state you have behaved towards a child or children in a way that indicates you may pose a risk of harm.'

Ali sneered. 'How is that even defined?'

Gina ignored his outburst. 'And in this case, behaved or may have behaved in a way that indicates their unsuitability to work with children.'

Ali jumped from the sofa. 'This is bullshit. What they are saying and what happened are two completely different things. How do you get from accusation, a ridiculous accusation, to unsuitability to work with children? Explain that, please.'

'I am not here to explain, Mr Morgan. I am here as an arbiter. I represent the school, but I also want to ensure you are aware of all aspects of this case.'

'Case? Now it's a case.'

He slumped back to the sofa. His arms folded in front of him, and he stared off into the middle distance.

'You really think all the options have been looked at?' Ali scanned the copy of the paper in his hand. 'Here. *Suspension should not be an automatic response when an allegation is reported.*' Ali spoke rapidly. '*All options to avoid suspension should be considered prior to taking that step.*'

'I understand what it says, Mr Morgan.'

Ali didn't stop.

'*The case manager must consider carefully whether the circumstances warrant suspension from contact with children at the school or college, until the allegation is resolved. It should be considered only in cases where there is cause to suspect a child or other children at the school are at risk, or the case is so serious that there might be grounds for dismissal.* Michael's known for causing trouble.'

Gina glanced towards Ladner, who nodded in reply.

'It's what we think. In regards to pupil safety.' Ladner pursed his lips. 'And in her position on the PTA, Mrs Addler has some sway with the governors. She has already pushed for dismissal.'

Ali stood and his feet sank deeper into the carpet. 'What is your rationale and justification? That you are so weak, you can't decide yourself?'

'Mr Morgan,' Ladner growled.

'You know this has no merit. You are bowing to the wishes of one parent.'

Ladner tapped his pen onto his palm. 'You need to calm down, Mr Morgan. I've had three emails since lunchtime. There are concerns.'

'Baseless concerns. Mrs Addler has obviously got on the phone and riled up her pit of vipers.'

'It seems they are upset.' Ladner let out a sigh.

'So, some parents don't like me. Big deal. I'm not here to be popular. Look at my results, Mr Ladner. With all due respect, this is a crock of sh—'

'All that might well help your case, anyway. The police may need to be involved,' Ladner added.

'But I don't think that is necessary at this stage.' Gina smoothed down her skirt. 'We will conduct a thorough internal investigation. Due to the age of the accuser, he is not technically a minor, but being a student at this school, any sort of relationship is, of course, illegal between teacher and student. A sexual relationship accusation such as this… Well, it really falls under a breach of trust and abuse of power.'

'Are you serious?' Ali spoke through gritted teeth. 'There is no relationship.'

Ladner rose to his feet.

'There is also this issue with the nightclub. It happened outside of school hours. But it might be a contributing factor in the case.' Ladner moved around from behind the desk.

Why were they not getting this?

Ali sat forward on the sofa. 'We are not dating. Or fucking. Whatever you think is going on here, is not. This has been cooked up in the mind of some messed-up teenager. And probably egged on by his mother.'

Mr Ladner raised his hand. 'That's enough, Mr Morgan. I understand you're upset. But there's no need to—'

'No need! Of course there's a need. To stop you and this ridiculous lawyer from ruining my life. I've been a teacher since I graduated. It's everything I've ever done—'

Ali put his head in his hands. His pulse beat through each of his fingers and pounded across his forehead.

'What if he's wrong? Or I mean, what if the *victim* is

found out to be lying? What will be the outcome?'

Gina flipped through pages of the folder, guided by small plastic micro-tabs affixed to chapters and chunks of pages.

Ali leaned against the arm of the chair. A damp, sick feeling settled in his stomach. He needed a beer.

'If'—Gina paced a path back and forwards on the carpet—'this proves to be malicious or there has been a deliberate act to deceive or cause harm to the person subject of the allegation, then he'll be in trouble.'

Ali rolled his eyes and attempted to hide his face on the side of the sofa.

'He's got it in for me… and I have no idea why.'

'This is where my concerns lie, Mr Morgan. You've either shared information or students have picked up on your personal details. And we all know Bridge Street is where—'

'Okay. I'm gay. I'm a gay man. I didn't realise it was subject to my employment here, and I know my rights. And I haven't shared anything. He followed me. You heard him.'

Ladner turned his back to Ali. Gina glanced down at the papers on her lap. Neither spoke for a moment.

Ali continued, 'Apparently, in this school, being gay is frowned upon. Which is odd.'

'Odd? How so?' Gina looked up as she spoke. Her gaze followed Ali's to Ladner as he returned to his chair. She nodded, chewing at her bottom lip.

'Odd, in the sense that this school professes to teach equality and diversity. That such narrow-minded bigots should be allowed to run the place.'

Mr Ladner turned as he sat and glowered at Ali.

'Now, that I won't accept.' His moderate tone remained low, but his hands moved up and down the edges of his notepad. 'We teach respect, love, and acceptance here at Haylestone.'

Ali rolled his eyes. 'And how is that working out for you?'

Ladner ignored his remark.

'As the case manager, I need to decide whether to hand this over to the police. The next step is to talk with the local authority designated officer.'

'And what about me?' Ali asked.

'Our school safeguarding lead, Mrs Sears, will be talking with the Addlers.'

'Can I continue to work?'

'With more information coming to light and your withholding of personal information, Mr Morgan, you have put the school in a very difficult position.'

'…being gay?'

Ladner bristled. 'This type of behaviour may offen— cause issues for members of the school community.'

'So this is about offending people? Is that legal?' Ali leaned in, incredulous.

'As an occupational requirement, not offending religious convictions of the members here is part of your responsibility.' Ladner cleared his throat.

'So I should have asked at the interview? Are you one of those nice schools or one of the queer-bashing hateful ones?' Ali looked between the pair, but they avoided his gaze. Gina looked conflicted but she didn't speak.

'And also, it's a personal hunch.' Ladner paused. 'There is also the nature of the way you presented at school this morning. We cannot and will not condone your drinking getting in the way of student learning. I will need to talk with the TRA. There may be prohibitions on future teaching.'

Ali's breath hung hot and heavy in his throat. His earlier headache had been replaced by a light-headedness, like this whole situation was a dream.

'For how long? Christ's sake.'

Ladner gave the briefest of shrugs.

'This process could take four weeks. It could be as long as twelve months.'

'Hopefully it won't come to that, Mr Morgan. We'll try our best.' Gina's tone had softened. Maybe she'd prove to be an ally after all.

Ali got to his feet, his heart pounding. The room seemed smaller by the second as the dark maroon carpet swirled beneath him. He couldn't lose this job; without it he'd not have a place to live. They'd take his flat. The place he'd worked with Trevor to build. There'd be nothing left.

'In the nature of this case, there are grounds for dismissal, so the only option is to seek suspension for the time being. You will no longer be allowed to make contact with students or access school grounds. I'm sorry this has happened. I can't condone anything you may have done, but I can sympathise, perhaps more than you know.'

Ali's heart thudded in his chest.

'Is that it? We're done? So, Mrs Addler gets exactly what she—'

'It is advised you keep your behaviour outside of school in line with the professionalism expected of an educator. If I'd known this type of thing was going on, and in your case, particularly with what I have learned just now, I would have intervened much earlier.'

Over the course of one afternoon, Ali had been stripped of his job and had no sense of how long until, if ever, he could work again. Losing his job meant losing his purpose, direction, and sense of self. At least he had Trevor by his side.

'I'll escort you out to the main gate.' Ladner's desk creaked as he pulled himself up.

Six

The steps up to the second floor flashed by, each one echoing the slap of Ali's work shoes on the concrete. Post-war apartment complexes of ruddy red brick, set at sharp angles—not a thing of beauty, but still their home. Ali steadied himself with the railing enclosing the outside hallway. He pushed the door, a red door, the colour of burnt copper. Locked and the lights were off. He fumbled for the key. The slot narrower than the last time he'd tried. Always something working against him, but despite that he chuckled to himself because of the couple of beers settled in his stomach.

The door opened inwards, banging against the coat rack. Warmth washed over Ali, his eyes heavier in an instant. Trevor lay stretched out on the sofa, his feet encased in fine-knit green socks. He needed to find that ring because giving it to Trevor tonight would fix this. Trevor wouldn't be swayed by the fucking Addlers.

Ali's bag thudded to the floor. His fingers scrambled with the zip before he fell back on his haunches and collided with the wall behind.

Trevor stirred, coming around from his nap, and sat

up. 'You're late. Everything okay?' Trevor's chestnut-brown eyes looked worried. Amber hues reflected in the lamplight while his gaze moved from Ali to the open door.

Fuck, he is handsome.

'I need to find it. Where the hell is it?' Ali's voice slurred, catching in his throat. Sweat beaded on his brow despite the December chill.

'Ali?' Trevor shut the door with a click. He squatted down next to Ali. 'Let's get your jacket off.' Trevor tugged at the sleeves as Ali lolled against him. 'Did you go to the bar?' Trevor added, hanging the jacket behind the door.

Ali steadied himself on the back of the armchair.

'I've had the worst fucking day...' His gaze locked with Trevor. 'And now I can't find this fucking...'

'There's beer in the fridge if that's what you're looking for?' Trevor eyed Ali, his eyebrows knitted together, a shadow of concern in his eyes. 'But haven't you had enough?'

'I'm trying to do something nice here.' Ali rolled his eyes.

'You don't need to do anything nice.' Trevor's hand left Ali's sleeve, and he returned to the sofa. 'You might have called or something. After you came into the staffroom'—he shrugged and picked up his phone—'I was worried.'

Ali's fingers scraped against cold metal at the bottom of his bag. It must have fallen out of the box. He imagined Trevor's smile, the corners of his eyes creasing up, and his excited yelps filling the room. The perfect start to their Christmas plans. He gripped it, the metal beginning to warm up in his pulsing palm, knowing a ring couldn't fix what was broken.

Ali got to his feet. Fatigue washed over him.

'What happened with Ladner and that kid?'

'Nothing. It ended up being nothing.' Ali slumped onto the sofa. It would blow over; nobody needed to know about this. If everything else could be compartmentalised, why not this? But it would be a mess—even he knew that much. His eyes ached, he needed some sleep. He'd wait and propose once things settled down, maybe after Christmas.

Trevor's hand rested on Ali's leg, his face pinched with worry in the dim light, the pulse of fingertips warm on his skin.

'Holidays coming. Are you excited?' Ali pulled Trevor closer into his arms, his hands clumsy, but things were coming into focus as he sobered up.

Ali examined Trevor's profile, staring at him. 'I…'

'Yes?'

Then he glanced at an old picture of them on the wall. 'Nothing.' *Accused, case manager, suspended*, all passed through his mind. The TV talent show blurred in front of his eyes. Tears threatened to flood down his cheeks.

'What happened?' Trevor asked, turning to face Ali. Closer than they'd been for a while.

'Doesn't matter.' Ali gritted his teeth. Hold it together—his father's words echoed. *Be a man and get your shit together.*

'You should get it off your chest. Whatever it is.' Trevor spoke matter-of-factly. The same logical tone he used when Ali had messed up in the past.

Ali grimaced. The images swirled on the screen, greens mixed with golds. He was stranded in a whirlpool of his own making, but an idea bubbled to the surface. Maybe this is what they needed, something like this to put them on the right path. For once.

He wanted to throw up. If he could get through this, then he could propose and Trevor would see he was serious about them. They needed to start living in the real world though, which meant no more hiding.

'I need to talk to Janet and my stepdad.' He sat upright. 'They don't even know about us, Trevor. How am I supposed to tell them?'

A frown creased Trevor's brow. 'Where's this come from?'

'I was thinking today, I can't keep living through lies. It's crushing me.'

'You always said they'd be okay with us.' Trevor ran a hand along his arm.

'But not like this. Fuck.'

Trevor studied Ali with narrowed eyes.

'You never make sense when you've had a drink. I thought you'd take it easy today. You were out last night, remember?' Trevor turned his whole body away from Ali.

If Ali could tell his parents about them, Trevor might stick around when all this shit came out. Everyone would find out eventually. It would be a total mess, but he might be able to keep him and Trevor together.

'Let's just go and see them.'

'Who?' Trevor looked confused, his brow furrowed.

'My parents.'

'You mean your mum, right? And Ray.' A look of concern creased Trevor's brow.

'Of course. My stepdad is basically my dad.' Ali sat up, his hands resting on Trevor's thighs. 'I think a night away would be good for us.' He knew his lies would catch up with him, but Trevor was in the other part of the school, so he might not catch wind of it. At least for a while anyway.

'If you really want to do this.' Trevor cocked his head to one side, raising an eyebrow. He shrugged and grinned. 'Let me make a list of what we need to take.'

Without waiting for a reply, Trevor jumped off the sofa and padded in the direction of the bedroom. Trevor was so organised, and he would never suspect Ali of anything, but that didn't make Ali feel better. Secrets and deceit; it reminded him of his father.

Ali ran a hand over his hair. This was too much. He needed to tell Trevor what was going on. Ali opened his laptop, but he didn't even need to send an email to take the day off. He'd been suspended. Fuck. His desktop screen glowed.

Trevor might up and leave. Ali wouldn't be surprised at this point, and anyway, what did it matter? He'd tell his parents about them, Trevor would be happy, and they could move on. Honesty would fix this. That's what his old man had always said, about most things.

Ali approached the bedroom. The low light from the

living room illuminated the empty room. Trevor wasn't there. Whispering came from the kitchen, a one-sided conversation between Trevor and someone else. Talking quietly, as if he didn't want to be heard.

Listening for a moment, Ali couldn't make out what was being said, so he moved closer. The dim lights and tension in his shoulders caused him to nudge the door harder than he had expected, and it jolted back, hitting the side of the fridge. The noise was enough to startle Trevor. His face recovered and in his regular voice he said, 'I've got to go. Talk soon.'

Trevor hung up and held his hand to his chest, acting out he was scared when Ali burst into the room.

'Was that Soph?' Ali flicked on the overhead light.

'Yes. She just wanted to check in. You know how she is.'

'Yeah'—Ali studied Trevor for a moment—'you didn't have to hang up on my account. I wanted to make you some tea.'

'Yes. I mean, it's fine.' Trevor looked flustered. Ali frowned for a moment before turning and walking across the kitchen to the sink. Sophie was one of Trevor's pals, so why was he whispering? Ali didn't like the sensation settling in his stomach.

'We'll stop in and see your parents for one night?' Trevor's question snapped him out of his thoughts. Why was he changing the subject?

'How's Soph?'

'Good. She wants to get together in the next few weeks if we've got time.'

'Oh. Well, I'm not sure where we'll be by then. I hope we can get those flights.' Christmas plans sounded ridiculous at this point.

'I said that.'

Ali pulled two mugs from the cupboard and threw tea bags into them. After adding the water and stirring in a dash of milk, he handed a mug to Trevor.

'You English people make weird tea.' Trevor grinned at him.

He liked making comparisons about the way Chinese people made tea "in a refined way" and Brits just chucked it all in a mug and stirred.

'Next time I'll make yours in the microwave.'

'Christ.' Trevor held the mug in both hands and walked towards the sofa in the living room. Ali joined him a moment later.

'Does Soph want to come over?' Ali looked over the rim of his mug and sipped the steaming tea.

'She's a bit busy.'

'What did you say to her, Trevor?'

'Just explained what was going on at school. She knows I had the final demo class today.' Trevor placed his mug on the coffee table between them. 'It went fine, by the way.'

'I heard you whispering.'

A pregnant pause followed.

'Really? Ali, you're being paranoid. She's my friend. I have things to deal with, too.'

'You can talk to me about it, you know.' Ali's words caught in his throat.

'No, I can't.' Trevor glowered. 'You *are* it. I need someone else to help get my head around what's going on. This drinking is getting silly. And you've just decided, out of the blue, now is the time to come out to your parents. It's a lot, Ali.'

'It's not 'coming out'… It's just having the truth out in the open.' Ali rolled the mug in his palms. 'I'm sorry. You're right.'

He had nothing else to say. Wanting nothing more than to pull Trevor close to him, to feel his arms around his waist and his head resting in the crook of his neck, Ali did what he always did and pushed the truth down inside him.

Trevor stepped to him, his arms outstretched.

Finally, a truce.

'It's okay. Things just feel a bit fucked up at the moment. Maybe it's because of Christmas.'

End credits and orchestral sounds enveloped the living room. Trevor's head lolled in Ali's lap as the movie finished. He rarely made it through a whole one. Ali stroked his hair and studied the rise of Trevor's nose.

Ali considered Trevor's parents. He hadn't seen them since they took a trip, on a whim, two years ago. It was the Christmas holiday in the UK, and China was gearing up for the Spring Festival. Trevor hadn't been home for a year or so then, and he'd wanted Ali to see where he came from.

Meeting Trevor's parents had been fine, if a little awkward. Ali was open enough about his sexuality, except with his mum.

Trevor was not. His mother, especially, held high hopes for him to get married and furnish their home with grandchildren and delighted screams. Nothing could be further from what Ali wanted.

His memories of Trevor's parents were vague. They were homely, and Ali remembered spending a lot of time in the kitchen or out taking walks to pass the time.

They had stood by the rocks near Deng Soul harbour. A short drive from Trevor's parents' place where the sea was calm. They had looked out over the steady rows of wooden spikes that held the nets for the seaweed farmers to drape the young seaweed that would eventually end up in Trevor's favourite pork bone soup.

'It's beautiful here,' said Trevor, ever the dreamer.

'I don't think I can do this.' The words twisted in Ali's mouth. A lingering bitterness taking flight once again.

'It's okay. We can go back in a minute.' Ali knew despite Trevor having flawless English, he struggled with some meaning that was not literal.

'I don't mean that. I mean us. I mean that… you're here.'

'What do you mean? I have two more years before I qualify.'

'That's exactly what I mean. You're not ready! You're not even saying you'll stay in Bristol afterwards. You're saying at some point you will come back here and marry some girl and have kids.'

Trevor smiled. His eyes twinkled. Usually this drove

Ali wild, but right there Ali felt he was being mocked.

'You don't want kids either. You told me they drive you mad and all that puking and shit. Did you forget all about that?' Trevor's grin grew wider, and he reached out a hand to defuse the tension between them. He'd always been the peacemaker.

'Don't fucking laugh at me. You don't get it, do you? I forced myself to be out. I came out when I was twenty-four. That's late, I know, but I did it. You're just living a lie and you're dragging me down with you.' Trevor frowned, seeming to not grasp Ali's point.

'It's not that. It's not worthwhile telling them now.' Trevor's odd turn of phrase ignited the spark that had been sputtering under Ali's surface for the last couple of days.

'You can't not tell them. You can't live your whole life in this… fake way. I worked so hard to come out.' Tears tickled the edges of Ali's eyes. 'So fucking hard. It nearly killed me a couple of times.'

Trevor spoke slowly, but with purpose.

'This has nothing to do with you, Ali. These are my parents. And I'm not going to tell them. Not now. My mum would be mortified.'

'How? You can't live your life like this. I want you to be free. I want *us* to be free.' Sobs burst up through Ali's throat. An eruption, days or even weeks in the making.

'I have to respect my parents. They live a simple life, Ali. You have to understand that. My mum doesn't even know what it means to be gay.'

'You can teach her.'

'You don't understand.'

'Of course I don't,' Ali shouted at Trevor's back as he began to walk away. 'Because you never let me in close enough to know.'

Trevor's green and black jacket caught the wind blowing in off the sea. His black hair, cut close at the sides and long on top, swept up towards the sky.

He turned. And took a step towards Ali.

'You haven't been honest with your mum, Ali. That's your business, not mine.'

'It's not the same.' She probably knew, but he couldn't say the words out loud. His father's words spun through his head once again. That door was firmly and tightly closed—he wouldn't be speaking to his mother because it would ruin her.

'You're here. I invited you here. What more do you want?' Trevor's eyes looked tired.

'I want you to tell them. Today.' Tears gushed over Ali's reddened cheeks. 'Or it's over between us.'

'I can't tell them. I won't tell them. It's not important. They live in another country. I just need to be there for them. To look after them. I don't need them to know every little detail about my life.'

'Is that all I am to you? A little fucking detail?'

'No! No, you're not,' Trevor shouted back, the wind rising around them making it harder and harder to hear. 'You're more than that. But you can't tell me what to do about something like this.'

'When? When will you? You're messing with my head, Trevor.'

'I'm not—' His voice dropped again. 'This changes nothing between us.'

'I need to know. I need a fucking plan or something to hold on to. You can't just ignore me.'

'Like you ignore me when I tell you you're drinking too much. If you must know, Ali, that pisses me off and I put up with that.'

The words stung Ali more than the salty air whipping up over the cliff tops.

'I don't think this is going to work.'

'You're making this more than it is. When they die. Then it won't be a problem.'

Thick black clouds forced their way across the sky from the west and the sun disappeared behind a wall.

'Fuck.' Ali grabbed Trevor by the arm, and they struggled up the narrow path between the sand dunes and grass back to the main road to Trevor's parents' one-storey house.

When they left the Zhang family a couple of days after, Ali said goodbye and sat waiting in the taxi watching Trevor say goodbye to his parents. They turned and walked back into their house. Trevor's sister, Mel, shook her head when he embraced her. Trevor frowned and looked around the small yard and walked to the car blinking back tears.

In the taxi to the airport, Trevor sobbed. She'd told him not to come back again if he was gay. Their parents couldn't handle it, not that they suspected anything; it was common to bring back friends during the holiday. But the way she'd looked at him, Trevor knew he would bring shame on the family. Trevor had cried for most of the trip back to the UK.

Trevor stirred on the sofa next to Ali. His eyelashes fluttered as if he remembered the moment on the clifftops. Ali had been scared then, too scared because he was falling for Trevor, and he didn't know how to handle it.

'I'll tell her about us first,' Ali whispered into the blackness of the living room. The TV hummed, its screen black. Warm air surrounded him, the sofa and Trevor's weight pressed against his side. He must have heard Ali muttering.

'Janet will understand. You'll feel better once you've told her.' Trevor's sleepy eyes held a warmth that could not reach Ali's heart.

Trevor's light snore returned and vibrated across the pillow.

Ali slid his arm out from under Trevor's neck.

'And then I'll tell her about Michael Addler.'

Seven

'Big day.' Trevor glanced from the road to Ali, who'd barely spoken since they'd left.

'I'm not sure this is a good idea.' Typical fucking Ali. He'd sobered up and now wanted to back out. Trevor gritted his teeth and concentrated on the road ahead. 'Do you think she's ready?'

'Are *you* ready?' Trevor snapped back. Ali slumped lower in his seat. He looked pathetic. The yellow winter sunlight pale against Ali's outstretched arm. The hair on his neck needed a trim, but they hadn't had time. It always felt like they didn't have time. Something always came up or one of them was in a rush.

Ali muttered in a low voice, 'I'll always be a disappointment to her. Always a fuckup.'

It sounded like Ali hated himself sometimes. Hated that his father didn't allow him to come out to his family. But maybe today would change that.

'It might be a new chapter for them.' Trevor wasn't convinced by his own words. It always seemed so simple: he'd threaten to leave, Ali would promise to quit drinking, they'd swear it would get better, but in the cold light of the next morning, they both lost their nerve.

This would have to be it. Trevor hated ultimatums, but Ali drinking himself to oblivion wasn't helping either of them. And the states Ali got himself into… wild eyed and frantic like he was trying to drown himself in the booze.

'You okay?' Trevor glanced at the side of Ali's face. Two days' worth of stubble in need of a trim. Grey lines from lack of sleep sunk beneath his eyes.

Their anniversary night, Ali had been sick, the worst he'd been for a long time. Trevor wasn't afraid of him, but something between them was dying.

'I'm sorry. I've got a lot on my mind.' Ali stretched his hands out in front of him. He was pushing Trevor away, the way he always did. Weren't they a couple, supposed to be involved and listening to each other? Because it didn't feel like it sometimes.

After they parked the car and got out, Trevor shook his head on the way up the path to the house. This was likely a bad idea.

Small, rectangular, and orderly—the little terraced house where Ali had grown up seemed normal enough. He glanced up at the window facing the street. Ali had told him he used to sit there and read when his parents fought downstairs. Sitting in the stars, he'd said. The greatest distance from the anger downstairs without actually running away. Poor kid.

Trevor reached out and brushed his hand against Ali's arm. He hooked Ali's fingers in his, but Ali jerked away and moved quickly up to the front door without looking back.

'Welcome. Both of you. Janet tells me your training is almost finished, Trevor.' Ray slapped him on the back. Ali's stepdad was always energetically pleased to greet people at the door. Janet took their coats and directed their shoes into the wooden shelves just inside.

The four of them settled in the living room after grabbing mugs of tea from the kitchen. Janet buzzed around, shuffling out a side table for the tea, then dashing off immediately for coasters. A moment later, she was up again and out the door for a cloth just in case any tea got spilled. Trevor didn't understand how Ray coped with her anxious energy.

They chatted about Trevor's training progress at school for a while. He handed over the last documents from his satchel to Janet, who placed them on the desk in the corner of the room. He'd get them back with her usual blunt remarks after the holiday.

As they chatted, Janet spent a lot of time studying her son. Trevor wouldn't be surprised if she already knew about them. She had been a pretty devout Catholic from what Ali had said, but this was her son after all.

'So, how're things at school, Ali?' Janet sat restlessly on the edge of her seat.

Ali placed his mug on the coffee table. 'What do you mean?'

'I thought there might be some… developments. I just heard something yesterday, that's all.'

Trevor shifted in his seat. Maybe someone gossiped about them, but this was her son. She'd understand.

Ali glanced up from staring at the back of his hands and met Janet's gaze.

'So, you know? It's all around the school already?' Ali sounded defeated.

What were they talking about? There's no way any students could know. They'd been really careful.

Ray seemed equally confused. 'Am I missing something?'

Ali studded his knuckle and dug it into his temple. He sniffed.

This was it. Their lives would never be the same, but hopefully Janet would get used to the idea quickly.

'There's a kid at school,' Ali said, his voice strained. 'And the little shit is out to get me.' The voice he used when he'd messed up.

'Get you? How?' Trevor's voice was husky in his throat. This didn't make any sense.

Janet leaned further forward and placed her hand on Ali's knee.

'Something about that new boy. Michael Addler, isn't it?'

Ali pushed his hair back from his face.

'Well, it's an assault charge. He was in the corridor, misusing his phone. And I had to take it from him. He's claiming it was an assault.'

'They shouldn't have phones on display in school, anyway,' Janet snapped back.

'I know, Mum.'

'I'm just saying.' She turned and raised her eyebrows at Ray, who looked like he'd rather be anywhere else.

'I tried to take the phone from him. And later on, Mrs. Addler went nuts.'

'Her? She's that one from the PTA. Holier-than-thou type.' Janet shook her head in Ray's direction. Ray's eyebrows shot up.

'After that, we went up to Ladner's office and basically…' Ali's sobs enveloped his words, and his shoulders shook. The words barely audible. 'He's made a serious allegation against me. I've been suspended.'

Trevor's mind raced. This wasn't what they were supposed to tell them. What the hell happened at school? Ali had kept this a secret all last night and this morning. Typical fucking Ali.

'It sounds like a misunderstanding to me.' Janet's tone was brusque and she waved as if dismissing the idea.

'That's not it. He also accused me of trying to…' Ali's bloodshot eyes blinked back more tears.

'Ali? What is it?' Trevor's hand twitched in his lap. He wanted to reach out and wrap his arms around Ali. Something worse had happened, he could sense it.

Ali straightened, brushing the tears from his eyes with his palms.

'He claims it happened on Bridge Street. There's some bars. That I tried to give him money.'

'It's one of those queer places, isn't it?' Janet cut in. 'If he's going there… Well, it tells you an awful lot about the type of person he is.'

'I'm really scared.' Ali held eye contact with Trevor. 'We were out near there last weekend, remember, Trevor?' Ali's voice was barely audible. 'His friend was with him, and he backed up his story.'

'It really disgusts me. Those bars basically try to attract kids with cheap drinks and then they wonder why this sort of thing happens. Why can't they just keep their *lifestyle* to themselves?'

'Mum. You're not listening—'

'There's no need to rub everyone's face in it all the time. I'm getting a bit sick of it, if I'm being perfectly honest. And that's part of the problem now. You can't say anything, it didn't used to be like this. Now I feel like I am offending someone left, right, and centre.'

Ali appeared to shrink into the sofa as Janet talked and fussed at the same time.

Trevor's mind slowed, the scene before him unfolding as if he weren't even in the room. At DV8 last weekend, he'd come back from the bathroom and Ali had been dancing with two guys. Two youngish-looking guys, but Ali had been wasted, and Trevor steered him away from them to some booth seats in the corner of the club.

'I can remember that night.' Trevor had pushed it to the back of his mind. Another not-so-great anniversary they'd shared.

Ali shook his head a fraction. Trevor could tell Ali wanted him to stop talking. Typical Ali—he should have known this would happen. He'd promise one thing and then do the opposite.

'We were out on Bridge Street—'

'The bar should really be taking the blame for this,' Ray languidly replied. Janet nodded.

'That's my view. I can't condone what they get up to, but it's really none of my business. The world isn't what it was when we grew up, but I wouldn't want any child to feel hurt or anything.'

Ray rubbed at her arm. She knew—in that moment, the way she pursed her lips, Trevor saw it. She knew Ali was gay but held back as if speaking it out loud would somehow make it final.

'Anyway.' Janet busied herself collecting the mugs on the table. 'Who needs another tea?'

Ali sank back into the sofa, his jaw tight. Whether Trevor felt anger or resentment towards Ali, he wasn't sure. They shared a common fear of coming out to their families, but why did Ali lie to him? Why not let him in? They could face this together.

'That's not really the issue, Mum.'

Later, in the spare bedroom at the front of the house, Ali leaned against the wall that lay parallel to the bed. A pull-out mattress was folded in the corner, ready for one of them to sleep on. The room had been Ali's but had been redecorated in muted cream and blue. The bed, a narrow single, remained in the position that Ali had said was his safe space growing up. Ali and Trevor stared at the screen flashing before them; neither seemed able to start the conversation they needed to have. Nothing registered but the canned laughter coming from a small TV screen. A numbness radiated off Ali which Trevor sensed even across the gap between them. What did he have to lose?

Trevor turned down the volume on the TV and faced

Ali. 'I'm pissed you kept that from me. Next time, we'll have to tell them because they can't keep thinking this is just friendship, Ali.'

'You think that's the most important thing right now?' Without turning away from the TV screen, Ali tensed his jaw.

Trevor frowned at Ali's quick dismissal. 'We'll deal with it. Like you said. It's just some kid. There's nothing in what he said.'

'Fuck, Trevor. Mrs Addler went to the police. And he has pictures of us. Of you and me on his phone.'

Trevor watched Ali from his position on the bed. They'd always been honest with each other. Ali appeared more bothered about being caught out as gay than being in trouble for the assault.

'Is there any truth in it, Ali?'

Ali's eyes blazed with fury when he switched his glare to Trevor's face.

'Wait. Wait. I didn't mean—' Trevor moved towards Ali with both hands outstretched. He needed contact to reassure Ali.

Ali lunged forward. He pushed Trevor up against the headboard. His arms flexed and the muscles in his neck strained as he hissed in Trevor's face.

'What the fuck do you think?'

The air in the room froze. The window curtain juddered and came to a stop, framing the glass against the glare of the lamp resting on the side table.

Trevor gripped Ali's arms and pushed him back. He wasn't strong enough to counterbalance Ali's rage.

'I believe you.' Trevor's face burned, but he wasn't sure now. He hated this side to Ali, but he'd provoked him. The lies between them. Too many to count at this point. Ali stumbling home stinking of some guy's aftershave, the stubble burn across his jaw when Trevor rolled over in the morning, always a seed of doubt resting between them. Both held back secrets from their families, from each other, and from themselves.

'You don't. We've been together for three years, Trevor. Does that mean nothing to you?'

'It's not like that, Ali. You lied to me.'

'What do you mean *lied*?'

Trevor slipped from Ali's grip. He wiped at the dry corners of his mouth.

'You didn't even mention this last night.'

'I'm trying to protect you.' Ali's eyes looked bloodshot up close, like he hadn't slept in a week.

'But these things don't just come out of thin air!'

Ali's face scrunched up. The corner of his eye twitched and his mouth gaped.

'You think I'm fucking a student?' Ali hissed.

Trevor turned away. His hands covered his face as he collapsed onto the bed. Curling up into a ball, his knees tucked under him, he didn't move.

A rock on the bed. The curtains took flight and cut through the thick air.

'I don't believe people just make things up like that.' Trevor's voice strained against the pillow.

'Everything alright in there?' Janet's tiny voice passed through the door. 'I heard some shouting.'

'Fucking fantastic.' Ali paced by the bed.

'I want to believe you,' Trevor croaked.

Ali loomed over Trevor's shrunken form. His hands hovered over the blue-knit jumper Trevor wore. He withdrew his hands, one at a time, and placed them carefully back in his pockets. He turned away slowly.

'You can fucking walk back.' Ali grabbed the car keys from the dressing table.

Ali yanked open the bedroom door to reveal Janet listening just outside. She jumped back, startled at being discovered.

'I… em, just dropped something down here.'

'For fuck's sake, Mum.' Ali brushed past her, almost sending her falling over backwards.

Janet glared after her son. 'I'm sure he'll be back in a minute, Trevor. I'm sorry for his rudeness.'

Trevor nodded, the room closing around him as he gently clicked the door shut.

Sitting with his knees drawn to his chest, Trevor tracked over what he'd learned in the past couple of hours. Should he have seen this coming? Sophie had told him to finish it last time. But here he was, sitting in Ali's bedroom with his parents downstairs.

Ali, who drank too much, was the guy who had looked after him when he first arrived and who he'd met on the first couple of days into his placement at the school. Michael Addler claimed Ali tried something with him, yet it didn't make any sense. Ali wasn't like that; he loved his students. The drinking had worsened, he'd admit that, but he must be innocent. The slivers of doubt scared Trevor, though, and the lies made it harder to believe Ali's side of the story. These things didn't just happen randomly.

He couldn't leave Ali like this. Trevor hadn't known anybody else for the first couple of months when he arrived in the UK, before he met Soph. He could help Ali. Fix him and make things better. Ali just needed to move beyond navel gazing and step out from the shadows and be honest with Janet. Trevor had initially agreed with Ali when he said they should keep it quiet. It wasn't like he hadn't spent his whole life doing the exact same thing. They'd been sneaking around for months before making it official between themselves. Ali always needed more time, wanted a bit more space to get his head straight before talking to Janet. They couldn't carry on like this.

Ali had caught his gaze during lunch one day not long after he started at the school. He'd lined up holding a tray, joking around with another teacher. Probably saying something funny—she laughed and rolled her eyes, then slapped his arm. Trevor stood in the back corner by the fire escape below a green exit sign. It was his third or fourth week at school and he was finally getting to grips with this new school and new country.

He checked his watch, a silver Casio, a gift from his sister before he got on the plane. She'd teased him about not needing it as he had never been late in his life. His heart had swelled as she pressed the box into his hands before he cleared airport security.

As he pulled his gaze from the display—he had about twenty minutes before getting his own lunch—he glanced over at the table Ali was on. This time their eyes met. Trevor's back prickled and a flush ascended his spine and over his pecs. His armpits felt clammy.

Trevor glanced away, but he couldn't help turning back and sweeping his eyes across the dining hall. Ali remained with his eyes firmly fixed on Trevor. A rush of heat ran up Trevor's legs and across his balls. Ali didn't blink.

Ali chewed slowly, and Trevor felt like he was being chewed on. He could feel sweat forming on his brow, so he reached up to wipe it away. His watch caught on his skin, and he winced from the dull scratch.

Trevor rubbed his temples again and by the time he looked up, Ali's back retreated towards the trolleys holding the dirty lunch trays. Trevor's gaze took in his wide shoulders and narrow hips that, under his navy-blue thin-knit sweater, tapered down towards a cute butt held in a pair of dark denim trousers.

Trevor munched his own food slowly. He wondered if that guy would go out for a drink with him. Perhaps they could meet up in the pub. He grabbed his tray and decided to ask if he saw him again later that week.

After depositing the tray, he exited down the hallway. The yellow walls of the art classrooms glowed, and he smiled as he studied some of the students' charcoal sketches and pastel prints.

A door opened to his left as he passed, and a face in the darkness hissed 'Psst.' He jumped but turned, and a hand grabbed his wrist and pulled him into the darkness of the classroom.

Ali gently closed the door. Trevor savoured the thrill of it.

They moved away from the door, circling each other in a dance, their feet stepping one after the other like they were dancing a tango just for the two of them. Neither one could stand still, and neither could their hands.

Ali's explored Trevor's chest. Slowly at first, and he didn't break eye contact. Then, he whispered.

'Is this okay?'

Trevor nodded, and Ali wrapped his fist around Trevor's navy-blue tie and tugged him nearer. So close, his hands around Trevor's waist, Ali pulled him in for their first kiss.

Eight

Ali stormed down the road from his parents' house, past leaves spread haphazardly across neat, frosty lawns that glimmered in the streetlight. Ali slammed the side of Trevor's car with his fist. A searing pain shot through his knuckles as the dark-green paint on the Vauxhall Cavalier barely registered the assault. He couldn't do it. Empty and filled with fear—his mum would never accept him for being gay. She wouldn't; there wasn't a chance in hell.

At the end of the road, a woman hunched against the side of a bus shelter. She was frail looking, her large blue eyes contrasted with her white hair, and she appeared tense until Ali approached. A smile unfolded, creasing her eyes.

'Visiting your mum?' She glanced down at his hand.

'Sure,' Ali sighed. 'Shitty week, Mrs Sanders.'

'It'll get better, dear. Look, here's the bus.'

Would it? Ali couldn't see how it could be much worse at this point. It would take two hours to get back to the city, but he couldn't be around any of them right now. Trevor didn't believe him, and he'd failed once again, his dad's words singing in his ears. He'd been right all along. Ali would never amount to much. Nobody would stick it out with him—he needed a drink.

He pulled himself up with the rail and slipped around the woman who muttered to the bus driver in her tan raincoat. The gentle rocking of the bus, the hiss of the doors letting people on and off blurred as tears fell from Ali's eyes and he sank into the seat.

Fuck him. Each time he thought of Trevor, Ali remembered something he had done for him. The birthday cake they made together before falling roughly to the sofa with chocolate sauce dripping from a spoon. The money Ali had given, thinking it would be shared by them both in the future—at the time, he hadn't cared as they felt unbreakable as a unit. Trevor laughing as Ali pretended to act out Janet's face when she found they were more than friends. Trevor had scuttled around their living room exaggerating Janet's quick and flighty mannerisms.

Like that was going to happen now.

Condensation trails ran down the window and pooled in a grimy black thread at the base. All Ali saw when he closed his lids were Trevor's eyes. Smiling when they initially moved in together, when they split the utilities and rent for the first time after Trevor's first pay check. Uneasy, an hour ago, when Ali asked him if Trevor believed the allegations.

Two steps down from the bus onto the pavement. The stop at the end of their road, or his road now, if Trevor decided not to come back.

Ali's head swam. Maybe gay guys didn't stand by their

partners. His dad had been right when he said, "They never have relationships that last." What would he say now if he had still been alive? Ali had confirmed Grant's suspicions on his deathbed, or death sofa as it was, that he was gay. In that shithole flat he rented after Janet kicked him out. His real dad was a drinker and had been violent. With his rotten liver, rotten breath, but he'd listened to Ali. He said he'd always known, probably, when he really thought about it.

'But don't tell your mum,' his dad had said. 'It'll break her heart.' He died a week later.

After nudging the door open and entering their chilly flat, Ali sank into the sofa where Trevor typed out his lesson plans. He'd tried to quit drinking many times before but failed.

He tossed the car keys onto the table. Another stupid and petty thing he did when he was mad. He couldn't handle his feelings sober or drunk. No better than a child.

Trevor said he lost Ali, couldn't find him in his eyes, when he'd been drinking. Ali didn't know what that meant, but it stung. Hurting someone he held so close mortified him. But Trevor had turned his back on him now, so what the hell did it matter.

But he lived through the torture of his own making. Clouded all through college and into university, he burned and boiled with something. Smashed, fucked up, off it, messy... he'd been it all. Week after week, Ali and his friends lined up bottles and lines of powders starting with ketamine, graduating to cocaine as they got older.

The powders burned, but they numbed, and that was the point. He'd quit them all, but the booze. It was crystal clear now like the vodka sitting in the glass Ali nursed on the sofa he'd once shared with Trevor.

Trevor was gone. All that sloshed about was the room and the glass he held. Ali mused on Trevor's lack of coming out and his own.

Trevor said he'd always known he was gay but kept it hidden, just the same as so many other guys.

Ali had noticed he was different from other boys and often found himself outside of himself looking in. Girls surrounded him, and he never felt nerves around them like some of the other boys seemed to. He relentlessly teased the girls in his class.

He thought about how his coming out had wrecked him. A bubble had burst, but he was released that day. Lying on a bed in his university dorm, sobbing and crying with tears drowning the pillow. The friends had quickly evaporated, unsure of who he had become.

Ali paced the living room. His thoughts clamoured, and the vodka, mixed with a tiny bit of cola, made him feel sick. He didn't want to go out because he'd patrol the bars, the back streets, trying to get some quick relief. He wanted more. He'd tried with Trevor, and he was all Ali wanted when he was sober. But the drink brought something out of him. A longing wound opened up, and Ali would search the night for something to fill it. He never could—there wasn't enough booze, dick, drugs, or escape to fill the void. Trevor had rocked his world once before, and now Ali had pushed him away.

'Fuck!' Ali screamed. Trevor was gone, and Ali remained isolated in the flat meant to be their flat. They shared towels there. They had picked out cushions for that sofa. Trevor didn't believe him. The one person he'd relied on, the only person he could trust, had betrayed him.

He took a pair of scissors from the drawer in the kitchen and began hacking at the curtains. He pulled down the rail and it crashed into his forehead. The burning pain drove him on. He stabbed the scissors into the cushions on the sofa. They popped back like fleshy thighs. The vodka thumped in his skull and the music pounded from their speakers. His arms stung, but he gripped and stabbed and pulled at the sofa cushions. He tore the heart from them, the yellow foam powdered and disintegrated in his hands. The dust and fluff rose in the air around the room.

Grabbing the vodka bottle, he poured a thick dash into the glass, and knowing he always felt better with some mixer—*he wasn't a fucking alcoholic, after all*—topped up the glass and swayed. Fuck, he swayed to the music. The yellow dandruff from the cushions misted his vision. Vodka splashed to the floor. It became sticky under his feet, but he didn't care. His arms moved above his head. He imagined Trevor stepping closer, putting his arms out on his chest. They wrapped into one another and moved. Their hips gyrated, and he groaned when they ground against each other.

He took a drink and moved to the speakers. The bass turned higher and began to pound and pound, a beat followed by another mouthful.

Fuck Trevor. Fuck him and his locked-in, closeted world. Ali was angry now. Face flushed, red cheeks burning, and the bitter taste of raw alcohol made his heart thump.

Trevor always put his fucking family first. He'd sacrifice his own happiness for their greater good. It was always about how they felt, how they came first. Trevor was the one with the loyalty problem. He'd let Ali down. Being disloyal came easy when your family took priority over your boyfriend. What they had, what was gone now, would never have worked anyway. Not with Trevor acting like that.

Trevor's iPad sat glowing in its charging station. Ali's gaze settled on the green light. It made him think of last Christmas, the first one they had spent together in a shared flat. They'd danced in the living room to old rock songs. Each bumping into the other and jumping on and off the sofa. They'd laughed and stripped down to their boxers; Trevor had laid back on the black sofa, his hands up behind his head. They'd been together for over a year by then. Not out or anything; Ali had wanted to take it slow and not be tied down.

It had been a front, really. Mr No-Commitment was secretly terrified. He couldn't get the image of Trevor, the first time he laid eyes on him, out of his mind. He pictured the exact shirt, black-and-white plaid and tight blue dress trousers. His hair swept back and a nervous grin on his face. He'd asked the way to the staff room at lunch or something like that. Ali was hooked at first sight and led him from the dreary corridor into the art room.

Ali's fingers tightened around the glass. Last Christmas had been fucked up.

Trevor's first real Christmas tree, and he'd stood transfixed in front of it, touching and feeling each gold and silver ornament.

Trevor had grinned as Ali fingered the edge of his grey boxer shorts, slow movements running up and down the elastic waistband. He pushed a finger in and then pulled it out. Ali's dick strained in his boxers. He kneeled in front of Trevor. The lights from the tree, small balls of white, green, and red flashed on and off. Swirling around the tree.

With Trevor's boxers kicked away, Ali moved his hand down his thighs. Running them over the sensitive inner skin sent Trevor shivering and his head rolled back. Ali swayed slightly from the alcohol he'd been drinking since before lunch. To get in the mood, he said, but it was a habit, and he didn't know any other way.

His hand gripped the base of Trevor's dick and he took in the firm length and also the purple line, like a graze, running in a diagonal across the softest part. It wasn't deep enough to be a cut but a scratch. The sort of fresh scratch done with someone's teeth. But not Ali's teeth. Trevor had been away for a week, to catch up at the course providers. This was their first time together since November.

He saw it now. It meant nothing, but at that moment, as the brandy and wine rushed together, all he saw was betrayal. The gaudy tree crumpled as Trevor was thrown into it. He crashed backwards and his head crunched into the slate fireplace beside the tree. The golden and silver balls shattered and lay discarded around Trevor's shocked expression. Ali hauled him up by his arm and shoved him again, but the fight had left him by then. He couldn't process Trevor seeing someone else.

'It was just a guy at the hotel gym. A fucking blowjob, Ali. That's all it was.'

'That's all it was to you!'

Ali's hands flashed around, searching for something to steady himself. He was drunker than he expected. Fuck, shoving Trevor into the wall and the tree flashed through his mind. He couldn't process that Trevor had ruined their Christmas. This Christmas, of all of them, the first one together. This one mattered, this one was important.

Later, Trevor had talked Ali down and said he understood. Who the fuck could understand a nutcase thinking he was cheating when they weren't even officially together? And now he was gone. Gone for good.

The light blinked again on the iPad like a green bauble. Ali couldn't look away, so he took it, and raised it above his head. The fucking iPad with all of Trevor's hard work. Well fuck him and fuck his stupid work. That always seemed to come first. Trevor barely had time for him. Ali hurled it at the floor, and it slapped onto the wood with a thud. He raised it again and threw it towards the corner of the coffee table. It caught the edge, producing a cracked screen and some thin scarring that threaded towards the corner of the device.

He fell forward and grabbed the scissors off the coffee table. Positioning the iPad against the wall at an angle, he stabbed down the pointed scissors again and again. Penetrating the screen, through the glass, each time a crunching when bits of glass flew out and scattered around the room. With multiple puncture wounds, the light died, unblinking. Ali cast it aside and sat with his back to the wall, his knees pulled up close to his body. He wrapped his arms around both legs, and the trouser material became sodden as he cried hot tears into his knees.

Nine

'Can you pick me up?' Trevor's voice trembled. A sob threatened to erupt—a bubbling across his chest, tempting his eyes at the edges.

'Where are you?' Sophie answered after a brief pause.

'Ali's parents' place.' His voice cracked.

'Did he hit you?'

…

'Trevor, talk to me.' Sophie's no-nonsense tone.

'He didn't. Can you come now?'

'I'll be there as soon as I can.'

Sophie's picture faded into the home screen when the call ended.

Trevor sat back on Ali's bed, his arms clutching his knees. He could hear Janet and Ray moving around downstairs. He needed to get out of here. Ali knew he'd be scared without his car keys. He'd stranded him on purpose. What did he expect Trevor to do?

Go downstairs and talk to his parents for him? That felt like something Ali would do. Tough talk, but when push came to shove, he'd crumble; he walked away or got out of his head, drunk. Typical Ali. He could be so petty sometimes.

Trevor stared out of the window. The moon hung bright in the sky. Why hadn't he just picked a guy in China and settled there? But the experiences there had been a form of punishment as well. Hiding in the shadows. He deserved everything he got. Mel had told him multiple times, and she would constantly remind him now. She was right—look at what had happened. It was never meant to be because it wasn't right, and it always ended badly. Two guys couldn't be together. The emotions were unbalanced.

In life, choices pushed and swelled like a seagull on the breeze. How had he ended up in England, in this mess?

Trevor scrunched his eyes, recalling his sister and China. Where had it gone wrong? The guy leaned up against a tree, a cigarette hung from his lips. He had on a dull orange T-shirt that dipped in and revealed a firm and tanned chest. It looked smooth, and with his hand rubbing slowly up and down the outside of his crotch area, Trevor had felt a stirring inside of him. An intense feeling gripped his stomach for the first time in his life. This was different to the kiss with Dee; this was the next step.

The guy flicked his cigarette away and it smouldered on the ground.

The attraction, unlike anything Trevor had felt before, crawled around his stomach and shot an ache across his balls.

The floor was spongy from layers of pine needles,

forming a carpet beneath their feet.

Under cover, the dappled sunlight fell across his shoulders, his white teeth showing through a curved smile. He stopped, turned, and pulled Trevor's hands towards him.

The guy kissed him roughly. The stubble of his beard like sandpaper against Trevor's cheek. He pulled Trevor's hair back suddenly and as his mouth hung open, more in shock than anything, the guy spat in his mouth.

The warm taste of saliva and cigarette coated his tongue. A sweet and bitter mixture, not unpleasant.

'Drop 'em.' His voice even gruffer than his rugged looks suggested. He didn't sound local. He pushed Trevor towards a fallen log, then stepped away and hung his black windbreaker up from a branch.

There was no foreplay, they didn't hold each other or touch.

The guy tugged down Trevor's sweatpants and his briefs at the same time in one motion. He loosened his own belt and released his throbbing cock. He spat on his hand, shoved two fingers into Trevor's hole. Trevor yelped, but it was barely audible compared to his scream when the guy plunged into him a moment later. A searing, burning feeling filled his lower back and anus. Trevor gripped the bark on the log, and bits of dry crumbling skin broke off in his hand.

Rough guys and rougher sex followed in the years afterwards. Always the same story: the guys Trevor attracted wanted one thing and one thing only. Expressing any sort of emotional vulnerability was seen as a weakness, and something to be avoided. There had been others, a few in China. But Ali presented himself differently, on the outside at least. Confident, sure of himself, and unafraid to be himself. Ali, conflicted about what he wanted. The loudest, brashest guy in the room, but a shrunken husk when faced with his own family or a discussion about the couple's future. Live for the moment, he'd said, be free, don't get tied down. But they were drifting along. Unmoored and unanchored.

Seagulls called in the wind outside the window. They cajoled each other. Ali would say it meant it was stormy at sea when they collected around the bus stop at the end of the street.

Sophie's car pulled up outside; the crunch of the gravel drew Trevor to the window. The car door opened, and she stood looking up at the house. She pulled her black jacket around her, stepping to the curb. Trevor waved and she beckoned him to come out. He made an *okay* signal, but he couldn't breathe; his chest constricted as he shrugged on his sports jacket.

A radio hummed from the living room. At least two voices held a casual exchange in the kitchen, the door slightly ajar. Even if Ali was still there, Trevor didn't want to talk to them. The sharp edges of the white fridge jutted out. Trevor took the final step onto the carpet carefully and slipped on his shoes. The white metal of the door handle was cold against his hand, and he eased it down as quietly as possible. The lock clicked but was barely audible. Trevor raised a boot to step out onto the path.

'Trevor? Is that you…?' Janet's voice. *Fuck.*

Janet held a cup in one hand. A white tea towel with a blue stripe clutched in the other. The edges of the crisp white material folded over her hand. 'You know he's always been like that. Quick to fly off the handle.' A smile played on her lips. Like she wanted to say something more. 'Like his father.'

The grey around her temples looked more pronounced with the overhead light. Ali always made her out to be a tough nut, but in her own home, she looked smaller than at school.

'I've got to get something from the car.' Shit. He'd just lied to her face. Ali had taken the keys anyway.

'I'm not upset with you. You don't have to worry.' Her soft tone didn't sit right with the hardness Trevor was used to. Ali had said she'd always smooth things over, or look the other way to avoid any sort of direct conflict. It had driven Ali mad and kept him firmly unable to open up to her about his sexuality.

Trevor willed himself to move and get outside. When he turned back to close the door, Janet's gaze didn't leave his face. Her eyes glimmered, she stepped forward, she came closer.

'What's going on, Tre—'

The door clicked closed. Trevor released his breath; it tumbled out, but the release barely touched his aching chest. He moved quickly, not wanting the approaching figure behind the mottled glass in the door to catch him. He didn't have the answers to so many questions.

Trevor glanced around outside, yet his vision blurred

trying to locate Soph's dark sedan. Ali was trapped. That house was suffocating, and it wasn't just because the heat was turned up so high.

The warmth of the car enveloped Trevor. He sank into the seat next to Sophie, his hands trembling.

'Just drive. Please.' Trevor cast a glance behind him. Janet, framed by the overhead porch light, stood in the open doorway. The car pulled out into the road, yet Janet remained staring out into the darkening street.

'You've got to end it with him.' Sophie didn't mince her words. 'You look like shit, by the way.'

She glanced at Trevor wrapped up with his jacket pulled tight around him.

'Something happened.' Trevor spoke through gritted teeth.

'Well, that much is obvious.' Sophie shuffled in her seat. Then lowered the heater. 'Talk to me, Trevor.'

Trevor blew out his cheeks, rubbing his hands together. Each digit moved of its own accord, like he'd lost control of them. His mind drew a blank, slate grey like the roofs of the houses.

The car pulled to a stop at a junction. The exhaust fumes of the vehicle in front rose in a grey cloud.

Sophie turned to Trevor, her gaze intense.

'I can't stand seeing you like this. You're like a dazed rabbit. It reminds me of… Last year—'

'Don't, Soph. This is different. Not like then.'

The traffic light switched to green and the car ahead pulled forward. Sophie eased off the clutch and crept forward into the haze.

'As much as it pains me to say this because I know it will hurt you…' Sophie gripped the steering wheel. 'Ali needs help. You went through all of this last year. Why are you putting yourself through it again?'

'He's going to need a lot more help now.'

'What do you mean? Can you stop talking in riddles, please?'

'A student at school accused Ali of trying to get them into bed.'

'What? You're joking?' Sophie alternated between gaping at Trevor and glancing back at the road.

'Well, only if they've got some evidence he did it.'

Sophie flipped the indicator light and pulled over into a narrow road on the left. She switched off the engine.

'Trevor. Start from the beginning. You're not making any sense.'

'It was our anniversary. You know I hate going to clubs, right? But I said fine, let's go.' The words tumbled from Trevor's mouth. 'And this guy, the one who's accused Ali. He was there.'

'You saw Ali with this kid?'

'He's hardly a kid, Soph. Ray said the bar's to blame more than Ali for allowing them in. Michael Addler shouldn't have been there in the first place.'

'Trevor, look.' Sophie's gaze flashed steel. 'This is serious. Whatever you think, he's a student. Ali's a teacher.'

'There were two of them, I can see it now. But it's hazy. You've been to DV8, you can barely see the bar from the dancefloor when it's packed.'

'Okay…'

'So I came back from the bathroom. And I couldn't find Ali, he wasn't in the place where we'd just been dancing.'

'This doesn't sound good, Trev.'

'I thought they were a couple. I think Ali was kissing one of them. His head was so close to one of them, but their backs were to me for some of it. Now I can't be sure. Like I said, it was busy that night. It's a bit of a blur…'

'Is he always like that?' Her forehead creased, her brows knitted.

'No.' Trevor's stomach clenched. Using the dashboard for support, he spread his fingers out—she didn't need to know everything about their relationship. It wasn't anyone's business. 'They were so close together. I mean, they could have just been talking.' He released a sigh. 'I don't know.'

Sophie pushed her hair back behind her ears. 'But it's normal for you guys to go and snog other people?' she said eventually.

'Ali said it doesn't mean anything.'

'Trevor. Is that what you think? Not that what Ali tells you is right or wrong. What do *you* want?'

Trevor bit down on the inside of his lip. The metallic taste of blood swam against his tongue. Each time he saw another man close to Ali, it cut him up deep inside. But the thought of being alone meant he dealt with it. He'd put up with the punishment.

'I mean, what's the choice here? It's either his

drinking or I've got to be his therapist. It's hardly the first time he's fucked around, is it? This is such a mess, Soph.'

'The first thing you gotta do is find out what's going on.' She narrowed her eyes on the road.

'It's whether I can trust him now. At all. He only mentioned it because Janet seemed to know what had happened at school with this Michael Addler. I don't know if Ali would have shared anything otherwise. We were going to tell them about us—'

'That's pretty messed up.'

'Yeah, like what the fuck?' Trevor's exasperated sigh filled the car. 'Ali's always on at me. "Tell the truth. Open up." But when it's him—'

'So, you've got to tell him. Or you've got to end it.'

Trevor sighed. Sophie didn't understand, and she never would. Ali had messed up, but Trevor needed him. What would he be without Ali? They'd come this far, so they should try to fix it.

'He needs my help, Soph. I think I can help.'

Sophie held Trevor's gaze. Neither one of them breaking the stare.

'You are part of the problem here, Trevor.'

Trevor's gut told him this wasn't Ali's fault—not that he was blameless, but his mind smoothed things over. There had to be some other explanation. Ali might have been flirting, but what did that matter? Ali said it was physical, that's all. He loved Trevor. Monogamy, just some more evidence of *hetero-social control*. It all sounded a bit dramatic to Trevor. He didn't see other guys in the same way when they were together; it hurt him that Ali still looked. It meant he wasn't enough for him.

'He's pretty messed up about his family. And some things always play on his mind.'

'A religious mum and a dead, drunk dad. Classic. It's no excuse for how he treats you though, Trevor.'

Trevor turned away and wiped his eyes with the sleeve of his jacket. The road ahead looked grim as cars streamed past. Whichever way he went, he'd lose. He didn't see any way out of this. Sophie's glare burned hot on his cheek. One of the most intense people he knew, she'd go out of her way to do the right thing for him, although, if that would extend to Ali, he didn't know.

Sophie slammed her hand on the steering wheel, snapping him out of his trance.

'Wait, if one of them was this Michael Addler, who's the other guy?'

'I don't know him.'

'I mean.' Sophie gripped the wheel with one hand and started the engine. 'Why would two straight guys go to a gay club and take pictures of men kissing? Think about it. Ali was drunk, hardly shocking… but you said Michael has pictures of you two. It doesn't make any sense… unless he's trying to catch you out? He already knew who Ali was because they are in the sixth form? He's seventeen, right?'

'But… Ali doesn't teach Michael Addler. He only joined the school in September.'

'Wait. I'm thinking. What use is a picture of you two? If he's trying to accuse Ali of something, then the pictures show you two as a couple. He's trying to get Ali in trouble.'

What she said made sense, but he didn't have the answers.

'Isn't it a violation of privacy?'

'I'm not sure that's relevant, but it looks like one of them has taken the picture *after* deciding to come for Ali. Or both of you.'

Trevor drummed his fingers on the dashboard. All around the car, exhaust fumes mixed into the bleak sky. Winter in the UK was nasty at the best of times, and being stuck in a cold car wasn't helping. Why would anyone want to harm them?

'Can I stay at your house tonight?'

'Oh, he took your keys. Again?' Sophie rolled her eyes and pulled the car out into the street.

'Yeah.' Another thing Ali did when he was pissed. He lashed out and wanted to hurt people. Usually it didn't amount to anything serious, but it still stung to be shoved aside.

'I'm proud of you, Trevor. You can stand up to him—you're both better than this.'

Ten

Ali cracked his eyes as the light from the window streamed into the room. It must be late morning. His neck ached from sleeping face down on the kitchen table. From the horizontal viewpoint, his eyes opening further, he took in the figure standing in the doorway.

Trevor squatted and picked up the iPad. He turned the cracked and mangled screen over in his hands, his mouth agape. Guilt and anger washed over Ali. Last night's anger dissipated like the fumes of alcohol, lost in the night, as he had tossed and turned.

'Why are you here?' Ali's voice stuck in his throat, his lips dried around the soft words.

'I came back to help you, and I wanted to talk,' Trevor said, his gaze on the iPad. He stood slowly and took in the scene of disarray. Bottles and cans lined the counter and kitchen table. 'But it might be best if I leave you to it.'

'*You* think that's for the best.' Ali's chair lurched back and banged into the wall as his fist came down hard on the wooden surface. 'Three years and the first whiff of trouble… you're out?'

Trevor clutched the misshapen iPad. His voice was measured and calm. 'It's not like that. It's hardly been peaches and roses up to this point, has it, Ali? Look at what you've done, this is our house. We were trying to build a home.' With his arm, Trevor threw a wide arc around the space. 'This is hell.'

Ali stood from the table. His hands clenched in fists.

'And how the fuck do you think I feel?' Ali spat out the words. He glared at Trevor. He didn't expect anything less from him. He'd always been weak. He hadn't suffered like Ali had. He'd taken the easy route out and left for another country.

'I saw it in your eyes last night. And I can see it now. I've had your back since day fucking one. I thought you'd fight for us—I expected you'd try harder.'

Perspiration prickled across Ali's forehead, all the alcohol breaking free.

Trevor blinked back tears, although his clenched jaw muscles demonstrated a sliver of steel rooted there. 'I just want to be sure.'

A salty droplet touched the edge of Ali's mouth. It tasted like a tear, or sweat, or one of Trevor's tears. Ali wiped his eye with the heel of his hand. Trevor looked miserable with his mouth turned down and a grey pallor across his skin. Ali released his breath, sending the saltiness from his mouth.

His vision blurred. Trevor didn't deserve this, didn't have to put up with his shit.

Trevor steadied himself and glanced about the kitchen, likely looking for somewhere to put the iPad down. 'It's not like I want this any more than you do. I've got my visa to think about.'

Ali stared past Trevor and the awkwardness grew, neither of them able to summon a word of basic conversation, unable to connect. Ali's mind tumbled with snippets of his father's vicious and inebriated words.

'I don't want to fight. I'm sorry.' Ali ran his hand over his brow, sweeping the sweat with it, and gestured for Trevor to sit in the other chair. Trevor placed the iPad next to him, his nail finding an edge that he nursed and drew convoluted patterns across.

'I want to ask you something about that night at DV8. And I don't want to fight.'

Ever the peacemaker. Ali attempted a smile, but through the headache it likely looked like a grimace.

'Can you remember Michael Addler being at the bar?' Trevor's voice sounded tentative. Talking of that night brought some focus to Ali's mind: a clear objective and a tangible goal.

'I can't remember. It's a total blackout. I know we went there. But when I'm trying to think of it, I can't.' Tension coursed through his jaw muscles, and it took all he could not to start crying. 'There's nothing.'

Trevor drew a breath and released it slowly. 'I saw you dancing with two guys that night. You kissed one of them. I'm sure of it.'

'I don't think anything happened…' Ali searched through the fragmented pieces. Each one a grey flurry, murky and unyielding to his probing.

'This time,' Trevor muttered.

Ali covered his face with his hands. They'd had a nice meal and a few drinks. He'd got more mojitos, followed by shots, then it was a blur. A blank space where happy memories of their anniversary should be.

'Why else would you be so close to one of them?' Trevor slid the iPad away as he spoke, turning it face down to cover the cracked and damaged screen. 'And you don't know for sure, that's the point. What a fucking mess.'

Light cracked through between Ali's fingers, piercing and unrelenting. He wanted to turn it off or move away from it, much like Trevor's questions. Each one another jab, another fingernail under the scab, yet they failed to illuminate anything further.

'Who's the other guy? Not Michael Addler,' Trevor asked.

'Simon something. Addler's henchman.'

'Henchman?'

'Sidekick. They're always hanging out together. You've seen the smoker's corner lot. These guys are the ring leaders.'

'What's his surname?'

Ali scratched his head.

'Smith. Simon Smith. I think, I don't—'

'We should find out more about him. He should be interviewed at least. I bet the police can pull their story apart.'

'I don't think he's got much to do with it. He was in my class last year. Quiet kid, scowls a lot, but wouldn't say boo to a goose. Michael Addler's the troublemaker.'

'I keep going over that night in my mind.' Trevor brushed a hand across the tabletop. 'We were dancing together, and I went to the bathroom. It took forever because some guy had collapsed in there and was blocking the doorway. The queue took about twenty minutes.'

Trevor picked at one of the cracks on the corner of the table.

'When I came back, you were dancing with two guys, and you had your arms wrapped around one of them. You were up close in his face, like you were shouting, but you were smiling. It was weird, now that I think about it, your face was really close to his.'

'It was…?'

'But it looked like he was holding you upright more than anything else. I don't know. It happened so fast and didn't seem that important at the time.'

Ali closed his eyes to a repetitive beat behind his lids. The drinking made the pulsation worse. Every time, he woke up like this. Every time, a piercing, nasty stabbing overcame his thoughts and consciousness. That night, their celebration, he'd drunk too much. Drink to celebrate, drink to forget. His dad's exact words.

'And then the next time this kid sees you, you're slamming him up against a locker.'

Trevor's voice elongated the words, in that way when he was puzzling over something and thinking out loud.

'He has pictures of us, Trev. On his phone. I was trying to protect us. Trying to protect you.'

'I don't need protecting, Ali. Look at the state of you.

Maybe you need to get help. You're always on at me. To come out. To be myself.' Trevor glowered. 'But I'm not the one drinking myself to death.'

That hurt. The words Janet had screamed echoed in his ears. His father was always dying for a drink. It was Ali's weak spot—an area of his life where he'd lost control. Trevor knew that—his words cut deep, as intended.

Trevor shoved himself up from the table and moved to the back of the kitchen. He slid two empty cans to the side and ran his hands under the tap.

'You believe him, don't you?' Ali stared at Trevor's back.

'I'm trying to make sense of this.' Trevor sounded flat and tired. 'I want to believe you.'

'If you did, you wouldn't need to think about it. You'd start trying to help me.'

Trevor grabbed a dish towel and bunched it before running it across his face. As the towel dropped away, a sneer crept over Trevor's lip, and a creased line raised his cheeks in disgust.

'That's it, isn't it? It's always my fault. You fuck up and somehow turn it on me. You're the one who's afraid, Ali. I can see that now.'

'I'm not.' The words stuck in his throat. His guts in free fall, Ali had never felt so afraid in his whole life.

'You are. Why the hell am I taking responsibility for the shit *you've* done? You need to grow a pair. That's what you say over here, isn't it?'

The skin around Ali's temples heated. But Trevor

continued before he could reply. 'This isn't normal, Ali. You've always pushed me into doing whatever you want. Do you ever stop to think, just for a second, how I'm doing or how I'm dealing with your shit show?'

'I do—'

'No, you don't. You're so wrapped up in yourself and getting out of your head.'

Trevor shoved the cans from the table with one motion and they clattered onto the floor. Trevor blew out between his lips. 'I'll make some tea.'

He picked up the cans, tossing them in the sink, before filling the kettle. Grimacing, Trevor leaned over the sink to open the kitchen window, all the while muttering about the stink.

Trevor seemed different today. Perhaps he didn't care what Ali thought anymore. After the mess yesterday, Ali could hardly blame him.

Trevor placed two mugs on the table. Dun-coloured liquid swirled and lapped at the edges of the mug like a miniature storm calming.

'I'm sorry about yesterday.' Ali swallowed.

Trevor held Ali's gaze. 'It makes more sense now. If your father was anything like Janet—It must have been impossible to actually talk about yourself. Why doesn't she listen?'

Ali scratched at his scalp and pondered the out-of-the-blue question. Where had this assertive Trevor come from? He'd barely confronted his past himself, let alone put it into words.

'You know about my dad. With Janet. They were

always fighting. I think they basically hated each other and couldn't stand being in the same room even.'

Trevor leaned back on the wooden chair. He stifled a yawn.

'Sorry. You've told me this before, Ali. It feels like we're going around in circles.'

Would telling Trevor make it any better? Ali's mind festered.

'I've wanted to. Ever since we met, I've wanted to sit Mum down and tell her about what's between us. But she's super religious. The things she said when I was younger… Horrible words about people like us.'

'It's not your job to make her accept you.' Trevor's hand extended across the pine surface of the table and wrapped around Ali's wrist. 'Because it's about you, isn't it?'

'She thinks what we are—what I am—is wrong. A sin.'

Trevor cleared his throat. 'You're never going to be better until you get over that.'

Ali nursed the mug. 'When I do tell her, I know she'll only say what she thinks I want to hear, but in her heart, deep down, she will always think there is something wrong with me. And I'm not ready to ruin that.'

'So, you intend to live your whole life like this?' Trevor pursed his mouth in that adorable way and waved his hand at the discarded mess in the kitchen.

Ali chewed the inside of his mouth. Nobody, before Trevor, could get under Ali's skin in the same way he did. Underneath, whatever feelings Ali had for Trevor, he sensed they could get over this and move on.

'That sounds like something I'd say to you.' Ali's eyes welled.

A smile crept into Trevor's eyes, crinkling the skin at the edges. They held each other's gaze for a minute.

Ali broke the silence. 'But with this case… I can't even begin to think about talking to her now.' Surely Trevor would understand. His family situation was equally tangled.

Trevor's fingers loosened from Ali's wrist, and he withdrew them. He sat back in the chair, his balled fist propped under his chin.

'So, if it comes out there is evidence… about the money for sex. Jesus… Ali.'

He still believes something happened. After all that, he'd tried to open up and get Trevor to understand. But he was just like the rest of them—

Ali swung his legs out from under the table, grabbing his coat off the back of the chair. He downed the remaining tea in the mug, and while keeping eye contact with Trevor, brought it down hard on the tabletop. It shattered on impact and sent shards of white china flying out across the kitchen.

'Ali!'

'Fuck you, Trevor! Fuck all of this. What is the point in doing this… any of this, if you don't trust me?'

Trevor reeled from Ali's outburst—the calm look and easy smile fell away.

'You're trying to turn this on me.' Ali's voice came out in a growl. 'You're letting your parents down as well.

Can't even come out to them, either.'

'What has that got to do with anything?'

'Everything. You're afraid.'

'This again?'

Trevor's fist clenched. He stood and leaned in towards Ali.

He'd never seen Trevor angry like this. Any peace between them a moment ago had evaporated.

'Why don't you sort your own shit out. Tell your mum you don't want kids instead of pulling my life apart. I'm sick of sneaking around, too. You've always thought you're so much smarter than me.'

'Fuck you. You're a piece of shit, Trevor.'

They stood facing each other. With the kitchen clock ticking up on the wall, the moment of anger slid by. Trevor moved to the cupboard where they kept the brush.

'All I'm trying to say is we need to figure out why they've decided to come after you. After us—'

'You don't need to pretend like you care. You've said your piece.'

'What else is there apart from those pictures? It's their word against yours—not that it makes it any better, but—'

'I don't fucking know. I can't remember a thing. Happy? Yes, I've fucked up and I don't even know what I've done.'

Trevor visibly wilted. The tension around his temples gone. It didn't matter what Trevor felt or thought at this point. It was over.

'You stay here. I'll find somewhere else to stay.' Ali gathered his keys and shrugged on his jacket. He ignored Trevor standing there, holding the brush handle, his mouth slightly open.

The cold air hit Ali's face as tears burned a track down his cheeks before he slammed the door on Trevor.

Eleven

Trevor stood in the playground, looking up at the school building as the wind caught the edges of his scarf and whipped it across his jaw. Red brick walls and Victorian-style windows formed a barrier blocking out the sun. He gripped the leather straps of his black satchel and moved towards the concrete steps leading up to the doors. There was no point skipping school now like he'd planned with Ali on Friday. There was no *them* now; Ali had made it clear what he wanted.

An emptiness settled over everything at the flat. They had gotten too close to the sun and burned their palms. A chain of events that had peaked and now tumbled towards its crumbling base. The ending of them.

Warm air rushed to meet him as he tugged the double doors open. The frozen faces, pointing fingers, and shocked expressions he had expected did not greet him in the corridor. It was a regular Monday. Nobody knew anything about him, just like before.

He breathed out slowly, pulling the door closed behind him, and absorbed the scene.

Students milled about by their lockers, a couple

wrapped up together in one scarf, and some boys shoulder-barged each other, laughing uncontrollably. The second bell would ring anytime now, sending a stampede of students to their classrooms scattered around the buildings and across the four floors out of sight.

Trevor wanted to get to the staff room, finish the paperwork to wrap up the observation classes needed to pass his training, and start figuring out where he might work next year. Staying in Bristol seemed like a stretch now, but he couldn't imagine a life in China either.

Janet's ashen face filled his thoughts. She had an uncanny ability to know what was going on with most of the students; she could spot a troublemaker from ten metres. Trevor hoped she would buy that he'd been stressed out over his friend. God, all the lying and sneaking about, why did they do it? One lie led to another, to another, to another. She'd stood in the street, that sharp, perceptive gaze never missing a beat. If he had to come clean with Janet, then he would. Well, clean without outing Ali.

After the winter holiday, he'd begin his teaching journey. It all felt like a blur now. Everything had been going so well, but with Ali in trouble, he'd barely slept the last few nights. Bristol didn't feel right without Ali beside him. The shine had begun to dim on this overseas adventure.

Keeping close to the lockers, with his head down and coat collar pulled up to his cheeks, Trevor caught a glimpse of his reflection in the glass partition dividing the middle school from the entrance way and the high school. His black hair looked neat enough, but his eyes… they were darker than he'd ever seen them, each a black iris burning to the edges of the white. Grey shadows had formed under them, and if his mother had been there, she would have said he looked haunted.

As he moved along the corridor, he thought of her, that she'd be getting ready to sleep in China now. She'd always lived there, but it had been their dream—the one they talked about on their weekly phone call—that she would visit him in England. His mum married young and had never left the small, rural area she grew up in. His dad barely spoke now, not two words besides asking for another cigarette, a cup of the local spirit bai jiu, or mumbling for another portion of rice. She wanted to go abroad, and Trevor wanted to take her, but something always put a stop to those plans. He winced. What would she think of this mess he'd gotten himself into? Flying back all the time was hard and expensive. He didn't mind the flight, but tearing up one root to transport to the other side of the world, attempting to catch up with family members again after so long, proved living across two continents to be a strain on everyone involved. "Be good," she would say. "Be kind."

The staff room door opened as he leaned into it. Trevor prayed, as his mother's soft voice left his mind, that it would be empty. Not many people came in this early if they didn't have the first class. He was hoping for an hour or two alone, to settle in and cover some ground before everyone else arrived.

But no. Janet stood by the kettle, gripping a mug in

one hand. She moved towards him.

'Trevor.' Her gaze ran his full length and then settled on his face. 'I didn't think you'd be here so early. How's the portfolio coming along?'

'Almost done. I think it can be finished by the end of the week.'

'Try and submit it before Christmas.'

'I will. Friday, I hope.'

Trevor placed his bag at the back of the room. Janet stopped him on the way to the kettle.

'Did you talk with Ali? His phone seems to be switched off.'

There was no point in pretending. She knew they lived together. He'd always suspected she was under the assumption that Ali was an angel looking after this lost guy from China.

'He moved out.'

She didn't hide her shock well. 'Has something happened between you two?'

'He needs some space. There's a lot he needs to deal with.'

'Where's he gone?' She sank into the sofa cushions. 'I can't believe he didn't call us. He should have come home.'

'He's doing it his way. On Saturday, he came by and took a few things. I think he's staying in a hotel.' No point in mentioning the smashed-up iPad and the mess he'd left the house in.

Janet tutted. 'I was quite upset when you both stormed out on Friday.'

'Sorry about that. So was I.'

'Trevor, did you hear any more about the case? I've been wracking my brain for anything I can remember about Michael Addler.'

'I don't know any more than you do now. I'm pretty certain his mother's a real bitch.'

Janet's eyes widened.

Trevor spat the words before pushing past her to the sideboard and small sink. His hand shook as he filled the kettle with water. 'Do you want some tea?' he mumbled, his head hanging low before he glanced to catch Janet studying him over the rim of her cup.

'I have coffee, thanks.'

'It's like the school doesn't give a shit about Ali. They don't seem to be helping at all.'

'Yes.' Janet mulled the words. 'There's a process they have to follow. You look exhausted, Trevor. Come here and sit down. Let me do that.'

Trevor turned the water on to boil and leaned heavily against the Formica drawers. His hands wouldn't settle, so he pushed them up through his hair and into his pockets. The small seating area created by an old wooden two-seater with scratchy fabric meant they faced each other. Their legs almost touched.

They sat awkwardly for a while. Both staring intently at the mugs gripped in their hands.

'I haven't seen or heard from Ali since Friday,' Janet started, shifting on the small sofa and turning her legs towards Trevor. 'I thought he might have called me or something.'

'There's a lot going on,' Trevor said. More than any of them wanted to deal with.

'I need to give a statement later today.'

'I understand that, but have you really not seen… Has Ali been in touch at all?'

'No.'

Her mouth turned down, and a sadness sat behind her eyes in a way he wasn't used to seeing. She usually looked steeled and ready to pounce. Now a fragility had moved in—not softer, but brittle, like the wind could catch her and blow her away.

'What can we do?' Janet sounded like she was under water, the words trapped in a bubble, fighting for oxygen, struggling to the surface.

What did she expect from Trevor? Ali once again passed on his problems to someone else. To Trevor, there wasn't much to cling to anymore. Rising in his chest, the bubbles became larger and pushed at his windpipe. A tightening sensation squeezed him from within.

'I don't know. I don't know what to do.' Tears streamed from Trevor's eyes and lashed down his cheeks, beating a path down to his chin. Sobbing, he bent over and pushed the tea away, his face buried in his arms across his knees. He continued through choking tears, 'I don't know what to do. About my course. About him. About anything.'

A shadow shifted and Janet's legs edged closer towards him, slats of light as she shuffled closer.

'You've got every right to feel like this. He's your

friend and you're hurting.'

She rubbed his back for a while, the slow motion calming him down and his breathing steadied.

'Trevor?' she ventured after a while. 'Do you think you should go back home? You're not in a fit state to be here.'

Trevor's mind sharpened. She had every right to know about them. This situation would get worse before it got better, and maybe she could help them. Perhaps Ali was wrong. She probably knew anyway, so what difference did it make?

He raised his head and shoulders, ignoring the throbbing headache forming at his temples.

'There's something you should know. About Ali and—'

Janet's hand snapped up and she cut him off.

'There's nothing I need to know about my son that I can't hear from him myself.' Janet lowered her hand. 'If I know my Alistair, he will have bottled it all up. He pushes everyone away because it's what he's always done. Especially, since his father passed—'

Janet seemed to catch herself. Trevor had never seen her this open and honest. It was unnerving.

He swallowed. A great stone stuck in his throat and rolled down to the pit of his stomach. He wiped his hands across his face, pushing the remaining tears away from his eyes, and wiped his hands on his trouser legs.

'You'll have to talk to Ali then. It's not my business anymore.' He'd tried, and if she didn't want to know, what could he do? His hand swept back and forth across the rough material of the sofa.

'I'm sure he will when he's ready. It's not like him to keep something from me for this long. Usually he blows up but will reach out eventually.'

Their eyes met and Trevor took in the creases and lines around her eyes. Her lips pursed, and he knew she could spit venom when provoked. He'd seen her in action in the classroom. All the kids knew not to cross Mrs Morgan.

Instead, her eye twitched at the corner, and a thin smile crept up into her cheeks. She placed a hand on Trevor's arm and gave it a squeeze. Trevor tensed but didn't pull away.

'If you've got something you need to get out, Trevor, then you should. But find the right time for you. There's some people in this world who are going to cause you problems. But one of them won't be me. I let people be themselves. It's their business, not mine.'

Her hand rested on his arm for a beat before she removed it and stood up. 'You've been a good friend to Ali.'

Trevor glanced around the room. His bag remained by the counter, but a sense of calm claimed him, and he leaned into it because he hadn't felt in control for a few days now. Obviously, Janet wanted to acknowledge Ali's sexuality—not from him, but it was good to know she wasn't a monster. And she was right, it wasn't his place to share it.

'I'm going to stay here for a bit. Get this work finished.' Trevor sniffed and pushed himself to his feet.

'Good. Good for you.'

Half an hour later, they'd settled into silence. Trevor had sketched out the reflection forms for the classes and chewed his pen, watching Janet tilt her head as she studied something on her laptop screen.

The drab staff room door thudded shut a few minutes after the bell rang. A few teachers pushed their way through and crowded around the kettle.

Trevor watched as some of the whispering stopped after a couple of nudges and widened side-eyes in Janet's direction.

'What's happened?' Janet levelled her gaze on Celestine's drooping shoulder pads. Trevor paused mid-chew, sensing Celestine bristling.

The drama teacher raised her eyebrows to the bearded, pot-bellied IT teacher who stopped whispering a minute too late. Janet stood and closed her laptop with one swift movement and approached them.

'Janet, we didn't expect you to come in today.' Celestine stepped towards Janet with her hand outstretched. She gripped her arm and pulled her closer. 'Is it true? About Ali. He had been seeing Smith and Addler from year eleven?'

Janet stepped back, her lips turned to a snarl. '*Seeing?* I think you're wildly off the mark there, Celestine.'

Trevor wanted to shout at them. Ali wouldn't ever do something out of order, especially not with a student. But something held Trevor back. Stopped him from defending Ali.

'Addler's mother was in earlier. Chewed out Ladner.' The IT teacher pulled a face and shrugged.

'I can't believe it,' said Celestine. Her face inches from Janet's. Celestine moistened her lips with a flick of her tongue. 'Ali never seemed the type to get into trouble. I mean, we knew he enjoyed a good time, but this…' Ali was known as a caring teacher, but he had definitely taken off more Mondays in the past year than ever before. Trevor's chest ached. They were saying Ali was closer to these students than he'd ever mentioned. He'd lied. Ali didn't even tell Trevor the day it happened. A pit sat sour in Trevor's stomach. If Ali could lie about that, then he could lie about anything.

'It's not true.' Janet swept her hand over her auburn hair, smoothing it down. Then she wiped her hands on her woollen skirt. She shook her head and glanced at Trevor. His jaw ached and he couldn't stop staring. Slowly, he lowered the pen to the table.

Celestine glanced Trevor's direction and lowered her voice. 'I heard the police are involved?' The sound bounced around the silent room.

'What would you know?' Janet hissed back. She began collecting her things from the desk and pushed some pens and her laptop into a shoulder bag.

'Someone said… you know, there's been something going on between some of the teachers.' Celestine remained still, her arms crossed tight on her chest, but her gaze caught Trevor's momentarily before she looked away. 'I wondered if Ali was involved.'

Trevor's mind cleared after the intense look in

Celestine's eyes washed over him. So what if she knew about them? The IT teacher and his colleague edged back by the other sofa.

Celestine's hand rose to Janet, but Janet brushed it away. 'And we just wanted to do what was right by the schoo—'

'That's my son.' Janet hoisted the bag onto her shoulder. 'And don't for a second try to wrap up your nasty little gossip in love and caring for this school, Celestine. Keep your nose out.'

It seemed Celestine could barely hide her disappointment, and she remained standing with her eyes on Janet. 'You'll call me, won't you? If you need anything.'

Celestine rolled her eyes to the two seated men when Janet turned her back for the door.

'Yes. Sure. Sure. Thanks, Cel,' Janet muttered under her breath, before grabbing the metal door handle. She glanced back at Trevor as she closed the door behind her. He raised his hand in a small wave. What else was there to do?

Once the echo of the closed door subsided, the two male teachers leaned together, nodding along. They both appeared enthralled by whatever Celestine was regaling them with from the sofa.

Trevor stepped over to the trio huddled together. Might as well find out what they knew. They seemed plugged in to all the gossip flying about the school. The others didn't appear to notice him, but he caught Celestine's attention.

'Do you know much about Simon Smith?' Trevor dropped the question casually.

'Smith? Addler's little wingman, right?' the IT teacher replied.

'Pair of troublemakers, those two,' the other one grumbled.

Celestine looked up at the clock on the wall and stood.

'I think he has an older brother who attended here. George. He was in my drama class a few years ago.'

The IT teacher smoothed his hands over his stomach and tucked in the loose ends of his shirt. 'He got bullied pretty bad, if I remember right. Weird his little bro starts hanging out with our current bully number one from the day Addler arrived here.'

It didn't make sense why Simon was wrapped up in this. Michael must have had a pretty big sway over him to drag him out to a gay club. He'd assumed they were straight, but now he wasn't sure—it didn't seem to add up. He mumbled something about getting his things together and moved away from the group.

'Bell's about to go. See you later.' They gathered their bags to leave.

Trevor's phone buzzed moments after the door clicked shut behind them.

The text said Ali wanted to meet him later outside the school. Ali had some questions to answer at this point. He needed to stop trying to protect everyone around him because he was doing more damage than any of them could handle.

Twelve

Trevor's eyes burned, and he typed up the last sections of the lesson plan on autopilot. All the excitement of the months leading up to completing the course had disappeared last Friday night. Each sheet of planning represented a day, a week, or a month on this teaching journey he'd taken. Getting through this meant more than just a certificate; it meant he'd succeeded, and he could go back to his parents proud that he hadn't let them down. They'd already be giving up so much because of how he lived his life. By being gay, he wouldn't be able to give them the grandchildren they craved. Returning home with a qualification had been his dream for the longest time, and Ali had stood next to him in all those dreams, but it looked like completing the course would have to do.

He should have felt elated, but an emptiness spread through his insides. The whole time in England had been a sham. As he stared at the dark brown rings left by the coffee mugs, his attention tossed about the room. The cheap pine cupboards, the dingy lighting, and grey upholstered sofas. He left his hometown for this? A wave of nausea washed over him.

The text from Ali said meet in the carpark. They could talk, and even get a chance to move things forward. They could get through this, they had survived the other stuff, this would be the same. But that all seemed like his dream. Being civil with Ali would be enough for today, but Ali had been bullshitting his way through life for too long. Someone needed to show him that lying to those you love wasn't good enough anymore. Janet wouldn't.

He knew Ali—or did he? His mind raced to that first guy in China. Guys could be jerks, utter scumbag assholes. They screwed around, took what they wanted, and anyone offended was labelled a boiler or a bitch because they expressed some sort of feeling. He wanted to be there for Ali; they should be facing this together, not alone.

Outside, the grey sky promised an imminent dumping of snow. The sharp corners of the Victorian school took the wind and threw it across both sides into the playground that extended out to the wrought iron railings before meeting the road.

Trevor bundled up his coat and gripped his satchel, but his foot shot out at an angle and he almost tumbled over. His fear of falling was a hangover from growing up in China where everything was a peril. His heart thudded in his chest. Every story from his parents or older aunts was wrapped up in some hidden danger in the air, the water he might drown in, or a stranger waiting around some dark corner to sweep him away. Surrounded by everyone living in fear—or perhaps they were just looking out for him—had left him ill at ease.

The thudding continued as he spotted Ali on the other side of the road wearing the coat Trevor had gifted him last Christmas. It was grey, woollen, and came down to his ankles. He'd said Ali looked like a millionaire financier. Ali didn't know Trevor had saved for two months and spent the last of his bursary money on it.

A blue knitted hat perched on Ali's head. His ears poked out, pink-hued against the dull sky behind him. His face looked thinner, his cheeks a little sunken. It had only been a few days since their fight, but Trevor didn't want to think about what had passed between them. It hurt too much.

'Hey.' Ali spoke first, his hands deep in the coat pockets and his shoulders up. An impassable distance at this point, so they stood the width of the pavement apart.

Trevor took a step closer because he wanted to wrap his arms around Ali's warm body and pull him closer under that coat. He wanted to bite his neck, nibble on his ear, and get out of freezing London for a few days, or weeks.

'You look tired,' Trevor blurted. He wanted to apologise but didn't know where to begin and didn't know if he should be saying sorry. It could all be smoothed over, but the shit between them hung thick and cloying. To know where to begin, which piece to balance first, seemed beyond them. Did they deal with Addler first and ignore Ali's growing drink problem? Or did they need to fix that first? They'd talked it over many times before and never got further than a week off the booze. A week later celebrated by a night worse than the previous month combined.

'Let's walk.' Ali jerked his head away from the school. He looked furtive, like a man on the run. Ali didn't hold eye contact with Trevor and looked at the school looming across the road instead.

Trevor jogged to catch up with Ali, who was moving at a rapid pace. The main road cut straight ahead and continued all the way down Easton Road. All the while, Trevor followed the hunched-up shoulders in the grey coat.

After a few hundred yards, the school now well out of sight, Ali slowed his pace and paused for Trevor to catch up.

'In here.' He tipped his head towards one of the rail arches under the sandstone bridge. A freight train rumbled overhead, but the grime—thick and impenetrable—didn't budge. The door to a small cafe shook in Trevor's hand as he followed Ali through into the brightly lit interior.

Small circular tables lined the space, all empty apart from an old man holding a mug of tea, and a black dog at his feet that jerked its head around as they entered. It quickly settled down, both paws supporting its head, and continued to ignore them.

'Two teas. Thanks,' Ali called to the woman in a floral apron wiping around the counter at the back of the rectangular space.

Ali took the seat facing the door and stared at it over Trevor's shoulder.

They sat in silence for a moment. Trevor felt his back heating up now they were indoors and began to shuffle his coat off.

'So,' Ali said, his gaze never leaving the entrance.

'So?' Trevor shot a quick look at the door over his shoulder and adjusted his coat on the chair. How would they ever get past this? Tension coursed through Trevor's shoulders, causing him to shudder. Ali licked his lips and tore a napkin into shreds.

'What's going on at school? Are they all talking about it? I bet they are. Fucking Celestine's having a field day, right?' Ali spoke feverishly, the words tumbling out in quick succession as he sucked on his teeth. Trevor had never seen him like this before.

'It's a bit weird...' Trevor began, but felt the steam being drawn out of him. He didn't know what to say. Ali had this effect on him. He planned out what he wanted to say and how he'd be strong this time, but his resolve fell away in the moment. Ladner had advised him he shouldn't be talking to Ali at all as he might be called as a witness.

'A bit... weird. huh?' Ali drew out the final sound like it was something unusual and he wouldn't have considered it such.

'Are you okay, Ali? You seem... I don't know. Are you eating?'

Ali met Trevor's gaze straight on. His eyes were red-ringed and bloodshot. His lips were dry and partially cracked. In the harsh light of the cafe, he looked much worse than he had outside.

'Am I eating?' Ali hung his head to one side and peered at Trevor. He narrowed his eyes and looked like he wanted to say something more.

He didn't.

Trevor continued. 'You need to look after yourself. Whatever happens. This could go on for a couple of months, right?'

'Yeah. Or longer. It's a waiting game and I've got fuck all else to do.'

'Like if there's a trial or something.' He covered his face with his hands. It didn't bear thinking about. 'God, I don't know, Ali. I've never been involved in something like this before.'

Ali's reply was cut off by the woman in the floral apron approaching and placing two mugs between them. She slipped their bill under the salt shaker before indicating the sugar packets in a little wicker basket.

'Why did you ask me here, Ali?'

'I wanted to see if you could remember something. I talked with a lawyer this morning and they said I need to get the facts straight. They said the police will be talking to Michael and that other kid this week. That's all I know.'

'I've already told you what I can remember. And Ladner took my statement this morning. They don't care about the club, but they think you propositioned him at some point.'

Ali chewed his lip, but the hard lines around his eyes softened slightly.

'The school put him up to it. His mother. You've

seen the state of things at the moment.'

'What do you mean?'

'They're out to get me.'

Trevor blew out through his lips.

'Is that what you were shouting at him? Some sort of crusade. Or was it about sex?' All Trevor could see was Ali's rapidly moving mouth and his lips close to the guy's ear. His eyes had looked glazed over, but that wasn't anything special. A smile had played on Ali's lips. He hadn't looked angry. If anything, he'd looked pleased with himself.

Ali narrowed his eyes and sat back. 'Why would I be shouting at someone about sex? Jesus, Trevor. Use your brain.'

Trevor winced and busied his hands with a sugar sachet. That hurt.

Ali flattened his hands on the table. 'Someone's put them up to it. I'd swear anything on it.' Trevor kept his gloved hands to himself and hid them behind the mug.

'Someone at school said he's got a brother,' Trevor offered.

'Who?'

'Simon. Simon Smith. He's the one you were closest to? I was talking to Janet about it—'

'What? When were you talking to her?' Ali's eyes gleamed. He sat rigid in the wooden chair.

'Just now. I didn't tell her anything. But she looked right through me. Felt like she knew everything.'

'Yeah. She does that.'

Trevor brushed away some sugar from the tabletop.

'You know what she's like. Anyway, you should call her, she's worried about you.'

Ali's gaze returned to the door, his mouth twitching at the corner as if he might burst into a great smile, but his eyes remained dark and unlikely to break out into anything positive.

'I will.'

Ali looked terrified, as if someone or something awaited him outside that door. Sophie's words pushed into Trevor's head. *Let him fix this, by himself. Being there and smothering him is only going to make it worse. Be rational.*

'So, they were both in the club.' Trevor moved the two cups towards the corner. 'And Addler at least knew you beforehand, from school. But why you? It can't just be that they hate gays and picked you at random.' Trevor tapped the knuckle of his little finger against the edge of the table. It didn't make any sense. Why Ali?

Trevor's gaze darted about the cafe. The dog raised its head and sniffed the air.

'So let's say, hypothetically, Smith thinks you asked him for sex in the club on the Saturday. What's happened or how is Michael involved so he confronts you in the corridor the next week?'

This was like a Sudoku puzzle, but one of the pieces was missing. Trevor hummed as he thought. He'd always had to visualise something to try and get to the bottom of it.

'You believe him, don't you?' Ali spoke, almost a whisper. He squinted at Trevor like he was trying to read his mind. Trevor shifted in his seat.

'Fuck's sake, Ali. I don't know what to believe.'

'I thought you would trust me. I thought you would believe me.'

Trevor scratched his nose. 'I did.' He corrected himself. 'I do.' He moved his gloved hand towards Ali's clenched in front of him. His fingers traced circles, each finger getting a workout from the other.

'You don't. You believe him. You wouldn't even stand up for me.' Ali's nostrils flared.

'Ladner said I shouldn't even be seeing you,' Trevor hissed. He glanced around, not that anyone they knew would be here, but because Ali looked unhinged and made him feel like shit. 'I've got to give my statement to the police after this.'

The waitress stopped whispering to the man with the dog, who turned at the same time. They were obviously talking about them.

'Fine. Fuck. What the actual fuck? You go back there, Trevor. Take what you want from me.'

'Why are you saying this?'

'I thought you'd be there for me. You broke my fucking heart.'

'We don't have to do this, Ali.' He grabbed Ali's hands, but one of the mugs of tea caught his wrist and tipped off the table. It shattered with a crash, sending tea splashing up the white painted wall.

The woman gave a tiny shriek, jumped up to grab a brush, and as Trevor stood frozen, Ali heaved himself up and pulled his coat up around his neck.

Ali grabbed his keys from the table. He missed, but

on the second try pulled them into his pocket.

He shoved past the woman and paused by the door. He stared at Trevor for a long time before leaving.

But as he'd shoved past and said, 'Goodbye, Trevor,' Trevor smelled it on him. He hadn't noticed before, but nothing could cover the smell of alcohol on his breath. He'd been drinking.

'That'll be two-fifty for them teas.'

Trevor pulled his own coat up around his shoulders and neck. The woman hovered around with the dustpan and brush propped up against the table.

'Here's a tenner. Sorry about the mug.'

She beamed at the crisp note and slipped it into her apron pocket. 'No problem, darling. These things happen. Is your friend alright?'

Trevor watched through the glass door as Ali turned the corner at the end of the road.

He saw now that Ali didn't need saving from anything Trevor had done. He needed saving from the fucked-up family who had never listened, let him get away with being a spoiled brat, and never told him he wasn't the centre of the universe.

'I don't know, if I'm honest. I don't think he is okay.'

Ali needed a good talking to. He needed to talk out so much of this unresolved stuff in his head. Ali rounded the corner, and Trevor turned to help the woman pick up the broken pieces of mug scattered across the floor.

'But I think he might get better.'

Thirteen

Ali closed the door behind him and headed out through the hotel lobby. Staying in the room wasn't an option tonight. After downing most of a bottle of wine, he was horny and needed to pick some guy up. To fuck, to forget, to not have Trevor swimming around and around his mind any longer.

As he moved down the street, a lightness, a freeness settled on him. Breaking up with Trevor was probably the smartest thing he'd done in a while. His dad was right after all. Men like him weren't meant to have relationships that lasted.

The corner bar came into view, its windows blocked out with rainbow flags and yellow light bleeding out onto the sandstone wall.

A familiar pulse shivered up his arm before he pushed open the door to the bar. Orange and purple lights washed over his black rain jacket as he entered the space. Twenty or so men milled about, some leaning on the bar, some with their backs to the wall, and a few spread out on the small tables dotting the space. Glasses lined the back shelves and a bartender preened himself in the mirrored wall at the back of the bar area. It looked busy for a Monday night.

'Vodka and orange, please, mate.' Ali slid a note across the bar. 'And a couple of shots of tequila.' The bar man gathered up the note and turned to pour his drinks.

Ali scanned the small club. Couples huddled in dark corners. Some stroked dimmed faces, some held hands or leaned casually into each other at the edge of the tiny dancefloor. A DJ raised their arm in a salute like they were tearing the roof off a club in Ibiza. This place was smaller than DV8, more of a place to hook up than dance.

'Hey.' A pair of legs, encased in tight denim, slid into the seat next to him.

Ali raised his gaze but was caught off guard by the eyes trained on him. A grin played out on the guy's face. The brightness of his bluish-grey eyes made Ali lean in closer for a better look.

'Wow. Your eyes are gorgeous.' The words were out of his mouth before he could think.

The guy laughed and extended a hand for Ali to shake. 'You can thank my grandma for her genes. She put all the effort in sending me over here from Ghana.'

'Well, thanks to your grandma.' Ali shyly raised his glass. 'What's your name?'

'Osei. But most people call me Osei.' He grinned at Ali. Their gaze locked, but he broke away to glance down to Ali's groin area.

'You single?'

'It's complic—Yeah, I am.' Not much use in holding

back now. Trevor had made his decision. It was time to move on. 'Give me your number.'

Osei raised an eyebrow. 'Fast mover.'

'In case I lose you later,' Ali winked. Osei thumbed in his number and pressed Call.

Turning over Ali's hand, Osei placed the phone on his outstretched palm and closed Ali's fingers around it. With their fingers intertwined, he pulled Ali towards the narrow strip of space that barely passed for a dancefloor.

They danced across from the bar. Their hips slid against each other as the music pounded around them. Osei's arm draped around Ali's back and pulled him in closer.

'Where are you staying tonight, Osei?' Riled up from the vodka drinks that kept coming his way, Ali felt fabulous. Osei's hands explored his backside, and he wasn't thinking about Trevor.

'I was planning on taking a taxi back home later.' Osei winked at Ali. 'Unless you've got other ideas?'

'I do,' Ali grinned.

Osei led him further onto the dancefloor, raising Ali's arms higher until he pulled his shoulders and used them to manoeuvre Ali into a kiss. Their lips locked, the sweet taste of alcohol and juice mingling together.

Ali pushed towards the bar and downed another shot, waving at the bartender for more drinks. He glanced at Osei's tall frame from the bar. His shoulders were huge and bulked out. This guy could carry two guys, one on each shoulder. A smile played across his lips when Ali handed him the drink.

'I'm going for a smoke. Don't go anywhere.' Ali felt a rush of warmth when Osei pecked him on his cheek.

Ali leaned up against the wall outside. The damp, cool bricks pleasant against his back. He leaned into someone's cupped palm for a flame; a moan escaped his lips when the nicotine hit the spot. Lights above his head burned bright, swimming in front of him like golden fish, thundering in and out of his vision. His heart pounded in his rib cage. His mouth dry. Ali patted down his pockets looking for his phone. He wanted to call Trevor. He'd tell him what he was missing by leaving him. It was Trevor's loss now. The cold bricks scraped at his back in the space above his belt and his T-shirt rode up, but his knees slumped him forward. The ground glistened with rainwater, and it coated the sides of his white trainers.

'Need help?' Osei dragged him to his feet. 'You're in a right state. Come on.'

'Fit. You look fit.' Ali leered and swayed in front of Osei. 'Come to my hotel.'

Osei stepped backwards, pulled him upright, and led him through the bar and towards a bank of waiting taxis.

***

Bright yellow light burned Ali's vision. He rolled over, his temple throbbing. He reached out to touch Trevor's neck. But his hand didn't run across familiar skin.

'Hey.' Thick eyebrows knitted together on a wrinkled forehead that ran into curly brown hair.

The guy hauled himself up on one burly arm as thick

as Ali's leg. Beefcake.

'My head. Jesus.' Ali reached out for the glass on his nightstand.

Fuck. What was this guy's name?

'You're not a big fan of the Almighty J, from what you said last night.'

'What do you mean? Ugh, what did I say?' Ali groaned.

'Those two guys. Jesus and… what was his name? Taylor.'

'Trevor.'

'Yeah. You talked a lot about them. Mostly Trev though.'

'I'm sorry. It was probably a terrible night.'

'No. But you should talk to him.'

'Who, Jesus? You think he'd listen?' Ali tried to smile and sit up. His head ached and the white cotton sheets were so bright, he felt his eyes might explode.

'You need to get some closure. You obviously still have feelings for him.'

'I do. But not like that. It's just too weird.'

'You said that a lot last night as well.'

'Just what I need. Someone who remembers everything.'

This man was hot. Ali couldn't deny it.

'Did we…? You know. Last night?' Ali's cheeks heated like an infatuated teen with a crush.

'You don't remember? It was the best.' He started to laugh. 'No. We didn't, you were too wasted.'

'Thank you.' Ali tried to hide behind the pillows

around the top end of the bed.

'For what?'

'For looking after me.' Fuck.

'No problem. Just talk to your friend. Okay?' He leaned in and made sure Ali kept eye contact with him. 'I think you'll feel better.'

Ali scratched at his head and scanned the floor for his clothes. All he could see was a pair of black jeans and a sock.

'This is cringe. But I can't remember your name.' Ollie, wasn't it?

'You've got a bad memory, man. It's Osei.'

'Okay. Okay. Let's see if I can make it up to you before we get something to eat.'

Ali rolled the duvet over their heads and pulled it down over the curly hair and beefy arms of the man lying on his side in the hotel bed.

After a shower, they stepped into the bright daylight and headed for some food around the corner from the hotel.

'What do you do, Osei?' Ali alternated between sipping from a large mug of tea and taking small bites out of a white bread bacon sandwich dripping with brown sauce.

Osei smiled and leaned back in his chair. He had a cute way of running his hand over his jaw.

'Let me show you.' He reached down into the pocket of his tan leather jacket hanging over the back of the chair. He swiped up to unlock the phone screen and thumbed through some photos.

He turned the phone to face Ali. After wiping his fingers on a paper napkin, Ali scanned a couple of the images.

They were all pictures of houses. But not fancy or smartly refurbished houses. Each image contained a room, or a couple of rooms, badly in need of repair. Paint peeled from walls, walls festered with stains or black mould in the corners. The final image showed a bathroom plastered in avocado shades, each surface dulled with grime and dust.

'What is this? You work in horror movies?'

'These are social houses, Ali. Across the greater London area.'

'Oh. You're a landlord?'

'Sort of.'

'They're a bit nasty looking, if I'm being honest.'

Osei took back the phone. 'Agree. They are a bit. They're not mine. We find places for homeless families, refugees, and people like that.'

'And you put them in those places?'

'That's the UK housing stock. It's a bit messed up. Especially at the moment.'

'Do you enjoy it?'

'I like helping people.' The words sailed from Osei's lips and caught Ali a left hook under his chin. He sat back. 'My grandmother moved me out of Ghana when I was in high school.'

'Because you're gay?'

'She saw the way I was different. And my parents were getting deeper into their religion back then.'

'That's fucked up.'

'Yeah.' Osei rubbed a hand over his head.

Ali's tea tasted cold on his lips. 'I've read about those laws. You were lucky to get out.'

Osei nodded.

'I've always felt I should help people. It's like I'm paying my grandmother back for saving me. If I don't, I'll let her down and let myself down.'

'You're a nice guy, Osei.' Ali had never been in danger for being gay. Osei could have been arrested, beaten, or worse. Tears pricked at Ali's eyes. A hangover's wave of emotion, but it gripped his chest. Trevor had told him of needing to escape and not feeling safe back in China.

Trevor would be getting his portfolio ready. Making those unit plans covered in multicoloured pen, tiny sticky notes, and scribbles that only made sense to him.

Fuck. What was he doing?

Ali missed Trevor.

Osei looked good; there was no denying that. But Trevor was a familiar feeling, an arm wrapped around his waist, a light shining in the darkness. The way his stomach hair grew around his navel and his leg hair was thick and black. Trevor hated it, but Ali loved tracing his fingers up the backs of his legs and feeling the muscles tense and tighten as he tried not to struggle against his touch.

Ali stared at Osei's hands. Osei clasped them in front of him, both hands wrapped around the phone. He looked quizzically at Ali, his eyes narrowed and head tipped to one side.

'Earth to Ali.' Osei's words snapped him out of his mind fog.

'Let's get another tea.' Ali scratched at his chin. 'I'm like a desert after all that drinking. Do you not feel rough?'

'You had a lot.' Osei chuckled before pushing his chair back and heading towards the counter in the cafe to order more drinks. He raised his hand to gesture at the blackboard and some desserts.

With his arm raised, his back muscles stood out against his black T-shirt. The arm cuff sat snuggly around his bicep as he motioned upwards with his hand.

This needed to be a one-night thing. *I can't get involved with this guy.*

Once seated again, Osei blew out a breath over the mug. 'Now that I think about it, I might need another few hours of sleep.'

Ali put his head in his hands. 'I fucked up real bad.'

Osei placed a hand on Ali's sleeve. He pulled Ali's chin up with his other hand. His gaze never left Ali's and, all the while, a thumb ran across his jawline from his hairline to his chin.

Ali shook his hand away and continued staring at the table.

'It was just a few drinks. You're gonna do the walk of shame right out of here and go back to bed. Just sleep it off.'

'It's not that easy.'

Osei frowned and tilted his head to one side again.

'How so?'

Ali took a deep breath in and ran his hands over his head. A soft groan escaped his lips. 'I've done something. Something bad.'

'Does it involve that guy? The one you wouldn't shut up about last night?' he grinned.

'Yes. And the school where I work thinks I did something with one of the students.'

'Fuck.'

The words hung between them for a moment. A soft muttering came from behind as an elderly couple entered the cafe and spent time finding a seat, scraping back chairs, and busying themselves taking off coats.

'I keep thinking about what I've done. How it's so fucked up.'

'Is it true?' Osei looked concerned and glanced around the cafe. The waitress had her back to them, talking to the couple, leaning in, and calling out the options they had for lunch.

'He won't forgive me.' Ali started to cry, his shoulders shaking as a million pieces of the puzzle from the last few days flowed up into his eyes.

He should never have let it go this far. From the outset, he should have seen it. Trevor had been beside him, in his quiet and calm way, but he had stood there. And Ali had pushed and pushed until finally, he'd broken away. Trevor was gone.

Ali's fingers reached together, but they shook and shook. He placed his hands around a silver container that burst with sachets of ketchup and brown sauce. His hands continued to shake, and the tails of the sauce packets shook like fans in the wind.

'He's too young. He shouldn't have to deal with this. It's my mess. I approached him in the first place. It's so fucked up—'

Osei pushed his chair back and stood up.

'That's fucking sick. You did that?' he hissed at Ali.

Ali's hands gripped harder on the sauce container.

'I thought I loved him. But I was too scared to see it through.' Tears streamed down Ali's face. Osei looked horrified; his mouth hung open. The couple had stopped talking with the waitress and were staring at Ali sobbing in the wooden chair. 'I do love him.'

'He's a kid. Fucking hell.' Osei clamped his mouth shut.

'We were meant to spend Christmas together. And now he's gone. And I don't know how to get him back.' The words came out spluttered through sobs as they stuck in his throat.

'You're a teacher, for fuck's sake. You're sick.' Osei spat out the words.

Osei backed away from Ali's table. He kept on moving backwards like Ali was radioactive.

'What do you mean? Teachers can't be gay? You think that…'

Osei's eyes looked suddenly haunted, framed with red around the white edges of his eyes. A dark shadow passed over his expression and he pulled away.

Osei bumped into the table behind and a chair clattered to the floor. The waitress moved over and tried to put her arm up like a barricade to the other tables.

'Sir. I am going to have to ask you both to leave. I'm sorry, but you're scaring the customers.'

Osei pointed a finger at Ali.

'He's sick. He took advantage of a kid.' Osei looked repulsed, and his eyes flashed. He grabbed at his jacket and bag. 'You sick fuck.'

Ali spluttered and coughed, drowning in his own tears.

'No. No,' he muttered through sobs, unable to get more words out to reply.

The elderly pair threw each other furtive glances, and the woman began to gather her purse and turned to pull on her jacket from the chair. She gestured and beckoned for the man with her to follow.

Osei stood for a second before backing away from Ali without another word. The waitress looked back and forth between them.

'Don't call me. Ever. You sick fuck.' He yanked the door open and pulled it closed with a bang.

Sunlight glided in through the open window and dust particles streamed by. The silence lay thick, and the waitress settled the couple back down with soothing hushes. She crossed to the counter, giving Ali a wide berth. The couple leaned in close together and whispered, all the while throwing glances at Ali's quivering form.

Ali stood up, pushed the chair back quickly. The metal legs scarred the linoleum flooring with dark scratches.

'I love him,' Ali said to no one. The waitress moved

her hand across to the white plastic phone attached to the wall.

Ali's hand fumbled for his phone. The room spun. If he didn't do it now, then he never would. His father had gone, but his presence hung over him. Wiping tears from his eyes, he stabbed his finger at the phone screen. The dial tone echoed back in his ear.

'Hello. Ali?' The tinny voice tickled his ear.

'Hi. It's me. Can you come down to the Westgate Cafe?' Ali's hand shook.

'Right now? Is everything okay? It'll take me an hour or so to get there.'

'That's fine. I can wait.'

'Okay. See you soon.'

'Thanks, Mum.'

Fourteen

'So you remember next to nothing?' The police officer leaned across the desk. A pen spun between his fingers. He pointed it at Trevor when he asked yet another question.

'Like I said, just two friends, and we'd gone out for some drinks to celebrate.'

'Celebrate what?' The officer's boredom was palpable.

'Coming to the end of my training.' They'd been over this twice now in the past two hours. This guy wasn't even listening. 'I did it part-time, so it took longer.'

It was second nature to Trevor to deflect questions about his personal life. There wasn't even a relationship anymore. They *were* just friends, they worked in the same building, and that was it.

'And Mr Morgan was drunk? Did he always get drunk when you went out?'

'Ali had a few drinks. I'd say he liked to have fun.' At Trevor's comment, the officer raised his eyebrows and wrote something on a pad in front of him.
'And you didn't recognise the students in the club?'

'There were these two lads in the club. I'd never seen them before. Even now, I'm not sure I could place them. We talked to different people all night.'

Just like friends would.

Trevor squeezed his fingers together. A chill had settled across his body over the past week, and he'd been unable to shift it.

'Nothing stood out that night,' Trevor continued. 'That place is full of cheap smoke machines and dim lights.' The three of them had stood out as clear as day, but Trevor wasn't going to tell the police about that image burned into his memory.

He couldn't identify them. *No* was what he'd said, and it wasn't a lie. But he knew Ali, and he'd been next to that guy. Their faces almost touching. Did they kiss? He'd said they'd been talking. Just talking from what he could make out, but Ali always made a move, always wanted to take it one step too far.

'Thanks for coming in, Mr Zhang. If we need to talk to you again, we'll be in touch.' Abruptly the officer stood up and motioned for Trevor to follow him out into the waiting area.

Sophie's face beamed when he caught her gaze. The smile didn't reach her eyes, but after he'd signed off two forms, sinking into her arms and warm embrace felt amazing.

Sunlight dappled across Trevor's trainers, but he turned his face away from the sun and shimmied across the bench towards Soph. The tall oak tree in the park opposite the station spread its arms, covering the grey sky with spindly fingers. Clouds, full to the brim with a dumping of snow, circled overhead. He wanted to sleep but getting into the bed alone scared him.

Fear. That's what had driven so many of his choices: leaving China, picking the first guy who glanced his way, and not standing beside Ali. He wasn't even brave enough to bring up his feelings when they talked earlier. He felt drained. It seemed impossible; they could never make it work.

'Earth to Trevor.' Soph's words filtered through the haze. 'What are you thinking about?'

'I've slept better without Ali waking me up multiple times during the night.' Soph looked at him, pity evident in her expression. 'Either he'd stumble in drunk, singing and laughing to himself, or he'd be out in the kitchen trying to be quiet but failing miserably.'

'It's for the best, you know that, right?'

'The bed's always cold in the morning and I'd reach out during the night to grab Ali's hand, but it wasn't there this morning.'

'It gets easier, babe.' Sophie meant well, but he could tell she was getting frustrated.

'Ali probably doesn't miss me. He said I broke his heart.'

'You need some space. Did the police say anything you didn't know?'

'Not really.'

A Christmas tree glimmered in the ground-floor flat across the street. He rarely saw them in China growing up, but they were everywhere here. A sign of coming together and family. They'd fought before. He hadn't realised how fractured they'd become even before this mess began. Between them, shouldn't they be able to talk about these things?

'The first time… the *only* time he hit me, the rage behind Ali's eyes boiled over. That night after the gym last Christmas.' Ali had always been a bit of a messy drunk. Usually he fell over himself trying to give hugs and express his deepest feelings clouded in beer or wine.

'You guys moved pretty fast. You'd only known him five minutes before—'

'He suggested we move in together. I thought w*hy not?*'

They'd both needed somewhere to live, and they halved their rents by sharing. Low pressure—that was how Ali phrased it when he floated the idea after a couple of dates. Friends with benefits. Trevor had thought they'd start their own family at some point and get their own Christmas tree.

'We moved too fast, that much is obvious now, and we were too casual.' In the back of his mind while the guy in the gym—the one who hogged the hand weights—took him in his mouth and pumped him in the shower cubicle, Trevor had thought of Ali. He would have committed. One partner was enough for him, or it had been. Ali's idea of a relationship was more flexible.

They had never really discussed it, but Trevor knew the sound the dating app made. Every gay person recognised it. They'd been eating spaghetti and Ali had checked his phone. He didn't try to hide it. Laughed that the guy was a needy bitch. But it felt wrong; Trevor, caught off guard, hadn't stopped him or said anything. So he'd decided to do the same.

'I never wanted an open relationship. I should have pushed back—stopped trying to make Ali feel how he felt. I should have talked to him and not tried to make Ali jealous.' Trevor wiped tears from his eyes. The fingerless gloves soaked up some of the tears and chilled his cheeks.

Sophie didn't speak but rested her head on his shoulder. Last Christmas should have been the worst moments of his life. They'd promised each other that was it—things would get better.

'The Christmas tree stood crooked and bent out of shape until New Year's and I threw it out onto the street. I couldn't stand looking at it anymore.'

'What did he say afterwards?'

'He flooded me with apologies and lamented his behaviour. He hadn't meant it, it wouldn't happen again, and he couldn't believe he'd reacted like that.'

Trevor could because he'd seen it before. The same hypocritical behaviour as his uncle. So he gave Ali one more chance. He told him if he ever touched him again, that would be it, it would be over. And he hadn't—things had been better.

'It's been good. Until our anniversary... and his dad's death. Until Michael Addler.'

'Oh, Trevor.' Sophie wiped away a tear. 'I hate seeing you like this.'

Clouds hung heavy on the horizon behind the buildings rising to the west. He'd have to head home soon and face the flat and start to get things in order.

Janet hadn't turned her back on him like he'd expected. There was something behind her eyes earlier. Something he'd never seen before, like he saw the young woman she'd once been. They shared a love for Ali, and they were both concerned—but they had both failed to protect themselves from being hurt by him. Ali's choices had swept them up, and they both lay discarded in his wake. This wasn't the love Trevor had watched in movies or read about in books. This love ached and gripped at his chest. They'd become desperate, but he couldn't sit back and watch it all fall apart.

Trevor gripped the edge of the bench. The cold dug into his palms.

'Ali said the school put those lads up to it.' Their school was Catholic, but it hadn't caused them any major problems. They'd stayed in the shadows, and the school had left them alone. That was never enough for Ali, though. He wanted to wage a war and battle against them. Mel, once she became Catholic, had become distant and he noticed how all her ideas became filtered through the ideas of the church.

'Do you think that makes sense, though? Why would some kids go after Ali?' Soph couldn't wrap her head around it, Trevor knew that.

The tips of his fingers turned white and stung, chilling him up through his knuckles.

Simon Smith was Addler's friend. He was in the club

on their anniversary.

'Did they know it was our anniversary? How would they know that? The only place we posted anything was our private Facebook. And we don't even use our real names there.'

Trevor wracked his brain about Ali's past. He'd lived in St Paul's his whole life. But someone close to them, most likely to Ali, knew about Ali and Trevor. And Michael and Simon had picked up on it.

'It doesn't make sense.' Ali wouldn't try to hide anything. That much Trevor knew for sure. Ali had no filter and flirted with anyone with a pulse, but he wasn't a creep. Ali was going through it; Trevor had never seen him suffer like he looked earlier. Maybe this was a test, something they had to get over. He pushed off from the bench—Ali was a mess—but he wasn't ready to give up yet.

'I've got to figure this out, Soph. I'm in too deep and I won't turn my back on him as well.'

Fifteen

Ali remained slumped in the wooden chair, while the air in the cafe froze—everyone moving in slow motion. The waitress looked across at the elderly couple every now and again. They exchanged wide-eyed stares and whispered between themselves.

'Can I get you anything else? Or the bill?' Smiling only with her mouth, the waitress wiped a cloth over the edge of the table, but Ali shook his head.

The door opened and a mother pushing a stroller, accompanied by two small children, entered the cafe. Janet followed close behind and held the door.

Ali glanced away from her as she settled into the seat opposite. His gaze followed the mother and her children. One dressed in a pink princess outfit and the other as Ultraman. The stroller bumped against a wooden coat stand before they moved towards a table in the middle of the room. Gentle noises bubbled from the boy while the mother expertly arranged him in a chair with a book, and the little girl hopped up onto her lap. The waitress sprang into action and rushed over; she complimented their outfits and took their order, asking about their plans for

Christmas before turning back to the counter.

'Ali.' Janet leaned in, her gaze running over his face. He swallowed, the lump of what he wanted to say stuck in his throat. He'd been transfixed by the display of normal family life. People who seemed to be getting on with things and didn't seem stuck in a rut.

Another person, a gaunt-looking teen, pushed through the door. Fucking doors. Always slamming in Ali's face. Every time someone left him behind or they ran away. Like nobody could bear his company for more than an hour. They upped and left.

'Is everything alright?' Janet's voice sounded dim. Distant. The couple's hushed conversation flittered at his side, but the sounds all ran together around him. In response, Ali's head sank down onto his crossed arms. A wave of nausea rolled in his stomach.

Ali jerked his head up, wiping the rough material of his jacket across his red cheeks and nose. 'What?'

'You asked me to come, Ali. You can at least be civil.' She tsked to herself and wiped at the table with a tissue from her purse.

Steam began to collect on the inside of the window from the barrel-drum kettle boiling on the counter behind them. Ali's shoulders tensed. His mind flashed red; she wouldn't help him, what had he been thinking? Irritation itched at his arms and coursed across his palms.

'You know.' Ali grabbed a handful of napkins from the box on the table. His eyes stung. 'All my problems come from you.'

Janet looked taken aback, but she narrowed her eyes.

'And which problems are they, Ali? The drinking or the—'

'You religious folk. You're all a bunch of god-bothering halfwits. Up on your high horses. Aren't you supposed to preach love and forgiveness?'

Janet appraised him. 'Everyone else is to blame.' She clasped her fingers together, but her thumbs remained rigidly pressed against one another. The pink flesh pushed to a pale shade of white. 'If you want my honest opinion, you need to confront what you have done. That's the first step.'

Ali groaned softly to himself.

'If you hurt someone or took advantage of someone. Then you need to own up to that.' Her teacher's tone. The one she used on him as a kid, and the one she used on his father. The one that made him feel about three inches tall.

'I know I fucked up, but I need to know you'll support me.'

'The bible says we should forgive. But I don't even know what's happened…' She lowered her voice, glancing at the couple and the mother who continued to fuss with the children. The little girl disassembled a bacon sausage sandwich, dropping bits gleefully to the floor. 'You stormed out on Friday.'

'Your precious book also says a lot of other things,' Ali retorted. 'A lot of things that destroy people like me.'

'It's God's place to judge, not mine. We help anyone, without discrimination. And, anyway, you are my son.' Janet crossed her arms. Her lips pursed, a look preserved for when she was digging in. Ali didn't know what she was thinking. How could he have thought she would accept him, or even understand him? She'd pushed their father to drink and now she'd push Ali away. All for her precious church.

'Well, I feel pretty discriminated against. My whole fucking life. And right now, I don't know which side you stand on.'

'I stand on the side of what's right.' Her fingers gripped at her elbows. 'Why are you attacking me? Is this about more than the Addlers?'

Ali slammed his hand down on the table. 'A student is making up that I abused him. Addler's fucking mother has started a crusade against me. To fuck with me and my life'—the words caught in his throat—'and I feel fucking powerless to do anything about it.'

Janet moved her purse closer to her. 'You're angry. And you're right.' Janet's smile froze in a grimace.

'Is that it? That's all you have to say?' Sweat broke out across Ali's forehead and the lights appeared to glow brighter. Everyone's champion, Trevor's fucking mentor, and one of the most respected teachers at the school, but being there for her son—fat chance. 'I don't need your fucking approval.' Ali's jaw ached from gritting his teeth, his hands clenched.

'Ali. Where has this come from? I thought you wanted to talk about what was happening at schoo—'

'Every time I walk into a room, I have to judge if these people are going to laugh at me, or beat the shit out of me.' Ali pointed his finger at the woman seated across the room. She shrank back. 'And every fucking time, I become so incensed with fear about what is going to happen. And you know what?' He lowered both hands to the table.

'I don't know, Ali. You're not telling me what's going on… so I can't help. You should try being kind to yourself.' The pained smile on Janet's lips did little to hide the hurt in her eyes. But Ali pushed on. This wasn't about him anymore; this wasn't his problem at all. It was them. They'd caused this to happen.

'I am this way because you dragged me to that fucking church every Sunday. And all my own mother has to say is 'be kinder to myself.' You. And him. Where was your kindness growing up?'

'What has that got to do with any of this? Ali, you're not making any sense.'

The air felt thick around Ali. 'Dad always made me feel like I was never good enough. Sat there on his high horse, he poisoned me, and you took me to that church and they poisoned me. I don't know who I am anymore. I'm scared that I've turned into him.'

Janet bristled. 'This feels like a rant. Your father and I did the best we could. You need to focus on moving forward. This is your problem.' The steeled look returned to Janet's eyes. 'Stop looking to blame everyone else.'

Ali's eyes screwed up like he'd received a sucker punch to the chest.

'How the fuck can I move on?' he gasped. Tears choked the words, but he couldn't stop. He'd dug into this wound many times before—multiple failed attempts to make sense of his past, but each time he came up short. His father was gone. His mother cared about her precious church and her reputation, basically anything but him.

'If you have done something wrong, you need to find joy again.' Janet's sharp intake of breath was audible in the stilled cafe. 'And maybe talk to someone.'

'I haven't fucking done anything wrong. It's you lot.'

'Then you should seek forgiveness. And be honest.' Janet's tone was steady. He knew she wasn't listening then. Even more than Trevor's parents, she would try to save face, to smooth things over and pretend everything was fine when it clearly wasn't. That same look—the squared jaw with damp eyes—Ali had seen face his father. It meant nothing. She wouldn't change her mind. As long as she could live in her dreamland, she didn't give a rat's arse about him.

'Fuck you.'

Ali kicked the table leg as he lurched to his feet. The table clattered as he pushed aside the surrounding chairs. One flew against the wall and crashed into the adjacent table. Sauce packets and two metal containers clattered to the tile floor. A high-pitched scream came from the waitress at the back of the cafe, and she reached for the phone on the wall. The girl dressed like a princess began to cry and her brother's lip trembled.

'Ali. Stop this.'

'You don't understand what you've done to me.'

Sixteen

Trevor scrolled through Facebook while lying on the bed. His phone pinged, and Ali's Relationship Status changed from *In a relationship* to *Single*. Great, dumped via social media. They'd kept things discreet in the real world, but online they had lived out a normal life as a happy couple. They hadn't met most of the people in real life, but what did that matter? They shared a part of themselves that nobody here in London got to see. Most of the connections were from guys they'd met travelling or at the bars about the city. A sad emoji already hung below Ali's post. The online world moved fast.

Trevor flipped over to Ali's main page where he'd shared his new connection with Osei. Who the hell was Osei?

From his profile page, the guy looked balding and had bug eyes. Ali was doing this just to prove a point. In two days, he'd moved on. What they had before really must have meant nothing to Ali. It was probably a fling they'd both strung out through familiarity and laziness. He shook his head. It was more than that. It was bullshit when people said, "move on" and "plenty more fish in the sea." Utter bullshit.

Trevor slammed his phone down on the bed and hugged his legs close to his body. He was stranded. He flicked back and forth between older photos on Facebook. The pictures of him and Ali caused his gut to tighten. There was nothing here for him now.

Maybe his sister had been right. Maybe two men couldn't have a proper relationship that lasted. Staying with that girl in China might have been better for him after all.

Min lay back on the lower half of the bunk bed in his university dorm room. Her head bobbed to music beating from Trevor's portable speaker balanced on a rung of the wooden bed frame. They sat close together, but her knees were raised, with her feet tucked up in front of her. It looked like a barrier to Trevor. He had wanted to kiss her. Now he saw he'd been shielded from seeing anything else as an option.

Her pink lips pouted. But before they made contact, she pulled back, tucking strands of hair behind her ears.

'Have you done this before?'

Trevor coughed. 'Yeah. A couple of times.'

She blushed and informed him it was her first time, so he would need to be gentle. With that, Trevor gulped and pushed her back slowly, and she sank into the pillow.

Their lips pressed together and they parted their mouths. Unsure of where to go next, Trevor pushed his face further forward and teeth clashed against teeth.

'Ow. Get off!' She shoved him back by the shoulders.

'I don't think this is what I want.'

After she'd left, he mused for a while about how easily his mates would have a quick fumble and move on. His mind wandered to the migrant worker on the path. His dick stiffened and he slipped his hands under the waistband of his running shorts. His first experience with a man.

He and Min met up again a few weeks later. Her persistence kept their relationship going. Trevor liked her well enough but didn't pay her much attention when she wasn't in the room with him.

'I don't think anyone gives a shit about love anymore,' Trevor joked with his friend, but a heaviness pressed on his chest.

Both sides of the family would bring up his own marriage soon. His mum had dropped some hints last time he was back. They'd insisted he focus on his study then, but he wasn't getting any younger. The older he got, the more questions there would be, and people would think there was something wrong with him—something wrong with his family.

Trevor dated, fucked men, and attempted to ditch his girlfriend a couple of times during their final year. Min was persistent and trailed with him back to his hometown before the last semester and their final year of university.

She asked him daily where he was applying to do his postgrad or work, as did classmates. Was he staying local or going further afield? What would he do next?

The questions hung over all of them.

An idea had been brewing in Trevor's mind for a few months. He'd been good at science for as long as he could remember. But he found the application and lab work dull and tedious. It seemed all the jobs were funnelling into tech and hundreds of graduates were heading south to Shenzhen and Guangzhou, to the blossoming factories and tech hubs springing up there. Tech pioneer Jack Ma was the talk of the campus.

Trevor stared around the grimy office of the Careers Department. Colourful posters were stuck all around the room. Tables and rankings of different national universities sat alongside crests and coats of arms of expensive overseas universities in England and America.

'So options are good for you. There is work in Shenzhen with Daiwoo or another entry position with HXWay down in Funding.' The college guidance counsellor sat back in his chair and rested his hands over a large gut that strained against his cheap black belt. After delivering his verdict on Trevor's future, he began to prod his smartphone screen with a beefy index finger.

Trevor's eye caught the red brick walls and ivy-coated windows of a university abroad. "UWE" it declared in bold white lettering.

'What about Bristol?' Trevor spoke abruptly and stumbled over the pronunciation. His English was okay, but he rarely got a chance to use it on campus.

The college counsellor swivelled around, his thick neck battling with his shirt collar to see where Trevor was looking and now pointing.

'England? Not many of ours go abroad. It's very

expensive. Do your, err… parents earn—'

'No.' Trevor screwed up his face as a momentary break for freedom flashed before him and then disappeared in an instant.

'All the STEM courses are very competitive and oversubscribed in many cases. Scholarships are limited.'

'I can imagine.' Trevor stared gloomily ahead, imagining his life panning out before him. Working in a sterile lab coat, in a white lab, wearing white gloves, and bound to a white computer.

'The only option is with the Confucius Institute, but it's not really tech based, so I don't think you'd be interested.'

'What is that?'

The man opened and closed a couple of his desk drawers, the metal clanging each time they banged shut. He finally found what he was looking for and slapped a few glossy brochures onto the desk between them.

'Teaching,' he proclaimed and spun the brochures towards Trevor. They rotated into view, and he read the headline: *Start your new life in England! Teach Mandarin.*

'Teaching?' Trevor rolled the word around in his head. The idea of standing in a UK classroom with loads of children staring at him had never crossed his mind.

Min lay propped up on the bed, a white shirt pulled around her bare shoulders.

'But you don't even like kids!' She looked at him with a puzzled expression. Tears welled up in her eyes. Trevor was too busy explaining that the whole thing was technically free. He just had to get the money for the flight and everything else would be paid for. It was basically a scholarship, but he would teach Chinese to high school students in England. The first year was training, and then he could settle there for two more years, or longer. He was racing through the information.

She met his bubbling excitement with a stone-cold glare. Her hand rested on top of the files he had spread out on the coffee shop table.

'You're running away, Trevor?' Her eyes cast down, her mouth a thin line. She pushed back from the round table and grabbed her bag.

'Not at all. This is what I've always wanted. What I need.' He couldn't contain his excitement.

'We had plans.' She spoke in a flat, monotone voice now. She flicked her hair behind her and stepped towards the door.

'Plans? You're supposed to be excited for me.' His turn to look miffed.

'I thought you were different. But you're not, are you? You're just a selfish scum bag like the rest of them. Use me and dump me.'

'It's not like that.' He stood and gestured for her to sit down.

'That is exactly what it's like. Now who am I supposed to marry?' Her voice rose. Trevor reeled back a little, unsure whether she was joking or not.

He stared at her for a moment longer. Their eyes locked in a battle of wills. Trevor broke first and sat down heavily into his seat.

Without another word she left, slamming the shop door, leaving a gust of cold air from outside.

***

Trevor left the house. Too many memories from his recent and distant past crowded him for space, each one crying for attention. He needed to focus on what he still had left, so meeting Soph would be a brief glimmer of sunshine in his shitty day.

Arriving at the office in the grey drizzle, it was difficult not to be impressed by the stone columns that flanked the expensive door and the glitzy decor that extended throughout the lobby. She had done well for herself.

'Congratulations, baby boy!'

Sophie, wrapped from shoulder to ankle in a pink military jacket and combat boots, met Trevor at the door and let him step into her office.

'Wow.' Trevor took in her appearance. 'You're really trying to tell the men of the world they shouldn't mess with you.'

She grinned and pulled him into a hug.

'I can't believe you passed! You survived!' She laughed. Sophie had dropped out of the teacher training course during the first month. Kids were not her thing, apparently. Being a model scout from Russia suited her much better.

'Lunch?'

'Give me ten minutes,' Sophie grinned. They would

often sneak out of the training college and take long lunches beside the River Thames on sunny days when they'd first arrived in England.

She settled back at her desk and continued typing.

Trevor chewed his fingernail and moved towards the window beside her desk.

Ali had moved on. Everyone at school seemed to think he was guilty, and his drinking hadn't gone as unnoticed as Ali claimed. Trevor should have stepped in and done something. But he'd believed Ali's excuses and naively been led along that it would get better, that this was the last time, and they had something special. Something nobody else had.

'You look like shit. And you're still moping. I could smell it on you when you walked into this office.' Behind him now, she poked him playfully in the shoulder. 'Sadness stinks.'

Trevor turned to her, blinking back tears.

'I do not.'

'You need to get over him.'

'Fine. Let's go.'

Sophie turned on her heel and slid effortlessly towards the door. She opened it with a flourish and beckoned him outside.

They linked arms on the main street in front of the grey and imposing office building, Broad Street was built for financial institutes and banks and gave off an air of confidence and wealth.

'I just want to know how he's doing.'

'Then call him.'

'I can't. He won't speak to me.'

'Well, it might be for the best. Maybe whatever you had—it ran its course.'

Trevor stopped. Pulled his arm out of the crook of her elbow. He squinted at Sophie's face in the glare of the late morning light.

'You think that?'

'It doesn't matter what I think, Trevor.' She reached out to him once again. 'But you have doubts, right?'

'I didn't have any other choice…' Trevor's sentence petered out. The wind caught a Coke can scrunched up beside a bin and dragged it noisily across the pavement in front of them.

'You were together for three years. And you just left him. You listened to your gut.'

'Is that what you think? It was that easy?' Trevor's face flushed. They'd had this conversation multiple times over the phone. Sophie had soothed Trevor—he thought he'd done the right thing then, but now? He wasn't so sure.

'Jesus. Just say what you think, Soph!'

They eased into a booth at a local bistro.

'You know, once'—Trevor swallowed a gulp of Coke—'I spent a weekend on Tao Bao.'

'What's that?'

'You know, it's like eBay.'

Sophie looked at him sideways in a way that suggested she had no idea what he was talking about.

'Tao Bao?' She sounded out each word. 'You were going to buy a boyfriend?'

'No.' He cracked a smile. 'No. Buy a wife.'

'Whaaat?' She leaned in. 'What the hell do you mean? You're nuts, Trevor.'

'It sounds crazy, doesn't it? But it's really common in China.'

'You guys are messed up. What if she found out?'

'She would know.'

'Your wife. Wait, let me get this straight. Your wife would know you are gay? And that's okay? Huh!'

'Yes. Well, it's mutually beneficial. She would probably be a lesbian.'

'Oh! I see. I get it. Wow. That really happens?'

'Yup. The thing is to make the parents happy. Do the big wedding and then get divorced a year or so later.'

'What the actual… That's mad.'

'It does sound a bit nuts.'

They shifted in their chairs, lost in thought. Sophie stirred her coffee.

'Wait. What I don't understand… Help me out here. Wouldn't it just be easier to tell your parents you're gay?'

'Wow. Smart. So simple, right?'

'Yesss. Surely. Easier than a whole sham-fake-marriage thing.'

'If only. It's all about face. Nobody would lose face if I were to get married. Parents, family, and friends all see the wedding. Everyone gets what they want. No real harm done.'

'But what about what *you* want? Isn't that important?'

A moment of silence passed between them.

'I would be happy. Because my parents would be

happy. It's basically *face engineering*.'

Sophie frowned. And then broke out into a smile.

'That's some messed up logic, Trev. But I sort of get it. It's quite sweet, actually.'

'They've done so much for me.' Trevor caught sight of an elderly couple shuffling down the street outside. The woman gripped the man firmly by his arm, holding him steady.

'True. So, you're basically a gay Avenger. Casting aside your true life to fight the system and solve the world's social issues by pleasing your parents.' She cast her hands around widely. Trevor giggled.

'You're so dramatic.'

'I know. You love it.'

Trevor wrapped his hands around his mug and brought his gaze back to Sophie.

'So, I've made a decision. I'm going back to China.' The finality of his tone caused Sophie to sit back heavily in her seat. 'You're right. You've always said I can't save Ali.'

'What the fuck? Trevor, you can't just run away…'

'I'm not running. For once in my fucking life, I'm standing up for something I believe in. Myself.'

'So you don't believe him?'

'There's nothing I can do about it. Wallowing around here isn't helping.'

She frowned.

'He's ignorant to how his family has fucked him up. I can't fix it, Soph, but I can make good with my own family. That's all I can do. I don't know where that will lead. Who fucking knows at this point.'

'Since when did you get such a filthy mouth?' She reached out, her hand resting on the dark blue of his shirt sleeve. 'I'm fucking proud of you, you know that.'

'It was always my plan. Finish the course and get back home in time for the Spring Festival. But now I'm thinking whether to bother coming back here. I need to fix my family before even getting involved in someone else's. Especially Ali's fucked-up family.'

Seventeen

Text messages popped up across the glowing screen as Ali tried to pay. In a haze, he shut them off by swiping the screen and held out his phone for the off-licence worker to scan. The phone vibrated in Ali's hand as the payment went through.

'All done. You go steady, mate. Merry Christmas.' The turbaned man smiled and turned away from Ali, who tucked the bottle of dark rum into the coat of his parka and shouldered the door open to get outside. The cold air wrapped around his cheeks, and he glanced at the warm interior of the hotel lobby but walked in the opposite direction towards Castle Park.

Fuck the both of them. Even if Osei didn't want anything to do with him, Trevor didn't need to know that. Saying he was in a new relationship would piss Trevor off. His mother had left him to rot, his drunk father was dead, and Trevor had turned his back on him. What did it matter, anyway? He would just be alone again to figure it out, that was nothing new.

An email arrived an hour ago asking Ali to appear at the police station tomorrow morning at ten. The cop shop on Christmas Eve, it was almost laughable. A week ago, they'd been planning the Japan trip. The cops obviously wanted this over and done with before the holiday started, so he might as well enjoy his last night before they locked him up.

Benches sat along the path, each one under dim lights that cast a pool across the tarmac. The darkness barely registered the attempt at brightening up the space. Castle Park, and the hills and mounds it contained, didn't care what time of day the guys came to hook up. Getting off in the park had been Ali's gateway into gay life in the city. Summer nights with his trousers around his ankles and not giving a fuck.

With a mouth full of rum, Ali sat back and stared up at the stars. Each one a diamond against black velvet, a softness he rarely had time for. This was what he needed. After all the shit over the past week, he needed to start looking out for himself.

The dance began long before Ali reached Castle Park. The dance between men cruising parks, across the world, a world where apps and mobile data made hooking up easy. Ali wanted sex now. No words exchanged. Just quiet, full-blown sex.

A shadow moved across the park in a section shrouded by conifer trees. The figure descended a steep path into the darker area behind the benches. It stopped, paused for a moment, and a flick of the man's chin caught Ali's attention. Ali lurched forward from the bench. He didn't need any more signs. A rush of excitement tensed his groin, and the pit of his stomach tingled. Half the rum in the bottle was gone, but he screwed on the cap and moved with heavy feet into the darker, wooded area.

The figure looked slim, with a narrow face and some scruff. A baseball cap hid his hair and most of his eyes. Ali reached him, grabbed the edge of his jacket, and pulled him in closer. The guy said something like "Steady, mate," but Ali just grinned.

His mind swayed. This was exactly what he needed. He tugged at the man's coat and led him off the path and into the bushes. Their legs bumped together, and a rough beard scratched the length of his face. The guy held Ali's jaw, firm fingers gripping his cheeks, creating a small circle with his mouth. Ali's eyes were barely open. The guy spat in his mouth and the saliva pooled on his tongue, bitter and tainted with cigarettes. He swallowed it down. He wanted this guy and clawed at his belt, tugging it open.

The rum warmed him all over and he wanted to be fucked. Ali rubbed against the guy's hard dick pressing into his hand. He found its length and moved to grip the tip, tugging urgently at the belt, but the guy pushed his hand away. Ali fell forward. Damp and muddy leaves met his palms, and he felt exposed on his knees with his jeans around his thighs. The guy was silent behind him and spat again, before he knocked Ali's legs further apart with a kick of his boots. He slammed into Ali roughly and he yelped, his hand knocking against the cold glass bottle. The burn filled him up to his chest, and the guy plunged fully inside him without pausing to find out if Ali was ready. The pain melted with the rum, yet the rough treatment wasn't the same as the summer nights he remembered. Cold, dead leaves rustled as the guy panted. The coldness extended up Ali's legs, his thighs, and into his stomach. The rum did nothing to chill the empty space nestled there. He'd wanted to be fucked, but not like this, not out here, not by this guy.

The man finished and pushed Ali away, zipping his fly before spitting again on the ground. Reaching into his jacket pocket, he pulled out a pack of cigarettes and offered one to Ali.

Ali leaned in to take it and put a hand on the man's cheek, attempting to draw him in for a kiss. The guy pulled his head back and positioned a cigarette in Ali's mouth. He flashed a cheap orange plastic lighter and turned against the wind to light his own with a cupped hand.

'Get home safe, yeah?' The guy turned back towards the path and began to descend the slope into darkness.

Slumped on a bench, suddenly feeling more sober than he wanted to and sore, Ali reached for the bottle of rum. The lid had come loose when the bottle was kicked over during the rough sex. Its contents wasted across the grass. Despite his blurred vision, he scanned his phone for the earlier texts. Two from Trevor. The first said he was going away for a while. Another sent an hour earlier said he was at the airport and hoped everything worked out for Ali.

Ali's chest lurched, and tears formed in his eyes. He drew his arms around himself, watching the figure pause at a streetlight to flick his cigarette into the small lake surrounded by black iron railings.

Through the overhanging branches of the tree above, the stars spun. The black swallowed each one and melted them against the inky backdrop. Trevor stood there in his black suit, the one he'd worn to a friend's funeral. White lights blinded Ali; Trevor's white shirt burned his eyes and melted into the inky sky.

'Where are you?' Ali screamed into the night. No reply came. The urge to move overcame him. To get another drink, to meet another guy, to forget this shitty moment. His career was over, whatever the police said tomorrow. He'd been alone for years before Trevor came along, and that light had gone out, so he'd face the police alone. Nothing they tried to pin on him could be worse than how he felt now.

He walked, then he broke into a run, his feet slapping on the tarmac and across the grass separating the road from the lamplights. The main road buzzed and the glare shifted across uneven surfaces. The bright beam of headlamps blinded him, and a car horn sounded just before he crashed into the headlight of an oncoming car.

'Fucking idiot. Look where you're going!' A voice trailed off into the dank darkness at the end of the road and the screech of brakes as the car hurtled around a corner. Ali swayed towards the orange globe indicating the pedestrian crossing he should take. There was another cruising area up on the left side of the common. He stumbled across the road to get there, and his heart pounded in his ears once he neared the summit entrance.

The hill tucked away behind a grove of trees. He leaned on the familiar handrail as he climbed, glancing down as the slope fell away sharply on the left hand side.

His knees shook from the motion of the wooden boards that covered the steep fall to the road below. The sound of traffic echoed up through the trees from the main road on the other side, mixing with the beating in his ears. *Thud, thud, thud,* Ali's heart drummed in his chest. Trevor's image coursed through his mind's eye. Ali's gaze fixed on the stars in the sky. A horn blared below, and *crack...*

The planks of wood that formed a barrier between the path and the edge of the sheer rock face gave way under his feet. Ali's grip failed to steady him with the railing, and he rolled down the pitch-black bank for a couple of metres.

Rock and pieces of wood scraped and scratched at his skin. Numbed from the drinking, he didn't feel the deep cuts on his legs and arms. His head thudded backwards, the base of his skull smashing into the collapsed edge of bricks and masonry work. The low running wall, spilling bricks and rubble down the bank, jabbed into the base of his neck. Ali's vision blurred as the searing pain cut off his breath.

Tepid water, stinking of decay and mould, seeped into the fabric of his shoes. Blinded by the pain in his temple, he moved his hand to check for blood, but it came away dry. A sharp pain stabbed, unrelenting, at the top of his spine, deep in the meat of his neck.

The slicked concrete and broken pieces of wood

surrounded him, but a thick pipe leaked warm water and he grabbed it, heaving himself to a squat position. The stench from the wastewater pipe hit his nostrils and he gagged, filling his mouth with rank, hot bile. Unable to make purchase on the ground, his legs gave out from under him.

Ali's hand slipped from the pipe, and he slid further down the embankment. His hands, unable to grip onto the clumps of grass and rocks, came unstuck and he tumbled down the steep sides of the slope. The edges of his vision began to twist and melt. Thudding intensified in his head and spread across his forehead, the bright light cutting his vision. He blacked out.

Someone called his name before he sank to the floor. The carpet was straw-like under his hands, damp with some give to it. His name echoed in the blackness. It grew louder and louder, becoming more desperate and higher pitched. Full of pain and anger. His mother screamed at his father, and it barrelled up the stairs to his bedroom. He dug his nails into the pillow and squashed it around his head to block out the sounds. The same bitter row between his parents, driven by drink until they'd finally burned themselves out and split up. For years, Ali had wanted to quit because of it. His mother screamed and berated his father who attacked back and blocked her way as she wrestled from his grip to escape out the door. The cat and the mouse fought with words. A thud meant one of them had a weapon. A bowl or the tin mug his father used for beer. It clattered to the floor. She called out, his name echoing through the dim space. He crept to the top of the staircase. A small square of land with three doors leading off. One into Ali's bedroom, one to the bathroom, and the last into his parents' bedroom. They wouldn't be snoring there for a few more hours.

He had to get closer. They were downstairs, and a shard of light peeped out from under the door. It nearly blinded him. She needed him. A choking sound, like she couldn't breathe. The growl from his father meant he was angry. She had flipped his switch, or he had flipped himself, but he would be drunk. To get physical with her meant she was filled with wine, lava, and danger because he didn't give a fuck anymore. Something scratched at the door.

Eighteen

Trevor had wasted so much time trying to fix Ali that he'd not been open, honest, and truthful about his own family. If being around Ali and the toxic situation had taught him anything, it was that family mattered. Trevor had been a hypocrite, Ali was suffering, and he'd been too afraid to do anything about it because his own situation scared the shit out of him. It made sense now; seeing your own life reflected back in a distorted fucked-up version of someone else's family did that.

Skidding to a halt on the concrete strip, the wheels of the plane squealed in protest. Trevor shifted in his seat and let out the breath he'd been holding since the landing gear tucked itself away. From the window, the flat ground surrounding the airport melted into mountains that soared off into the distance. The cities in Fujian were babies compared to their sisters Shanghai and Beijing. Smaller in size and still, once the surface was scratched, very traditional and conservative in many parts.

Trevor took the cigarette offered by the taxi driver, and after cracking the window, he inhaled a lungful of the expensive cigarette. The driver must have been to a wedding recently to get his hands on this brand. The red packet gave it away. Nobody actually bought Hongtashan cigarettes, they just stockpiled them from the tables at weddings.

Around the airport, the city landscape became blocks of eight-storey apartments, interspersed with towering thirty-storey modern developments. Trevor eyed a whole block or more that would be gradually reduced to rubble and rebuilt with soaring skyscrapers, malls, and wide roads. The narrow alleys and densely packed urban villages were being pared down and developing skywards rather than sprawling messily sideways.

How would the family take his news?

The last time Trevor returned home was for a cousin's wedding, one of the many cousins he met infrequently. They'd danced all night and played drinking games until the groom collapsed. Everything about China was busy compared to London, but comfort resided in the chaos.

They pulled into the carpark. A head leaned into the passenger doorway the moment they stopped. The stout woman grumbled about the price offered and gestured to Trevor to hurry up and get out. Her thin, quiet husband smiled weakly. Clearly patience wasn't a trait she wanted to instil in her children, and the taxi took off with them inside. Trevor scanned the bus depot and settled his suitcase on the tarmac.

A woman, decked head to toe in denim, leaned from a minivan doorway, and through her shouting at a friend across the station yard, they figured out he needed to take van number sixty to get to the village where he grew up. The numbers changed every time he came back. Everything looked familiar but bus stops, road names, and even viable routes changed year to year.

The minivan creaked and groaned as the road ascended and twisted up the new tarmac, and fields took over and became the only landscape on either side. Passengers disembarked and hauled off huge water buckets containing fish, frogs, and crabs from the coastline. The minivan appeared to pick up speed, and before long they arrived at a wide archway signalling the entrance to the village.

Roaring off down the road, the minivan bounced along, sending dust and small stones flying into the surrounding grass. Trevor stretched his neck and adjusted his backpack and small suitcase. A familiar scent of burnt paper and fireworks hung in the air—typical for this time of year. Celebrating the New Year meant setting things on fire.

Red lanterns and banners hung from the archway alongside gold lettering proclaiming political affinity. The village name sat next to a roaring dragon's head extolling the virtues of the tea grown in the region and surrounding mountain terraces.

The coarse track threaded up from the main road and split into forks disappearing behind beige stone buildings in all directions. Trevor followed a familiar path. An occasional greeting rang out as he passed, before he turned the final corner and a shadow fell across his path. Something blocked his way. He squinted into the bright sunlight to see what, or who, prevented him reaching his home.

'Son of Xu, is that you? Well, I never!'

His mother's older sister's voice boomed out, and he paused by a blue plastic barrel stinking up the passageway with food waste more than ready to be hauled away.

'Auntie! It's me. Let me pass, this bucket of fish slop stinks.'

Her laughter cracked and boomed like thunder. 'Where is she, then?'

'Who, Auntie?' It amazed him every time he saw her that she wore the same peach T-shirt, stretched tightly across her arms and chest.

'Well, well, returning home empty handed and without a girl. Whatever will your mother say? She's been waiting forever to meet her new daughter-in-law.'

'Not yet, Auntie.' Trevor shook his head. She was joking around, but it started an ache in his stomach. He knew his mother would be disappointed. 'No girl. But I bought some snacks from England for you all. And for my favourite auntie...'

'For me?' She grinned and took a couple of steps closer to meet him.

'I said my favourite auntie. Auntie Xin, my mother's youngest sister, of course.' He enjoyed getting his own back, and they joked back and forth as she swooped in to help him haul his suitcase and backpack up and around the corner to his parents' home.

He looked around the dim kitchen as he stepped inside. A central table dominated the space, its sturdy legs thicker than a fence post, the surface polished from years of chopping and being wiped down. He stood in the gloom for a moment, soaking up the silence, and traced his fingers over the scarred tabletop. The marks were deep and ingrained with black. In a grooved block next to the table sat a steel butcher's knife. Frayed blue tape wrapped around the handle and the tarnished blade ran to a wicked edge. Trevor's mother had prepared meals with it throughout his life, and he stroked the handle affectionately. His mother entered as he placed the knife carefully back down. Her face cracked into a smile. She greeted him from across the room with the usual 'Have you eaten?' and moved towards the stove, regardless of his answer. It was almost time to cook, to begin chopping onions, washing rice, and peeling ginger ready for the nighttime meal. He reflected on the bear hug Ray, Ali's stepdad, would have given Ali at that moment. Trevor's parents didn't do that. Physical contact kept to a minimum, but light touches to the arm and heaving plates of food ensured Trevor felt loved. Trevor's father, looking smaller and paler, sat staring at the small, dusty TV in the corner of the kitchen.

'Hey, dork.' Trevor's sister walked into the room backwards carrying an armful of battered textbooks. 'Help me throw these out, would you? There's another pile in our old room.'

'Got it.' Thankful for being given a task, Trevor moved through the small kitchen and stepped onto the worn staircase. After eight steps, he was up in the roof space. The area was separated by a wooden board draped with fabric and patched with layers of old music magazines and newspapers. Someone's idea of decoration, or they'd decided the bedrooms needed another layer for warmth.

He moved across the space once shared with his sister. She was a year older, and boy did she like to remind him about it. The room had been cleaned out bit by bit. Moving the piles of books, school uniforms, and other teenage paraphernalia exposed the two low beds side by side in the room. Built from the same tree, the logs had been split on the concrete courtyard behind the house. The scratchy blue blankets remained, and they tickled Trevor's knuckles when he bent to collect the pile of green and white bound textbooks on the bed.

As he pulled them to his chest, one slipped from the top of the pile and splayed out on the bed. A piece of graph paper tumbled out and the neat, folded edges and immediately took Trevor back to his maths class in eleventh grade.

The final weeks before the stressful gaokao exams that would assign students to their future path by way of numerical scores and a multitude of tests were filled with last-minute cram sessions. Trevor's classmate, Dee, had leaned into him where they sat slumped at the back of the cold classroom. The other students had trailed out, and Dee wanted to sit for a moment before going out to get some fried dumplings. They had kissed once before. An awkward moment that neither of them pulled away from, but neither knew what to do with. Sex education in public schools then consisted of what older classmen told you in dirty jokes or rhymes, or someone else's uncle bragging at the annual family gathering about the loose women he'd pulled on the road. Trevor and Dee felt close, but they had no model for what they felt between them.

Dee held the note out to Trevor. His thin, slender fingers seemed to bleed into the stark white paper. Dee never went out in the sun. He said he hated sports, but it seemed more like he wanted to preserve his smooth, unblemished complexion. There was a huge stigma in having a tan of any kind. It meant a low-skilled agricultural worker, or someone who worked out on the rice harvest. For most of the girls, and Dee, they barely stepped into the sun and would scuttle along the edge of buildings holding umbrellas, flaps of cardboard, or their hand to protect themselves from the disfiguring sun.

Trevor took the paper and started to unfold it.

'Not here. When you're alone.' Dee spoke in a low tone and glanced around the empty classroom.

'Fine.'

Trevor read the note later in his bunk bed. Dee outlined his feelings for Trevor. He talked about them settling down and owning a house. How they could run away together. He wanted to spend his life with Trevor, but Trevor wasn't ready to admit he was gay, to admit he was any different than everyone else. Dee's ideas stuck in his teeth like cheap gum. He couldn't fit himself in with Dee's view of being gay.

They ignored each other for the rest of the school year, but once they brushed past each other in the school yard. Trevor swept along with his group of friends, laughing, hollering, and joking. Dee stranded in the centre as bodies circled around him, a frozen island with a glum face. His paleness framed by a shock of black hair and wide, scared-looking eyes. He stepped forward and smiled for a moment on seeing Trevor. Trevor glanced away, turning his body from Dee. The boys moved him along with back slaps and jeers. Dee remained rooted to the spot. Ignored by the jostling and elbowing happening around him. When Trevor looked back, he was gone. Years later, a friend of Dee's uncle told Trevor, when he returned one New Year, that Dee had killed himself. Cut his wrists and bled out in the showers during the second year at university.

The steps leading up to the musty bedroom creaked and Mel entered the room, picking at a cobweb tangled in her hair.

'Look at this.' His sister picked the strands from her hair. 'It wants to make a home in my skull.'

'Plenty of space for it up there,' he teased, and she crunched his shoulder, slapping him on the arm. She scanned the room and moved into the back corner before crouching by another pile of books.

'Mum wants to know when you're bringing your girl back. Glad you didn't bring another foreign guy back, anyway.'

Trevor's cheeks burned, but he ignored her.

'How have they been? Dad seems weaker this time.'

Mel lowered herself to the corner of the bed and flicked through a pile of papers in her lap. The lines around her eyes and mouth were more defined than the last time he'd been back.

'The doctor said his right eye won't be good for much longer. His hearing is getting worse as well.' Mel glanced up. 'But Mum's okay. They miss you.'

'But you're here.' Trevor tossed the book in his hand and slumped to the bed, his shoulder pressed against his sister's exposed arm. They used to sit for hours reading books and doing homework like that.

'How long are you back for?' Mel turned to face him.

'A couple of weeks.' *Unless they kick me out.*

She sniffed, her eyes fixed on the book in front of her.

Trevor stared at the book, at the note tucked inside. 'Do you remember Dee?'

Mel scratched the side of her nose and sighed. The sounds of their mother chopping and talking to their father, an endless stream of comments about the price of pork, or the predicted weather, and the occasional grunt in response, filled the space.

'His family never got over it, you know?' Mel's mouth turned down a fraction like a bad smell had entered her nostrils.

'He was a sweet guy.' Trevor's gut tingled again.

Mel brushed at the dust stuck to her trouser legs. The book, grimy and discoloured from years sat rotting in the attic room, spread on her lap.

Mel dropped her voice to a whisper. 'Apparently, he was a gay. That's what Mum heard from Chen Lu at the night market.'

So they knew. Trevor's fingers itched.

'I mean, it's to be expected,' she continued. 'It's not right, and the shame it brought to his family. Carrying on like that, he acted like a little girl. It's the parents we felt sorry for. Why do you ask?' Mel's eyes narrowed for a moment, her gaze moving over Trevor's face.

The same look she'd given him before he got in the taxi and returned to the airport with Ali last time.

'These books made me think of school. And it's sad, don't you think? Everyone just turned their backs on him.' Trevor's guts ached and his jaw clenched. He stood and moved away, pretending to check something in the corner. He'd picked Ali over Dee—his leaving must have played a part in Dee deciding to take his own life—and now he had nothing. And nobody.

Mel tutted and let out a sigh before pushing herself from the bed.

'Okay, it's sad for him. Sad for his family. I'd have taken him to church if I'd known. Got him some help.'

Trevor rolled his eyes. Since converting and becoming a Catholic, Mel's answers to life's problems always led back to her precious church.

'They're part of the problem,' Trevor muttered under his breath. 'I thought you lot were meant to be nice to everyone—'

'Not this again? Grab those books, come on. You've got all these funny ideas in your head since going to England.' Mel dumped a stack of books in his arms and whispered, 'Are they all gays over there?' She snorted and seemed pleased with her joke.

Trevor ignored her.

'I'll head back in a week or so. Depends on how long I can stomach you.'

Mel mock gasped. 'So rude. Move it.'

Trevor's foot scraped the top of the stairs. He met his sister's gaze. 'Dee was a good guy, Mel.'

'Move! You're getting a lot of white hairs, little bro. I can see that now.'

After they'd eaten and darkness seeped in from outside, Trevor hovered in the kitchen with his parents.

'Mum?' Trevor spoke in the local dialect to his mother, who did not understand Mandarin.

She busied herself with wiping off the table. 'I'm glad you came back for the Spring Festival. Family should always be together for the new year.'

Trevor felt a dip in his stomach and down through his groin like he was riding a rollercoaster at maximum speed.

His father sat in his chair off from the stove. Trevor kneeled down in front of him. The cold stones of the floor chilled his knees.

He placed both hands on the edge of the chair, the wood warm under his fingers, his father's eye rheumy and unblinking.

'I need to tell you both something.'

Nineteen

A wall, topped with razor wire curled in concentric patterns to keep people climbing up from the road, loomed in the dark below. Ali slid until another pile of masonry, and a ditch cut into the rock, prevented him from falling further.

He steadied himself against a fence post and kicked out at the wire in an attempt to flatten it down. In his struggle, the cable flicked back and dug into his leg. Designed to capture and hold on to its prey, the sharp barbs scratched and cut up his back. He twisted away with one foot to step over it, each time stamping the coils down to make space. Once it flattened enough, Ali launched himself off the wall to the road below.

He landed on both feet, and his hands dropped to the ground to steady himself. Grey flaps of shredded T-shirt tickled his ribs, the other half tangled in the wire at the top of the thick stone wall. He turned to face the shrouded slope he'd come down. Every part of his back and legs ached. His muscles screamed from the pounding of the rocks and debris he'd crashed over.

Silence surrounded him, but for a solitary orange

streetlight that hummed and glowed against the black street. No cars passed on this section of the road. Fuck. Fuck. Fuck. Ali crouched at the base of the wall. His head throbbed, his torn, bloody fingers smeared and pressed at the screen of his phone. He needed to get out of there.

Ali sobbed as the dial tone vibrated against his tender ear. The stars taunted him from above, his vision blurred. The voicemail stated nobody was there for him.

'It's me.' He wiped at his eyes and grunted, snot running from his nose. 'You don't want to speak to me. I get that.' His jaw ached.

A taxi approached from the darker end of the road. Ali waved his arm.

'I'm staying at the Bath hotel. I hate how we left things… Osei, but I'm going to the police station tomorrow.'

The taxi pulled up. The driver's mouth turned down at the sight of Ali.

'I just want to talk to someone…' He retched before leaning on the taxi door. The driver shook his head but pointed his thumb to the back seat. Ali tugged on the door, his bloody fingers slipping on the handle.

'I hurt Trevor. He doesn't deserve any of this.' The static crackled back as the only response. Tears blurred Ali's vision. 'I'm sorry. I've fucked everything up.'

Ali hung up and slumped into the faux leather seats. The driver's eyes framed in the rearview mirror looked nasty perched above his sneering nose. A sinking feeling mixed with the rocking of the taxi; nauseous bile rose in

Ali's throat.

The taxi driver grunted when Ali passed a fiver through the glass partition and stumbled to the curb, retching.

Ali approached the lobby and the receptionist, who had checked him in, avoided his gaze. The lift delivered him to the eleventh floor where he fumbled with the zip on his gym trousers. He patted down his pockets and found the key card. *Thank fuck.*

The water from the shower hit his skin, turning the liquid at his feet a dull pink.

Ali sank to the floor of the shower, his head in his hands. He had to be at the police station in ten hours.

Ali awoke with a start. A familiar panic crept up his chest, and he squinted at the curtains as the sun filled the room and cast its light across the grey-and-white striped bedspread. An ache ran from his shoulders down to his shins. Something pulled on his leg hair. Throwing back the sheets revealed tracks and lines of blood congealed across his leg in a smeared pattern. His tattoo of a Chinese symbol for luck, *xing*, was caked, dark and dirty, in dried blood.

Ali looked around in a daze, also taking in the room. A wine bottle on its side, a glass of something brown and sticky by the small oval mirror. Every item in the room was a flashback of flying high last night. He'd been dancing before he went out, using that bottle as a microphone at one point, or crashing into the dresser with vodka and Coke in hand. Vodka and Coke. A bad idea hours and hours before he'd even gone to Castle Park.

He grappled for a bottle of ibuprofen from the vanity mirror by the bed and tipped three into his hand. Throwing them to the back of his throat, Ali dry swallowed the pills.

A fog hung dense and heavy across his scalp. Every time, each and every time, a shame he needed to process. It had to end.

He grabbed a pen and wrote on a piece of hotel stationary.

This is it. The last fucking time. I am sick of this. Who the hell am I? What have I become? I am acting like my fucking father. I deserve better than this, and Trevor deserves better than me.

The scrunched-up piece of paper hit the wall.

His phone blinked to life, and a message popped up on his screen.

Fun night? You OK? Ali hated those side-eye emojis; they implied he was a skank. And at that moment, he was.

Osei. Fuck. What had he said? He must have called him. Osei, out of all the people he could have called, why him? Ali wanted Trevor there. Trevor never made him feel alone.

From his suitcase, he pulled out their picture. Its golden frame sparkled, but it was cheap wood. He held the frame in both hands—they stood in front of an ancient townhouse in the village square by Trevor's family house. They had travelled for days to get there, and that trip had been the catalyst to breaking them apart. Ali saw red. Fucked off and angry at Trevor for leaving him again. For not being there when he needed him.

It came apart easily as he smashed it against the headboard. A thick shard of glass came away and landed on the bedspread. He tugged at the picture of him and Trevor. Ali's fear tainted anything between them—that one day he would wake up and be alone. He'd always be alone. Even surrounded by people, he was alone.

The corners of the photo tore easily. A jagged cut ran between the two smiling men.

Ali's tears fell onto the bedspread and he sniffled, unable to hold back the gulping and gasping sobs that overcame him. As he tore through the final fold, one piece rose, fluttered down, and turned over. In small print on the back was written, *I will always be happy with you.*

Trevor's distinctive cursive.

He slammed both hands over the message. Pushed them into the mattress. It relented under the pressure and sank deeper.

He squeezed both eyes shut and tried to recall Trevor's image. The feel of his hands across his shoulders, stroking both cheeks, kissing Ali's earlobes one after the other before he fell asleep. All gone now. Vanished and torn apart like the photograph. His father taunted him then. *Keep it to yourself, you'll never be good enough.*

Ali's eyes snapped open and looked at the shard of glass on the bed. He picked it up carefully. It curled like a glass tooth, snarled and curved to a fine point. It weighed nothing in his hand.

Trevor squeezed his shoulder.

Ali applied pressure on the wedged end of the shard in his fist. At first, it met resistance, a dense cushioned pillow pushing back against the sharp edge of the glass. He winced but didn't stop pushing.

Trevor moved a hand across his leg.

Ali tightened his grip, a burning kicked in as the glass sliced through the palm of his hand and bit into him. Through gritted teeth, he grumbled under his breath. Blood bubbled up between his fingers.

Trevor always said Ali was his lifeline.

Ali squeezed. He wanted Trevor there with him, but all that came was more blood. It spilled onto his leg and the white bedsheets. Hot, scalding redness spread out, threaded and veined across his leg.

Ali pumped. More of the glass disappeared, swallowed up into his fleshy palm. He gritted his teeth once more and pushed down, feeling a fire shoot to his wrist and into his face. His cheeks burned. A metallic taste filled his mouth.

Trevor rejected him and had gone back to China for good, and Ali could hardly blame him. What a fucking mess he'd created. He was no better than his father. He'd drank to the point that people couldn't stand being around him.

Ali twisted the glass icicle into his hand one more time. The flesh of his palm tore, shredded into ribbons, and still he pushed.

He cursed under his breath. Trevor stared at him from the photo, taunting and mocking him from thousands of miles away. Ali's body went limp, and his hand opened. The glass shard didn't fall for a moment but stuck out of his palm, rigid. Turgid flesh ballooned around the wound. Ali shook his arm, and the barb came free. It tumbled, caught his little finger before ending flat on the bed. The light caught the corner that hadn't been embedded in his hand.

Ali stared at his sliced palm. A release like something he hadn't felt since being fucked hard by Trevor. He tried to close the bleeding hand, but the flexibility was gone. The fingers barely flinched around the base of the swelling.

A knock at the door startled him. The sound echoed across the narrow passageway from the pine door, past the cheap white kettle and mini fridge. His eyes shot to the copper-ringed peephole. Another knock, and a muffled voice came through the door.

Someone called his name. Ali's good hand held the wrist of the other. He wanted whoever it was to go away. His eyes flickered like a roll of film in an old movie projector. Each image over-illuminated and moved quickly across his line of vision.

He slid his knee from under him and swivelled on the bed. Purple bruises crept up and around his ankle. Any protruding part, like his knees, ankles, elbows, and shins, was black or blue. A purple-to-plum rainbow tinged with the yellow of a rotting plum stone.

The side of the bed and sheets and up and across the

pillow were stained with patches of blood or streaks of dirt. His hand dripped blood.

A third knock, and a muffled shout of his name sent Ali shuffling for the bathroom. Grabbing a small face towel, he stretched his hand and fingers out as much as he could, wincing at the pain, and wrapped the towel around the bleeding wound. The white terry cloth quickly turned crimson then began to drip.

He leaned against the door, his shoulder and the bandage concealed from whoever was outside. He used the other hand to attach the security chain. Opening the door a crack, he intended to slam it shut after telling the housekeeping to leave him alone for a while.

'Ali.' Osei's face filled the gap. 'Are you alright?' He glanced up and caught Ali's gaze. 'Your face.'

Osei's gaze softened, and he reached out to touch Ali's neck.

'No.' Ali instantly drew back. A shudder ran up his body. 'Not now. I'm sorry.' He pushed the door back, but Osei shoved the narrow part of his shoe into the space at the bottom of the door.

'What the fuck, Ali? Did you get attacked? You look awful…'

Ali stared down at Osei's foot. His running shoe wedged in the door wasn't moving anywhere.

Fuck. 'Did I call you last night?'

'This place is a mess, Ali. Did someone come to your room and beat the shit out of you?'

A pregnant pause enveloped them.

Osei sighed. 'You don't remember calling me last

night, do you?'

'I blacked out.' Ali's voice was a whisper. 'After I fell, it's a bit of a blur.'

'Yeah. You sounded pretty wasted.'

'Probably,' Ali mumbled. His hand throbbed through the towel. Suddenly, the weight of the entire day and night pressed down on him, and he slumped into the door.

'Open it, Ali.' The pressure from the other side didn't let up. Ali blew out a breath, his jaw continued to throb. *What a fucking mess.* He released the chain, allowing Osei to step into the room. He looked tidy with a well-fitted black polo shirt buttoned to his neck.

'How did you even get into the hotel?' Ali pulled back the curtains.

Osei glanced around the room. 'I asked them what number the wasted guy stayed in. But you told me you were here.' He filled up the kettle in the bathroom sink and shook his head.

Ali folded the worst of the bloody sheets into a ball and shoved them, alongside the glass shards, up to the head of the bed.

'You can't hide it, Ali. It'll wash out. Whatever. Are you okay? Your forehead is all cut up.'

Ali's head swam and his stomach turned hot, bile rising in his throat.

'It's fine. Now is not a good time. I'm sorry.'

'You need to go to the hospital, Ali.' Osei pulled back and began searching in the inner pocket of his tan leather jacket for his phone. He turned away from the door, raising the phone to search for a signal.

'I don't. I need to go to the police station. I've got to give a statement.'

'Fine. Let's see if we can clean you up a bit.' Osei picked up the kettle and a white towel before stepping towards Ali.

Osei pulled out of the hotel car park. They'd be a couple of minutes late, but they could blame the traffic. Sunshine covered the dashboard, mocking Ali's beating headache in its radiant brightness.

'Why are you helping me?' Ali glanced at himself in the sun visor mirror. The scratch on his temple looked angry.

'About what you said in the cafe. About taking advantage of someone. It was about Trevor, wasn't it?'

'Yeah, who else would it be about?'

'Never mind. I thought something else—'

'That doesn't answer my question.' Ali threw a glance at Osei.

'You know what's odd?' Osei caught his gaze, grinned, and turned back to the road.

'What?'

'You make a lot more sense when you're wasted. I thought you were a decent guy that first night. Hung up on your ex, clearly, but okay.'

'So, you haven't written me off, then?'

'There's something under all that bravado and boozing. You're a nice guy.'

'Wow.' Ali stared out of the window.

'And anyway, my church says help yourself, and then help others.'

The car slowed, and Ali processed Osei's words. The police station, a grey oblong, came into view and they pulled into the carpark.

'Christ. You're religious.'

Osei switched off the car and turned in his seat. 'You didn't see this?' His eyes glinted when he reached into his shirt and pulled out a gold crucifix. Ali's eyebrow twitched.

'It makes me feel good to help people. I feel useful. And it's what my grandma would want me to do.'

'Fuck.' The daylight stabbed at his temples. Ali covered his eyes with a hand. 'Are you saving me?'

A deep throaty chuckle escaped Osei. 'You are something else, you know that?'

'I'm scared they'll keep me in there.' He twitched his head towards the building.

'I'm not here to save you. You just need a bit of help right now.'

'I'm a teacher. If I hadn't been so wasted… None of this would have happened.'

Osei's mouth pinched.

'It happened, Ali. You've got to deal with it now.'

'Will you wait out here for me?'

Osei's hand reached up behind Ali's head, his fingertips warm against the back of Ali's neck before his blue-grey eyes filled Ali's vision.

'You're gonna be okay. I'm not going to let you fall.'

Twenty

Trevor's mother turned from the stove and narrowed her eyes. She didn't look mad, but she might be soon. If they had a problem with him then it was on them. He'd read countless articles on how to handle the situation but barely any applied to parents who might not understand the concept he was about to deliver.

Trevor swallowed. 'Since being in the UK, I have realised something…'

Both parents turned their heads, catching each other's eye. They weren't subtle about it.

'What are you doing? Get up off the floor.' Mel paused in the doorway, a mound of clothes piled in her arms. Trevor got off his knees. She continued, 'Spit it out, then.'

'I've wanted to tell you something for a long time…'

Mel's jaw tensed; it looked like she had gritted her teeth. She already knew anyway. Since she'd met Ali when he visited, she'd been different and treated him like something was wrong with him. Time stood still for a flickering moment.

'…I'm gay.'

Mel's lips parted, but her mouth closed without a sound and she shook her head. Trevor looked from his mother to his father. Both had their heads bowed, as if searching for answers.

His mother spoke first. 'You will bring many problems to this family.'

'We have always known you were different from other boys.' His father pulled himself forward. The armchair creaked under the shifting weight. 'We can tolerate this, but it will be difficult for us. And for you.'

'I know.' Trevor's grip fell from the back of the chair. It was going better than expected. No plates thrown, the knife remained on the chopping block surface—only Mel's face, fixed in a scowl, caused his stomach to flutter.

'But we can't have you telling other family members.' His mother's gaze travelled from Trevor's face to Mel's.

'It helps that you are living away from here. The family won't be so affected by it.' His father stood before him.

Always thinking about what other people thought. They'd rather cut off their own limbs than lose an ounce of face in front of the neighbours.

'Give us some time to decide what is the best way to approach this. You will return to England soon.' His father placed a hand on Trevor's shoulder for a moment. Their eyes met and a wisp of a smile caught his father's lips. Of all the people he needed to tell, Trevor had worried about his father. A man he'd always looked up to but felt worlds apart from. For the first time, he saw his father for the man he was. One who'd raised his family and wanted the best for them. Even if they would never see eye to eye, they were his parents and they loved him. They'd deal with it their way.

Trevor ran his hand through his hair and across his face. He wanted to bolt from the room and call Sophie. Now his parents knew, he'd be happier. Trevor had needed to be honest with himself about his family. Coming out wouldn't change what had gone between them, but he'd done something Ali hadn't: he'd been honest with his family.

Mel hadn't moved from her position by the door. She hugged a pile of sheets to her chest and stepped forward into the kitchen.

'Trevor, I can't take this. I'm sorry,' she said.

His mother murmured into his father's ear. Trevor turned away from his parents.

'Do you hate me?' Trevor put his hands out to Mel. She met his gaze but didn't move.

'No. Of course not. But I can't approve of what you do. My church is against it,' she shrugged.

'What does this have to do with your stupid church? Is this some new thing? You used to be much more open-minded.'

'I still am. But I can't see this as normal.'

'Great. I'm not normal. Thanks a lot, sis.'

He stood close to the blackened top of the cooking area their mother had used for years. The backboard covered in oil spots, yellowed by the meat fried every New Year that spat oil up the wall. The sizzling of rice thrown into the pan with eggs and garlic. Beside it was a bottle of soy sauce—forever being filled from the larger bottle. Trevor ran his finger over the ridged outer edges of the bottle. Mel cleared her throat and placed the bundle of clothing on a chair.

'I talked to the priest about it. He said you won't be fulfilling your nature. I think he meant what God intended you to do.'

'You talked to him about me?'

'Of course. I am still trying to understand it all myself. I don't hate you, Trevor.'

'But wait. You knew I was gay?' Trevor whispered the last question and released some of his pent-up disbelief.

'When you came back here with that foreign guy. I noticed how you looked at him and I guessed he wasn't just your friend.'

Trevor dragged a hand through his hair. A newfound understanding of his sister overwhelmed him. She might not understand, but she still loved him. They could fix this.

'I hope you can accept me one day. I'd like to be happy, and I think you would want me to be happy, too.'

'You are my brother.' Mel played with the gold cross hanging on a thin chain around her neck. She fingered it for a moment before tucking it back into her shirt. 'But I can't give you my blessing. Not now. And that won't change.' Her face crumpled and her mouth slumped, her eyes brimming with tears. 'I'm sorry, Trevor.' She paused for a moment and placed her hand on his shoulder. They locked eyes, and Trevor's tears bubbled up at the edges and his bottom lip quivered. Mel broke free, and in two steps she was at the base of the staircase and ascending to the small rooms upstairs. She didn't look back.

Trevor watched the empty staircase for a moment before a rustle and the sound of the front door being pulled back caught his attention. His mother called him.

'I'll come with you.' He heard his own voice replying to his mother, and he turned and walked away from the staircase.

Trevor and his mother walked in silence, entering the narrow maze of streets around the central pond area that housed most of the shop fronts selling vegetables. They were soon surrounded by piles of carrots stacked next to nets of cabbages, leaning up against dusty wooden crates spilling over with herbs, and sacks of rice and flour.

Trevor's phone buzzed in his pocket. 'You go ahead, Mum. I'll just take this call.'

She squeezed his arm. He hadn't realised how little they used to touch, but she'd held his arm the whole way from the house—a closeness that hadn't been there before.

'It's me.' The line crackled, but there was no mistaking the accent. It must be midnight in the UK. Ali was likely drunk. Maybe he'd come around and seen that Osei was a mistake. Ali would say it didn't matter what they thought, but he'd done it. He'd told them. There was a chance they could figure things out now.

Trevor stepped out from under an awning covering the sprawling vegetable stands and turned his back to his mother. She'd stopped by a woman selling tomatoes.

'Is everything okay?' Trevor paused, waiting for Ali's drunken rambling to start.

A murmur and a whispered exchange he could barely hear.

'Ali?'

'I wanted to share some good news with you. Osei said I should share it.'

Trevor shut his eyes. *Osei*. His lids were heavy like he could lie down and sleep for weeks. He'd caused this; this was the god's way of getting revenge on him. I brought this on myself—Mel would say that, and more. Messing about with guys in England. *What did you think would happen?*

'Can you make it quick?' Trevor imagined them sitting on the sofa at home, arms around each other, making fun of him.

Ali took a breath. 'I've been at the police station all day. And there's no charges. They decided there's no evidence for a criminal investigation.'

'That's… good. You must be thrilled.' The words came heavy. Each one an effort. He should have felt relieved, elated even. It proved Ali wasn't a predator.

A pause.

'You don't sound pleased.'

'I am. What happened?'

'There's camera footage of Simon and Michael trying to get into DV8. So the bouncers are in trouble for letting them in. Addler has some pictures on his phone. But they just showed us dancing. Well, and one of me and you kissing. But whatever.'

That night again. Ali had his arm around the guy's shoulder. Trevor was sure they'd kissed. Or it looked that way. The evening had been arranged for their anniversary. A celebration. But Ali had been all over everyone that night. He saw the image again: Ali's mouth close to the guy's ear. Trevor had grabbed his arm, to save the guy from Ali's shouting, or that's what he told himself. But he was jealous. A similar feeling cooked his guts now. What was he making so much noise about that night, anyway?

Ali sounded thrilled, but something didn't sit right in Trevor's stomach. He hadn't given the case against Ali much thought since he left. Not really his problem. There wasn't any evidence, and it boiled down to Addler and Smith claiming Ali had offered them money.

'What about the assault charge in school?'

A rumble of thunder in the distance caused many of the stall keepers to glance up and begin covering their produce.

'That's the next step. Ladner wants me to go to school next week. Osei thinks I can get my job back. And we can move on.'

'That's great, Ali. Look, I can't really talk right now. Haven't you got someone else to call? Osei, perhaps?' Trevor grimaced at the malice in his own voice. He didn't care. He didn't owe Ali anything at this point. What did it matter now? He had bigger problems to deal with. Mel being the main one. And Ali might be able to switch into happy mode and ignore the whispers around the school—it would be common knowledge by now—but

Trevor didn't move on so easily.

'I'm sorry. I wanted to let you know. It's Christmas Day tomorrow.'

'I know.' Trevor's gut twisted. They'd fucked that up. Better they moved on; there wouldn't be any reason to celebrate another Christmas with Ali.

Another silence. 'Osei's here. He says hi.'

Trevor looked to the sky. Grey clouds gathered at the edges of the horizon. They'd be getting a downpour soon.

'Great.' Was Ali in some sort of rehab programme? He sounded like he was trying to make amends with the world. A few months too late at this point. 'I hope you get better. And I hope you're happy.'

Another pause. Trevor regained his composure. Just get through this call, don't show them you're bothered. Ali's problems were not Trevor's anymore. He'd been there for Ali when they had started this together. But it looked like they wouldn't finish it together.

'I've let you down somehow, Ali. I should have believed you.'

'Don't say that. I'm seeing now we had a lot of problems. From the beginning.'

It felt like a slap to the face how quickly Ali had moved on. Barely a couple of weeks and some other guy had taken Trevor's place. It was for the best.

Ali continued, and he sounded more together than he had done for a while. Annoyingly cheerful. 'I'm going to pass you over quickly. Wait a second.'

What?

'Trevor. It's Osei. Look, I know I'm probably the last person you want to talk with right now. Anyway, I pushed Ali to tell you. To talk with you.'

'Thanks, I really appreciate it.' Trevor's robotic voice came out with the breath he'd been holding. *Who is this guy? Someone Ali picked up and now he's Ali's life coach or something?*

'You shouldn't turn your back on a friend. He needs you.'

'What?' It caught him off guard. Another punch to the gut. Happy fucking Christmas.

'I said he needs you.'

Trevor gripped the metal pole that supported a shop awning. The canvas rippled and caught the wind coming in strong now. The pole shook in his hand. Was he for real?

Ali's seeking atonement and yet again it boiled down to Trevor to make amends.

'I've gotta go. My mum's waiting for me.'

Trevor hung up.

Twenty-One

Ali sat outside Ladner's office. An hour ticked by, measured by his tapping foot drumming against the leg of the narrow double sofa. The lights above the corner of the secretary's desk blazed. Each one a small circle of light. Things had to get back to normal soon, whatever normal was at this point.

Ladner explained that all those involved should meet on "neutral ground," i.e., his office, before the final meeting to decide if and how Ali would return to school now the police charges were dropped. Ali hoped Janet and Mrs Addler wouldn't cause a scene, but knowing they both were stubborn meant anything could happen.

Janet had been a soft-spoken mother apart from when she opened the white wine after work, to "ease her aches" as she had said. The sun would set, and she became sharper, the wine flooding her bloodstream, expanding her capillaries until they burst across her nose. The radio turned up louder while two glasses were sunk. Plates and bowls banged down, and a spoon rattled as it was tossed into the sink. Regular Janet did not toss spoons into sinks.

Ali's foot thrummed back and forth on the wooden chair leg. The light above the secretary's desk burned a little brighter. Despite it burning his retina, he continued to stare.

As a kid, Ali would sit at the four-seater table, dreading his father's arrival. Inevitably, he would arrive shortly before seven. His hand ruffled through Ali's hair when he passed by, planting a kiss on top of his head before moving towards the garage. Ali hated the garage, with its sodium lights that blazed towards the rear, away from the doors opening out onto the driveway, but most of all he hated the back corner on the left. If he kicked the boxes on any given morning, they would rattle and chink with bottles and tins. Lava from his mother mixed with self-entitled, boiled molasses from his father. Two liquids feeding off one another. Molasses creeping, following the path burned through by the lava.

His father's thick voice and pointed fork identified an issue with the dinner. It always seemed to be about spaghetti and meatballs. The sauce should've been cooked longer, or it wasn't cooked enough. Janet sneered. Sometimes words were enough for them. Back and forth it would go, hour after hour. Chasing each other from room to room. Cat and mouse, but in this case, the mouse had a toothpick and determination to peg the cat. The mouse knew the cat bore softness between its claws and behind its ears. To gouge and enter, in the hope of causing a free flow of blood. They were equally nasty drunks.

And so was he. He'd played cat and mouse with

Trevor. Fuck. The thoughts slid into his mind one by one, stacked up against one another. A family curse, and he'd pressed replay on their relationship. Acted it out with Trevor. *Fuck.*

'Fuck.' Ali's face itched like the floor with the scratchy straw carpet grazing his skin. His cheeks burned and his lungs tightened from the screaming in his head. 'Fuck.'

A door slammed, and Ali startled on the standard grey office sofa. Footsteps shuffled behind the door in front of him. Ladner stood with his arm out, beckoning Ali inside. He couldn't respond and felt his vision blurring as he slumped to the left on the sofa. He'd spent so much time navel gazing that he'd missed what was right in front of him. Trevor. He'd pushed him away and caused him to get on a plane and return to China. Pressure pounded on his temples. He wouldn't become his father, not for a second.

'Come on. Take a seat in my office.' Ladner crouched beside Ali. With his help, he hauled himself into a seated position, but before he could orientate himself, a voice Ali hoped he'd never hear again said, 'What are they doing here, Mr Ladner?' And Mrs Addler walked into the office reception area.

The four of them sat in a sullen silence. Ali, Ladner, Janet, and Mrs Addler. Arranged around the low circular coffee table. A collective scowl shared by the entire group. Ali clutched a glass of water handed to him by the receptionist. He couldn't stand the look of pity that she cast over him. Likely, he looked like a wreck, and face planting in the sofa hardly made him look like he had his shit together. Did he want his job back? Was that even an option now? He needed Trevor; he always knew what to say to make him feel better.

'I didn't realise this was for everyone. I'd have brought my lawyer if I'd known.' Mrs Addler sniffed and reached for her bottle of mineral water.

'This is a preliminary meeting. I wanted to get you together to see if we could reach a consensus before the board meeting tomorrow.' Mr Ladner looked tired. Dark circles ringed his eyes, a puffiness settled on his jowls. 'We can't decide here, but we can discuss the options.'

Janet smoothed her skirt. 'I hope there will be some compensation for the victim. Or at least a public apology.' She gestured to Ali. His temple ached, but the burning behind his eyes had subsided.

'Victim?' Mrs Addler scoffed. 'You seem confused, Janet. My son is the only victim here.'

'Your son, Helen'—Janet gripped her leather purse— 'is a nasty, spiteful little runt. Just like you.'

Mrs Addler's mouth opened, and she threw a horrified look at Ladner.

'How dare you? Your son is at fault here. Not mine.'

Ladner shifted on his feet and edged around the corner of the desk before sinking into the leather chair. He placed his hands flat on the desk and looked happy to have a large solid piece of furniture between himself and the sparring parents.

'What exactly are you trying to achieve here?' Janet's

voice came out husky. 'Chris? Why are we here?' She jutted out her chin.

Mr Ladner dipped his head and reached into the drawer of his desk and retrieved a manila folder. 'Ali told us at the first meeting with the school lawyer. She noted, let me see, what does it say, '…as a gay man.' We want to ensure we follow the correct procedures and treat everyone fairly. However, an assault charge on school property is still being looked at.' Ladner cleared his throat.

Ali met his mother's gaze. Her lips pressed tightly together, and she looked ready to explode. He hadn't wanted her to find out this way.

Mrs Addler reeled off from a clutch of papers she opened on her lap. 'He might still pose a risk of harm. Is he suitable to work with children after all this?'

Ali spoke for the first time. 'I've been cleared of all charges.'

'By the police.' Mrs Addler dismissed him with a wave. 'It doesn't change the assault in the corridor. And whatever the police may say, I believe Michael.'

'That's enough.' Mr Ladner raised his hand.

Janet was silent, but her hand found Ali's, and she squeezed his fingers.

'Can we focus on the issue and the facts at hand? We need to hear Ali's side of the story.' He gestured towards Ali with the stack of papers in his hand.

Mrs Addler ignored the headmaster and continued. She leaned forward, her eyes gleaming. 'Another boy has come forward. He was seventeen, Janet. Seventeen.'

'So'—Janet took back her hand and folded her arms across her chest—'he's a legally consenting adult in the eyes of UK law.'

But still illegal in Ali's position as a teacher. Who the fuck were they talking about?

Ali cast a glance at his mother. Her eyes narrowed with Mrs Addler taking all of her attention, but her hands were clenched tightly in her lap. What other student was Mrs Addler talking about?

'But Ali is a teacher. This boy was a *child.*' Mrs Addler hissed the last word.

Mr Ladner sighed. 'Helen, let's deal with the facts, please. He *was* a teenager. He claims to have known Mr Morgan when they were both sixth formers.'

'George.' The word tumbled from Ali's mouth. His first kiss with a guy. His first everything. They'd met online through a basic chatroom. He'd been between Ali's legs—

'I remember him.' Janet turned to Ali.

Mrs Addler startled. 'That's right. George S—'

'For god's sake, Helen.' Janet cut her off. 'That boy, you say, was seventeen. Nearly eighteen, actually. And Ali was nineteen. And it was years ago.'

He stared at his mother, but her gaze remained rooted on Mrs Addler.

Mrs Addler's lip curled in a bitter, jagged line. 'Isn't that what they call a—what is it, Chris? An abuse of power?'

'Well, yes. In his teacher's role, that sort of behaviour is illegal—'

'What the hell are you talking about?' Janet cut Ladner off. 'Ali wasn't a teacher then. You must be talking about Ali's friend. George, that was years ago.'

Ladner's gaze moved from Janet to Mrs Addler.

She scrunched her face before replying curtly. 'He was still a boy and remembers Mr Morgan very well. Apparently, he wanted to be a teacher back then.'

'Oh, my good Christ. Sorry, Chris.' Janet raised her hands. 'She is insane. And he didn't come forward, and you know it. You hunted him down. Probably crawled through Facebook for hours, didn't you, Helen? It was probably Myspace, going back that far.'

Mrs Addler's face flushed at the remark, but she remained resolute, her arms folded across her chest.

'I wanted to know if he made a habit of approaching minors.'

'Stop. Just stop before you make yourself sound any more ridiculous. George was not a minor. Ali is not a predator.'

Mrs Addler blanched. Stood. She reached for the door and wrenched it open. She gripped the handle as she bent down to grab her handbag, resting by the foot of her chair. She hissed at Ali, her face centimetres away. 'Stay away from my son.'

'It'll be my pleasure'—Janet's nostrils flared—'if you and your son stay away from mine.'

Mrs Addler slammed the door.

Ali blinked. This was more than he could process. Janet had known all along. She hadn't said anything though, after all this time. Typical Janet. Did she know about Trevor? She hadn't rejected him. Yet. But she looked ready to tear something apart, her fingers moving rapidly across the hem of her skirt. He might be next, but Janet remained rooted to her chair, a faraway look in her eye like she was contemplating what to do next. Frozen, apart from her thumb that worried the knuckles on her left hand now she'd stopped bothering her skirt.

Ali gripped his knees. He pushed himself up from the sofa and walked towards the window. The trees at the edges of the playing field, tall cedars with narrow branches ending in spindly tips, swayed in the breeze. The afternoon gloom settled in as the sun sank lower in the sky.

When Ali turned back, Mr Ladner was writing something on a pad.

'You remember him after all this time?' Ali said.

Janet smoothed her skirt and snapped out of her reverie. 'George Smith. I'd never forget that name.'

She beckoned Ali to come and sit on the sofa beside her. The whole time, her gaze remained rooted on Ali's face.

Twenty-Two

Trevor knew tonight would be the last night he would spend in China for a long time. Being back, he'd seen there wasn't a life for him here. He'd have a job in Bristol for a couple of years until he decided what he wanted to do. But staying there depended on his visa; without it, he was screwed.

Trevor's parents, wrapped in thick padded jackets, chatted animatedly in the kitchen, their feet steaming in giant bowls of hot water. The curling smoke from his father's cigarette rose and filled the air with a bitter fragrance from Trevor's youth. He remembered his uncles pulling him into their jackets roughly, with the same smoky smell, but they hugged him in a way his father never did.

He watched his father now. A man of few words, but he had worked hard when Trevor was growing up, and they'd moved a couple of times when he was very young. When one business died and another one of the family members opened a new market stall or had a shipment to fulfil of the newest fad in the US or Germany, and they needed extra hands to fill the order—they'd move to the next town or county. Those were happy times. He remembered the buzz of machinery and lights glaring all night in the workshops where he would settle down after finishing his school homework. His mother would tuck a blanket around him and then return to the factory floor to continue on the pressing machine and working to provide. Once in Hunan, when they were in primary school and slept on the dusty wooden floor, his sister had handed him half a steamed bun.

'Eat it,' she said. 'Go on, Trevor. Eat it.'

'Whoa!' Trevor snapped out of his dream. He'd dozed off in the small living room next to the kitchen. The blaring TV lights, the chatter, and the warmth of a blanket wrapped around him.

'You were snoring.' His sister didn't take her eyes off her phone.

'I was thinking, actually. Remember when you fed me that steamed bun in Hunan?'

His sister's gaze flicked up and caught his.

'You really enjoyed eating that baby cockroach I put in there,' she guffawed.

Their mother hushed and tutted through the doorway. 'Ha. Ha. You were such a horror. Bullying your poor, starving brother.'

Trevor side-eyed his sister.

'Poor? Maybe. Starving? Hardly. You were the fattest kid in your class. By a good few inches!'

Trevor opened his eyes in mock horror and shock.

'You're evil.'

'Okay, favourite boy. You need to get over that. It

was twenty years ago.'

'Whatever. It was a dream.'

Mel returned to her phone, and Trevor watched the flickering TV, but his eyes returned to his sister. Her face, a narrow nose and defined cheeks like his, illuminated white from the glare of the phone screen. Her fingers tapped away on it, quick-fire rapid movements.

'What's your dream, sis?'

Trevor leaned over and away from the TV to get her full attention. She continued to tap on the phone screen, ignoring him. 'Hey!'

'What?' She turned to look at him.

'I asked you a question.'

'I know. It was lame, so I ignored it.'

'You are hard work. I've got to go back to England in a few days. Actually, the day after tomorrow I leave for the airpo—'

'I won't change my mind, Trevor.' She cut him off. She put down the phone, thumbing the power button until the light turned off. The room lit from the yellow hue given off by the ancient TV and the glow of the electric heater positioned between them.

'My dream is you'll see things how I see them. The church I attend is very clear on this. The priest has told me to stick to my guns. And I will, because it's what I believe is right for you.'

'I'm gay, Mel. I'm not the devil.'

'It's not really about being G-A-Y. Well, it is. The priest said, 'intrinsic moral evil.' It's a disorder, Trevor. Like those people are sick. They need help.'

'So you can't ever be happy for me?' Trevor shifted in his seat. He didn't want to have this talk with his sister now, thinking she would cool down after a few days, but she hadn't. She hadn't been afraid to use a fist or object to show Trevor she was upset when they were kids. Her favourite weapon had been her hairbrush, and their mother could never understand how a little girl could break so many plastic hairbrushes into two parts. Their mother would tut about having to spend more money that they just didn't have.

'I am happy for you, Trevor. You seem content working overseas, but I can't forgive you committing sin. There is no other way to see it. It's a sin. Unless you are celibate. That's the way the priest sees it. And that is how I must see it.'

'We won't agree on this. It's who I am. I was born like this. Why can't you just accept me for who I am?'

'Live your life how you want to.' Both their voices rose and filled the small room. 'I just don't want you to rub my face in it, that's all.'

'But you can't help with my dream? That's it. Your precious church is more important than your own brother.'

She stood up and in one swift motion crossed the room then closed the door between them and their parents in the kitchen.

'Don't you ever say that!' She pointed her finger at him. 'You have always put yourself first. You were always the favoured little boy. I was the mistake. The sister. The girl. Do you think they were happy when I was born?

When little me popped out. No, they wanted you and your little dick. You've never thought why we're so close in age? You have always been put first. Your fucking feelings have always been on a pedestal. Since day fucking one.' She towered over him, shaking.

Trevor's eyes filled with hot tears. 'Sis, I—'

'Don't. It doesn't matter. And just so you know, I am the one living here. I look after Mum and Dad while you swan around whatever country you fancy, getting up to fuck knows what. Don't forget us, Trevor. Your family is here. Not there. Not with him. Whoever he may be.'

She sank back into the overstuffed armchair and pulled the white knitted blanket up high to cover the bottom of her chin, as she had when she was a little girl.

And turned away from him.

Trevor didn't know what to say. He stood, feeling empty, and walked out of the room, closing the door behind him. His final glimpse of the room showed Mel staring straight ahead at the TV.

Trevor's mum approached him in the kitchen. She smiled and rubbed his arms through his sweater.

'You must make us proud. You know that, don't you?'

A tight-lipped smile twitched his lips.

He wanted nothing more for his parents than to ensure they were looked after until the day they died. Neither would ask for help, yet it was his duty as the eldest son to ensure both had everything they needed.

'I will. You might even get to visit England one day.'

'We'd like that.' Faint tears glistened at the edges of

her warm brown eyes. His parents would never fully understand how he'd manage living in England, or living as a gay man, but they didn't have to, and sharing this part of him with them could only bring them closer. She released his arm and moved back to the chair beside her husband.

Trevor wished them goodnight. Taking everything in as he climbed the stairs. Home, but since being away it felt different somehow. Everything was in the right place yet twisted at an angle. The chairs didn't fit right, and the lamp glowed a touch dimmer than he remembered. He'd grown up and changed; it was unrealistic to expect his home to move at the same pace.

From the bottom of the narrow wooden steps leading upstairs, he turned to look back at his parents sitting side by side. His father's body seemed smaller and sat a little lower in the chair. His mother's hands looked daintier than they had before. Both parents worked hard, but they were safe here. He had nothing for them, but he would help them build a new house in the future. The walls here sagged a little, the doors stuck in the frames, and the kitchen roof had leaked since he could remember. A tin bucket echoed through his high school dreams.

Trevor wept that night. Big, salty tears dampened the bedspread in his old bedroom. He took a small picture from his wallet and unfolded it. A passport photo of Ali from when he was in his late teens. His hair flopped down and almost covered his eyes, but swept back in a way that made him look like he had dashed into the photo booth and was surprised by the photo being snapped. Trevor had found it in Ali's room one afternoon, back when things were good between them. At that point, he'd wanted nothing more than to take Ali with him everywhere he went.

Trevor ran a finger over the rough edges. This guy… who was this guy who'd caused him so much pain? If it wasn't love, then why did his heart ache so much?

He scrunched up his eyes and balled his hands into fists. Where was Ali now? What was he doing?

It was the middle of the night back in England. Trevor sighed and bit his lip hard. But Ali must be fine, wherever he was right now.

Trevor toyed with his phone for a while. His fingernail dug at the shiny black surface and he thumbed through some photos on Instagram. There were a few of Ali with his parents. His sister. None of Trevor—the two worlds kept strictly apart.

Those moments before coming out to his parents felt wasted. What had he worried so much about? Hiding hadn't helped him or Ali—they should have leaned into their relationship and used the support of their parents and friends around them. Instead, they'd pushed their parents away. It wasn't Trevor's parents' job to validate him or tell him his worth. He had to do that. He needed to find his focus.

He thought about Dee and about the guy on the forest path. The furtive fucks and knocks on doors. Gays were still in the shadows here. He didn't want to repeat that—but could he make it work with Ali? Not if he'd moved on with this Osei. Trevor had always believed in fate, and going to England was part of his journey. His thoughts mixed together and looped back and forward.

A Pandora's box had opened for him in England. He should settle there; that part seemed clear at least. There would be other guys like Ali. Maybe Ali was a monster. Trevor just didn't know at that point. His mind was a ditch. He dozed off.

And, a while later, he awoke with a start.

His phone clattered off the bed. Why not try? Just to hear Ali's voice, to see if he was okay.

The phone rang silently in his hand. After six tries, he scrolled through Ali's Facebook. His thumb smudged each picture faster and faster, the years of Ali's life blurring by. Way beyond the years before Trevor met him. He wanted to see if he could work out where it went wrong. The last row of pictures stopped his scrolling. Ali looked about twenty. Still clutching a pint in one photo and held up by someone else in another. He had changed little in ten or so years. A bunch of lads. Had he come out by that point? It was impossible to tell.

Trevor's gaze cast across the pictures. Laughing girls squeezed Ali's arm. Ali face up on a bed with writing all over his neck and ears, definitely drunk. A guy crouched down, running a hand over his back. Could be a mate, but they leaned into each other.

Trevor paused. Scrolled back a couple of photos. The same blue shirt in about five different pictures. Maybe a boyfriend? He looked pretty young.

Trevor's eyes widened as his finger hovered over the

name.
   George Smith.

Twenty-Three

'Well, that went well.' Janet rolled her eyes towards Ali. 'She won't be involved in the board's decision, will she?' She directed the question at Ladner.

'We will do our best to seek a fair judgement and outcome. But I have to warn you, working here afterwards might not be an option. Historically, it's advised teachers move from the county where allegations have occurred.' Ladner steepled his fingers under his chin.

Ali shook his head. No job in the middle of January—pretty bleak.

'So, George Smith. He used to be a student here. Late nineties. Quiet boy. Complete contrast to his brother.'

'Brother?' Janet swivelled in her seat.

Did they really have to go over all this now? The headache persisted across his temple. 'Mum, can we not?'

'Simon. That little twerp is George's brother?' Janet's gaze moved between the two men.

Ladner kept his gaze on the paper in front of him. 'It might just be a coincidence. But with the allegations coming from Michael, we'll have to look into how Simon is involved.'

Janet clutched the tea mug and turned to Ali. 'He's more than a little involved. And I want to know why.' She drew a sharp breath through her teeth, her mouth scrunched up like she was thinking.

'How did you know?' Ali drew a breath. 'Before George, I mean.'

'We had the internet, Ali. And you didn't delete the search history often enough.'

Ali sat back, stunned that Janet had known about his illicit browsing for so long.

'I pushed it to the back of my mind,' she said. 'I thought it was a phase. It was illegal for teachers to talk about any type of gay sex ed then. Section 28, you probably don't remember it.'

'I do.' Ladner's head shook slightly from side to side. 'A horrible bit of Tory legislation. The effects carried on for years.'

'I feel let down. Why didn't you tell me earlier?' Janet leaned in closer. It seemed she didn't want Ladner to overhear them. Fat chance it mattered now anyway.

'I don't know why I didn't tell you. I was scared.' Ali eyeballed her.

'Oh god, I think I've always known.' She sat back in her chair. Not bringing up George between his legs was all Ali could wish for at this point.

She continued. 'But I didn't ever want to admit it to myself. Or anyone else.' A thin laugh escaped her lips, and she brushed back her hair. 'And you and Trevor are more than friends? Ray said you acted like a couple sometimes, but I told him that was ridiculous.'

Ali didn't know what was worse. Keeping secrets from his mother or discussing them with her.

'We are just—'

Janet said, 'How would I have told people then? You know what your uncle is like.'

'Can we talk about this later, Mum?' Ali's cheeks itched. The room became smaller all of a sudden. 'And you won't have to worry about Trevor anymore,' Ali muttered under his breath.

'Isn't that right, Mr Ladner? How do they expect us to get our heads around it? You just can't tell nowadays.'

Ladner toyed with the gold wedding band on his finger. 'My sister. She was different.'

'Cathy? I'm sorry, I didn't mean to upset you,' Janet responded quickly.

'No. You haven't.' Ladner's gaze didn't leave Ali's face. A softness crept in around the edges of his eyes that hadn't been there when he was tearing Ali a new one.

'I remember her. So full of life. The life and soul as they'd say back then. It wasn't a party unless Cathy Ladner was invited.' Janet's eyes misted.

He chuckled. 'She would have loved to hear you say that.' Around his mouth, lines drooped, and he ran a hand around his chin. A glazed look frosted his grey eyes facing the window, and he blinked rapidly. It appeared Janet wanted to change the subject; she had always been good at reading people's faces and likely noticed that this turn of conversation was making him uncomfortable.

'Thanks for the tea. But we best be off. We'll see you

tomorrow. Thank yo—'

'She was gay.'

Janet's mouth froze around her words.

All this time—Ali's mind swam—most of the people around him knew someone gay or had seen his poor attempts to hide his own sexuality. And they'd still loved him and still given him a chance…

Janet stared at Ladner as a smile crept onto his lips. He returned her stare over the rim of his mug, his eyes glistening with tears, but he didn't try to wipe them away.

'The system was always unfair to her. Back then, in the late seventies. Where did she have to go? Who could she turn to? You remember her, that side of her. Partying and being social. She was the light of the party.'

Janet placed her mug down carefully. 'She was, she really was. Did she find someone? I lost touch with her when we all moved off for university.'

'No.' He sounded resolute, and Janet leaned in because it appeared he had more to say. 'She didn't. That light in her began to dim. It was one of the most painful things I have ever seen.'

'I heard she suffered from depression. And dropped out of her course.' Janet spoke in a small voice. They both stared into the middle distance for a moment.

Ladner let out a sigh, placing his hands behind his head.

'It was more than that. She went to college. We kept in touch, we were always close. She was my big sister. After the first term, she seemed different. She'd met a girl. She was in love. They'd been partying and became close. So, she wanted to tell me and my parents that she was happy and gay.'

Janet ran her finger along the edge of the mug. Ali tried to read her expression, but her face remained stoic. Why was Ladner bringing this up now? He'd hardly been helpful and gay-supporting barely a few weeks ago.

'But when she returned… I remember getting home from school, and there was shouting coming from the kitchen. My father had her back against the wall. He was holding her there. I'll never get that image out of my mind. After all these years, it was like she was an animal. You know, when they are trying to catch a feral cat, or a wild animal, and they use that pole. He was trying to crush her. My mother just sat at the kitchen table, sobbing.'

Janet covered her mouth, her eyes wide.

How had he ever been afraid she would react like that? She had strong opinions, but she wouldn't have been brutal, and she would never be unkind. So much had gone on in his head, and so much of it wasn't true.

Ladner continued. He spoke in a calm levelled voice like he was retelling a mundane story.

'I can still see them now when I entered the room and he dropped his hands from her throat. And she pushed back from the wall, her face red, her hair over her eyes. She ran up the stairs. It felt like I had walked into a war zone.'

'And they never came around?'

'Never. They were too deep into the church and religion. I think the priest even came over that night or that weekend. It's all a bit of a blur.'

'My god.'

'My mother told me months later. She was drunk then, drinking almost every day, like the shame or guilt was too much for her. That Cathy died in a car accident.'

'I'm so sorry.' Tears streaked Janet's cheeks.

Tears pricked at the edges of Ali's vision. He'd felt the same—not so long ago. The shard of mirror and his drinking… he'd tried to drown out a part of him that he should have celebrated.

'But it wasn't true. She killed herself. Because they abandoned her.'

They sat in silence for a few minutes. Janet's wrapped Ali's hand in her own.

'I've been thinking about her a lot in the past couple of weeks. How the system was stacked against her, how unfair it can be, but ultimately how sometimes we answer to a higher power and it's out of our control. But I should have done more.' Ladner wiped a single tear coursing down his cheek. 'Mrs Addler went too far. I'm sorry. I should have done more for you.'

Ali watched them both brush away tears. Times had changed, and things were supposed to be better now. Ali hoped for students now that it was easier to come out, to be themselves.

'I don't know what trouble you're going to end up in'—Janet turned towards Ali, her cheeks flushed and eyes reddened from the tears—'but we will stand by you.'

Ali waved Osei into the flat and closed the door behind

him.

'Thanks for cleaning just enough so we can find somewhere to sit,' Osei grinned. That fucking positive attitude again, in response to everything. If only it was contagious.

Ali threw himself onto the sofa, chucking the dustpan and brush on the floor. 'I can't afford to live in a hotel any longer. Trevor's gone, anyway. I'll deal with this shit-tip tomorrow.'

'So what about your job? It's a goner?'

'I'm not sure right now. My mum thinks I'll get struck off. And she seems to be right about everything at the moment.' A stream of air escaped his lips.

'You okay about that?'

'I'm scared. I've worked in schools for as long as I can remember. Teaching has been my life. Everything I've worked towards has been for that school.'

'It'll work out. We talk it through…' Osei's intelligent eyes, the ones that had captured Ali's attention that first night, narrowed like he could read Ali's thoughts.

Turning his body to face Osei, Ali spoke without looking away. 'I've been thinking. Before this goes too far, I need to get out of here. I don't think I'll be around for a while.'

'How long will you be away?' Osei's gaze roved Ali's face.

'I mean, I can't see you anymore. I hope you understand…'

Osei's left eye twitched, barely a flicker, but it seemed he'd registered the words and the meaning behind them.

'I don't get it. I thought you were going to jail.' Osei laughed, a deep chuckle that he must have felt in his belly. 'Too soon?'

'Yes. Too soon.' Ali raked a hand through his hair. 'I'm sorry, but I have some things to work through. It's the whole—'

'It's you. Not me, right? I get it.'

'You're a sweet guy.'

'You're still in love with that Thomas, or whatever his name is, aren't you?'

Ali's cheeks burned. 'I need to find Trevor.'

'I knew since that first night.'

Ali covered his eyes. He tensed, expecting a slap, but Osei's hands cupped his hands from the outside; his warm palms pressed up against Ali's cold skin. Not everyone responded with violence—Ali was learning that.

'Was I that obvious?' Ali peeked through his fingers at Osei, still staring at him, and snapped them back as soon as he caught sight of the deep blue-grey eyes waiting for him.

'I guessed I was just a rebound.'

'You're a good guy. And hot. You've got a great dick.'

Osei chuckled again. He gently lowered Ali's hands and smoothed down the front of Ali's shirt.

'That Facebook thing was a bit much. That was for him, wasn't it?'

'Oh, good Christ. I'm deleting all social media from now on. Note to self: do not drink-post online.'

Osei's grin vanished. 'You should get a handle on the drinking. You'll never move on if you don't.'

'Okay, okay. I know.'

'I'm serious. You lash out, Ali. You hate yourself in those moments, and you take it out on others. I saw it in your eyes that first night.'

'Say what you feel, Osei. Jesus.'

Self-entitled prick. But he wasn't wrong—

'Fine, you're right. I hate myself sometimes. Happy now?' Ali sat back, his arms folded.

'Where does that come from?'

A shudder moved through Ali's back muscles. A tension settled in his neck, a familiar scratching feeling touched his palms. He knew this day would come. The conversation he'd had with himself every morning waking up with a splitting headache, a dry mouth, and a sickness in his stomach.

'My father.'

'I guessed as much.' Osei's smile reached his eyes.

Here it came, the lecture from someone who didn't know shit about what it was like, how much he'd gone through, and how it would never get better.

'Don't repeat his mistakes. Forgive your parents and move on.'

Ali's eyes clouded with tears. *Fuck. Like it was that easy.*

'Talking to someone, somebody objective who's outside of your shit, helps.'

'It wouldn't work. I hate talking to people about stuff like that.'

'You liked talking about Trevor that first night. A lot, actually.'

'I'll figure my stuff out first. Trevor will have to wait.'

'Go get him back, Mr Desperado.' Osei gave Ali a light shove to his arm.

Ali swatted at him before taking a deep breath to steady himself. He moved to the mirror and smoothed down his cheeks, tears wetting his fingertips.

'Too late for that. He went back to China.'

'If it's meant to be, you'll find him.'

'We have the internet now.' Ali laughed through the tears. 'And Google Maps.'

'You know what I mean.'

'I do. And thank you. If this had been the other way around, I would have been such a jerk about it.'

Osei just smiled. He reached over to collect a notebook and a jacket, and unplugged his phone charger by the coffee table.

'I know.' Osei smiled again and pulled the shoulder bag up before slipping on his shoes. 'I should say thanks to you.'

Ali laughed. 'Now who's talking shit?'

'I mean it.' Osei punched him lightly on the arm again. 'You showed me being a selfish jerk doesn't mean I'm not good enough. That I should put myself first. Life's too short to spend it trying to please other people. Especially those who were meant to be keeping me safe. My parents rejected me—I could be dead now.'

Fuck. Ali had been so wrapped up in his own shit. He'd barely listened to Osei's story about how he escaped Ghana.

'You are wanted and loved, Osei. Fuck your parents. They turned their back on you. You are good enough.'

Ali believed this but had failed to see it for his own shit.

Osei nodded. 'I don't need to deny my own needs. I'm always trying to help—putting my value in how much I can please other people.'

'Like your grandma?'

'Exactly.'

'I need to touch base with her. I'm going to try and see her again this year.'

'And your parents?'

'It's too dangerous to go back. But I'll see how we get on. From what my grandma says, I suspect they've gotten worse. Those beliefs don't disappear overnight.'

They sat in silence for a moment. Osei had a ton of shit to deal with as well. Masking his own demons, same as Ali. Everyone was fighting something from their past.

'I got sober too, you know?'

'You did?' Ali had sworn Osei drank with him that first night.

'No vodka in my OJ, mate. You'd have noticed if you didn't always have your head up your arse. Excuse my French.' He winked and moved to collect his phone.

'I used to drink to hide from my parent's negativity. I wasted so much time trying to make sense of them, to be enough, but it was never enough.' Osei's words sounded determined. 'But now… I am enough. You showed me how destructive I'd been.'

Ali's world sat opposite him on the sofa. Every word of shame, every moment when they'd both been rejected by their parents. They'd come from different places, but they'd always share that.

'We're too similar.' Ali stroked the fabric on the sofa. 'We're always seeking approval. When we are enough already.'

'Exactly. We are good enough, Ali. I see that now. My value is not just helping others. My value is helping myself.'

'I've gotta go to rehab.' Ali stood. 'I can't expect Trevor to pick up my pieces anymore. I need to get away. He's not here, and that's good for me.' Clarity. For once in his life, Ali saw a way out of this.

They lingered at the door for a minute. Ali scratched his head, trying to avoid eye contact.

'So, see you around, perhaps?' Osei backed away from the door and towards the lift going down. Ali was pretty sure they'd never cross paths again. They'd both gained something, but sometimes leaving things in the past was for the best.

'Sure.' Ali gave a small wave as the lift doors slid closed.

Ali sank down once Osei was out of view, his back resting against the ridges of the wooden door panels. He stared around the empty apartment: the curtains catching the breeze, the wilting flowers in the vase, and the messed-up cushions strewn around with a pizza box lying open next to the TV remote. How far back would he need to go to undo the damage he'd caused? How much time would help him heal? Trevor would have a fit if he saw how much mess there was. Ali would make amends if the chance came. If Trevor came back.

Osei had a point. The buzz had worn off drinking.

All he ever did was wreck things, that much was obvious now. There wasn't a single soul around to stop him or prevent him from doing anything.

He caught sight of his laptop.

'Fucking Facebook,' he exclaimed, jumping up to delete his relationship status posted the other night.

Twenty-Four

Expansive white beams stretched across the airport ceiling. Trevor stared at the intricate criss-cross patterns and mulled over where he was headed. Things hadn't gone badly by all accounts. His parents still worried him, but he'd done what he could with them. They'd wanted him to be someone he couldn't be and do things he couldn't do. He'd accepted that and, for the first time, he felt calm. Telling them about his true self had been the best decision. A crushing weight had ascended from his shoulders. The world hadn't opened up and swallowed him like he imagined it would.

Still, his mother's voice rang in his mind. He'd take a partner back one day. He'd be the first, and it would blow her mind.

He'd been afraid to talk, to tell his parents who he really was. Without role models, or even a sense that being gay could mean being happy, he'd made some bad choices. Dee's face reflected back in the window and the tarmac shimmered in front of him, from the heat, from his tears. There was no point in beating himself up about that. Nothing would bring Dee back, but he could make better choices going forward.

The plane took off and bumped and rolled him into the sky. The first time years ago, he'd been hurtling towards Ali. Not knowing it at the time, only knowing he needed to escape. He'd been on the run. Now, his hometown wasn't scary, and all because he'd lifted the veil and allowed his family to step a little closer to him. He didn't fit in with the close-knit village life. After a few years away, he didn't belong anymore.

The clouds outside the window crumbled away, and Trevor's thoughts moved in and out of focus. Everything he'd dreamed of growing up had come true.

And he hurtled back towards Ali now. Or the place Ali came from.

Ali was his life there. With school and the training, pretty much all his time and attention had been spent with Ali.

Time away from Ali would be best for them both. He'd let Ali take over his life in many ways. He'd quickly tied himself to Ali and then became stuck. That was clear now. He'd expected Ali to be perfect and hold everything together, and never questioned that Ali wasn't the idealised version he saw or had even forced on him from his own dreams.

Mel's words hurt the most because she'd put her church above him. The air steward nodded as if understanding his thoughts and handed him a glass of water. As the plane dipped and passengers murmured, Trevor thought about what he did have. Found family. Those he'd chosen and didn't turn his back on. He'd let

Dee down, and if his sister didn't want to know him… She couldn't relate, but he'd found someone who lived the same experience as him. Someone who had done so much despite his own issues and one mistake.

Love didn't conquer all. It could hurt, and it dulled your senses, but stepping outside and returning home gave Trevor clarity. Ali needed to go to rehab.

He needed professional help. Trevor's parents showed him relationships took work but both sides needed to contribute. People didn't fix others. People couldn't forcefully change others. He could fix only himself.

His uncle hadn't changed for anyone. And his auntie—she'd been hurt for a long time. Nobody had stood up for her. It wasn't Trevor's fault.

Sophie had told him to leave Ali, and she was right. But without Ali and the Addler case, Trevor wouldn't have re-evaluated everything that was important.

Without Ali, Trevor never would have analysed his relationships in such detail. He wouldn't have picked over Ali's family and seen his own issues. What held Ali back was also holding him back.

They were one and the same—different in that Ali feared his parents for the violence and negative abuse they had doled out, but Trevor feared his parents too. He'd feared their disapproval, and his sense of shame had grown since he turned his back on them. He'd been running scared. Like Ali. They'd been running from reality.

The blue sea stretched out under the clouds from the

window. The horizon and endless possibilities stretched further than he could see.

He'd been meant to meet Ali—not to complete or make his life better, but to test him, to push him to face up to his own fears. Sophie had been right, but not in the way she thought.

Trevor's love wasn't meant to come from Ali. It wasn't about Ali completing him or saving him from his past. Ali had helped him through his own grief, to see that what he had wasn't so bad and he needed to be brave, to face his parents and not seek their permission or forgiveness but to demand their acceptance of his existence.

And Trevor played a role in Ali's life. He couldn't save him, nor should he try, but he did hold power to change Ali for the better through his own actions and love.

They'd have to get him into rehab. He couldn't do this alone; they'd become toxic, and ending it was the right thing.

The pain caused by Ali's drinking—Trevor had let it go on. But since he'd told his parents, he felt a nudge it wasn't all his fault. It wasn't his fault that Mel felt the way she did. And, like any addict, if Ali wanted to drink, he would.

Trevor was in love. A love he hadn't felt before, but when he was away from Ali it felt stronger. Burning brighter than when they were together sometimes. Maybe he was more in love with the idea of Ali than anything else. Love wasn't a complete and final solution to anything. Love was hard work, took time, and needed to be nurtured.

But he knew deep down, Ali hadn't done anything with that student.

Simon Smith. The name didn't ring any bells, but there was something there. He'd read enough crime and mystery novels to know the suspect was always known to the victim. People didn't go around randomly accusing people or jumping folks they didn't know. It did happen, but it was rare. Something closer and much more insidious was going on. Trevor suspected Ali of some sort of fuckup. But Ali wasn't bad, he wasn't evil. Trevor had spent time observing Ali in class and his passion couldn't be faked. Kids were unforgiving in their ability to spot a fraud. They saw the kindness in Ali. The kindness he'd drowned in drink to cover his shame.

The seatbelt lights flashed and switched off again. Blinking on the screen in front of Trevor, the map showed they were flying over central Europe now. He'd come a long way. And even if they couldn't work things out, if this relationship wasn't supposed to be, he could stand by Ali. He could still be a friend, and Ali needed a friend right now. When loneliness crept in, it hurt. And his mum always taught him to be a good friend.

A seed had been planted in him, and his feet touched solid ground for the longest time. If all the possibilities of the universe branched out around him, as the plane soared through the sky, then anything was within reach. Nothing excused Ali laying his hand on him, but it had happened once—and Trevor didn't blame himself now, but saw that it was barely about him in the first place. Ali was sick and needed help. They'd both made choices and each one had a result.

Trevor had stooped to Ali's level. He should have remained strong and said that no, he wanted an exclusive relationship. He didn't want to fuck around. He'd tried to live by Ali's rules, thinking it would please Ali and pull him closer. But he'd lost himself and pushed Ali away.

They had created a fertile ground for mistrust, and he saw that now. Hindsight was a fucker. He was strong, he was powerful. Ali needed to get better before he could grow and move on. Trevor had.

And until Ali could catch up, there was no *them*. They'd been co-dependent, like his aunt and uncle. Their families had been there, flashing warning lights of how not to have a relationship. Love didn't conquer all and it shouldn't. His aunt shouldn't have put up with that. She should have walked away. Ali should have known better, seeing Grant raise his fists to Janet.

A tear slipped down Trevor's cheek. In that alternate universe, Trevor screamed for his auntie to run, run away, and never look back. They couldn't go back, only forward, and while he knew that goodness existed in Ali, somewhere, deep down, he couldn't give up. Mel had turned his back on him. She'd caused him that pain, and if Trevor was only going to be there for Ali as his brother, he wouldn't turn his back on his found family.

A man in the seat over the aisle caught Trevor's gaze and smiled.

Trevor looked away. They'd messed up, but fuck it,

life wasn't going to get better by pretending everything was okay. Their families had fucked them up, but if they looked carefully enough, they also held the answers to getting better. Janet had stepped away.

People fucked up in the real world. Trevor had fucked up by hiding himself for so long.

People had tiptoed around Ali.

He couldn't save Ali. That wasn't his place. But he could help him.

And he wasn't hiding anymore. So, the world better fucking watch out.

Twenty-Five

Ali hugged himself as he shouldered the double doors open to enter the school hall. He was already chilled by the cold air outside, and the atmosphere in the assembly hall did little to warm him. His hand tingled from the cuts—they'd leave a bumpy scar. A memento to never be so stupid again.

Gina, the school lawyer, stood filling a small thermos flask from the water dispenser on a side table. Steam rose from the spluttering tap, disappearing into the lights glaring down from the lighting rig suspended above the space. Ali had missed the Christmas show this year, and he didn't know if he'd be allowed to show up for the next one.

Gina adjusted her black suit jacket with a free hand and moved to a chair at the end of the row. Each chair stood empty for the moment. She set the flask down, checked herself with a small compact mirror, and settled into the chair. The rest of the room held a few PTA members, including Mrs Addler. As always, her husband didn't show up, but she busied herself adjusting a tray of flapjacks and brushing some sugar off the tablecloth.

Were snacks really necessary for a school board meeting when firing a teacher was number one on the agenda? Ali shook his head, catching Janet's attention.

Janet rose from her chair at the back of the hall. Michael and Simon sat facing the half circle of chairs where the main board members would sit. They jostled each other. Ali looked away.

Janet approached him, and they met silently a few metres away from the staging area. She stroked his cheek, following it with a worried look.

'You look thin. Are you eating enough?'

'I saw you yesterday.'

'I'm just asking, that's all. Me and Ray were talking abou—'

'Mum.' With one word, Ali let his mother know he was fine, and she should stop.

'Okay. Okay. Come over here and sit down.'

'I've got to sit up there.' Ali jerked his head towards the chairs that sat apart from the others. One each for him, Gina, and Ladner, he assumed.

'It's a shame Trevor can't be here.' Janet hooked her arm through his. They stood still for a moment, and she leaned into him. Although she was a foot shorter than him, it was nice to have her close. Closer than she'd been since he was a child.

'He's not coming.'

Beneath her woollen hat, pulled down so the brim covered her eyebrows, Ali knew her brow was creased. She'd get over their breakup—just another Ali fuckup to deal with.

'He worked hard. Now that I think of it, he's never missed a deadline, despite all of this.'

'Yeah. He's good… was good for me. But don't get your hopes up, Mum.' If he could move on, then so should she. Eventually, they'd see each challenge for what it was. People came along at different times, but his chapter with Trevor was done. Best for all concerned to get over it.

She tutted in response, released his arm, and grabbed his hands again, patting them together between her woollen mittens.

'I know you hate me arguing with you.'

'Yes.'

'But, well, I have to say. He seemed like a nice fella. I hope you know what you're doing.'

'I do.' More than likely he didn't have a clue, but he needed to keep it together, to get through this meeting at least. Things had fallen apart since Trevor left, Ali equally to blame for their relationship failing; he saw that now. He'd lived in a world of excuses, clouded by alcohol, fuelled by anger at himself. He'd pushed and pushed Trevor away, terrified at what it meant for them to stay close to each other. He owed Osei a world of favours because Osei had helped him see what he really wanted, and getting wasted wasn't the answer.

'I'm glad you've decided to get sober. It never suited you.'

Following a deep inhale and slow exhale to steady herself, Janet edged away from him towards the back of the room.

Ali rolled his eyes. Since Ali's coming out, Janet had become open about everything and didn't hold back her opinions—not that she ever had a problem speaking her mind.

The seated panel looked grim. Each one shuffling papers and rearranging pens. Three parent board members had joined Ladner, Mrs Addler, and Gina. Ali's chair, noticeably separated from the group at the end of the semi-circle, dug into his back. This didn't bode well. Hopefully, it would be quick.

'Mr Morgan. If we could get started now.'

'Sure.'

Gina rose from her seat and read from a piece of ivory paper.

'This meeting is called to order. The police report indicated a lack of evidence to suggest that Mr Morgan poses a risk of harm to children, or behaved in a way that indicates he may not be suitable to work with children.' She glanced around the group. Nobody moved. She continued, 'Assault allegation. On December twenty, Mr Ladner, present, witnessed what has been labelled an assault against Michael Addler. This meeting is to conclude the investigation and move on from this incident.'

Ladner turned to face Gina. 'It wouldn't be classed as an assault. The school does have a 'no show' phone policy.' Ladner caught Ali's attention and nodded. 'Any member of staff would be right to remove a phone should a student refuse to hand it over.'

'Further evidence showed Michael had inflamed the

situation by taking unauthorised photographs of Mr Morgan without his permission,' said Gina.

'With another teacher in the school,' Mrs Addler grumbled under her breath. Ali's relationship with Trevor, and the photos, were irrelevant to the police. All they showed was Michael's use of a smartphone and lack of respect for others' privacy.

'In this instance, following the local board LEA guidance and investigation, taking into account the police information clearing Mr Morgan, the subsequent accusations appear to be malicious or even invented. Therefore, we move to strike Michael Addler from the school's register. We also advise the social services to comply and intervene with a full investigation and disciplinary action for Michael.'

Mrs Addler's hand shot up to cover her mouth, failing to cover her whispered conversation to the woman on her left.

'But he's been under a lot of pressure.' Mrs Addler stood, her hands wringing out in front. 'He's just a silly boy.'

The lawyer ignored the interruption and continued. 'As per the school's behaviour policy in such circumstances, Michael Addler will be unable to register with a school in this local catchment area.' She turned to Mr Ladner. 'Do you have anything more to add?'

'Well, I am—'

'No.' A voice from the back of the hall snapped Ali's head up. On the other side of the doors leading into the hall, a figure stood, wrapped up against the cold in a thick ski jacket with a zigzag pattern across the chest and arms. Ali knew only one guy who would buy such a loud jacket. Trevor.

Ali's heart raced, and he wanted to jump from the raised staging area, but something held him back. Too much had passed between them. But why was he here?

'That's not going to fix this.' Trevor's voice echoed through the hall. His boots clomped forward. The entire hall pivoted; a collective gaze followed him to the front.

'I'm not sure this is appropriate—' Gina stepped forward, but Trevor raised a hand.

'Just give me a second, please. This isn't only about Michael Addler. It's about Simon Smith, also. Look at these pictures. And this one.' Trevor held his phone out to the PTA members. Some frowned at the images. 'It's very clear these are two brothers.'

'We already know this information, Mr Zhang. George Smith is Simon's brother, but I don't see what relevance—'

'But if you don't know why, then you're missing the entire point.'

Trevor stopped in the centre of the semi-circle of chairs.

A murmuring started at the back of the hall, moving forward row by row, as neighbour and neighbour turned to each other.

'He detests the fact his brother is gay. And egged on by Michael Addler, they targeted Mr Morgan. I think they found pictures online and started their campaign against Mr Morgan.'

Michael and Simon sat immobile on the third row. Simon stared straight ahead. How did Trevor know anything about George? It had been years since Ali had talked to him.

Gina huddled with the chair of the PTA. They both shook their heads.

Something stirred in Ali. If he didn't speak up now, then the Addlers, and people like them, would win.

'These boys are so intolerant to anyone who is not like them.' Ali's voice was loud in the echoey hall. 'Most likely poisoned by their own family. Kids aren't born to hate others. They learn it.'

A gasp from Mrs Addler.

'You turned my brother gay!' Simon's voice sailed to the front. The fifteen or so parents present moved their heads like they were watching a tennis match.

Mrs Addler looked confused by this and more so when Trevor pointed towards her.

'As an employed teacher here, alongside my colleagues, Mr Morgan'—and indicating Janet—'and Mrs Morgan. As the school governor rules state, with three teachers, in accordance with the headmaster, and with school legal representative present, I move to strike Mrs Addler from the school PTA. Michael should stay.'

Michael and Simon both stared open-mouthed.

Ali felt a flicker in his gut. A warmth travelled up through his groin. Trevor had blown off his shy and retiring previous self. The man stood in the hall gesturing like a lawyer from a TV drama was filled with something he'd rarely witnessed before: confidence.

Gina straightened up from talking with the PTA chair and cleared her throat. The rustle of papers audible in the condensed silence that sat over the hall.

'After discussions with the PTA chair, for Mr Zhang's motion to come into agreement, with immediate effect, we need the headmaster to agree for it to be a passing motion. What do you say, Mr Ladner?'

A beetroot colour crept up his neck. His hand shuddered across his forehead.

'I'm not sure this is correct and above board. In addition, the boys should still face consequences.'

'In fact, it is, Headmaster.' Gina slid a paper across the mahogany table and placed a pen on top. 'You just need to sign here. And the boys can be issued community service as a penalty for their poor decision making.' She winked at Ali. 'Perhaps a local LGBTQ+ charity could show them there's more similarity than differences between people. Mr Morgan?'

This couldn't be happening. It was over. All eyes in the hall remained rooted on Ali, but his mind crashed with conflicted thoughts, mostly filled with Trevor's brown eyes and the smile reaching them. He struggled to connect his brain and jaw.

'I suppose so.' Ali's words tumbled out before he could process what the fuck Trevor was doing here.

'Okay.' Gina dropped the pile of papers to the table. 'Let's take a fifteen-minute break.'

Ali walked over to Trevor. A grin played on Trevor's lips and his hands went to hold Ali's hips but dropped to his sides when Ali gestured with his head for them to find some space. They walked from the staging area and stood by the main doors, away from everyone else. But it was obvious by the glances cast from the tea table that they would be people of interest for a while. Trevor didn't stay still; he relayed the details of the flight and how he'd come out to his parents. In Ali's stomach, oil and water mixed together; a thick smear occupied the space where Ali, in his head, should feel happy and elated. He hadn't expected this and wasn't ready to deal with it. Trevor continued to talk, said he was sorry, sorry for not believing in Ali, sorry for—

'I can't do this. I need to get away.'

Ali removed Trevor's hands from his cheeks.

'You can't run away.' Trevor's jaw muscle stood out.

'Run away? I need some space… I'm the fucking problem.' Ali's voice faltered.

From the corner of his eye, people nudged each other and glanced over their shoulders. Ali shook his head. He couldn't put into words how he wanted to bear hug Trevor more than anything, but because he was terrified of hurting Trevor again, he had to let it end. He didn't trust himself to come back and not fuck it up again.

'I told my parents.' Trevor's urgent, hushed whisper choked in his throat. 'I've lost Mel. I don't want to lose you as well.'

It did Ali no pleasure watching Trevor's smile fade, and he pulled him in for a hug. This was best for both of them. They could get a clean break.

'I'm sorry. I can't.' Ali's head spun.

Over Trevor's shoulder, across the room, Janet took a tissue out of her pocket, one she always had balled up there, a crumpled thing, probably dry. She would always save them and hated wasting money. For years, he watched her getting beaten down. Less physically, but his father's words a constant battle between them. It continued when they were sober, simmering under the surface. He never understood why they stayed together. Ali watched her now, her gaze meeting his across the hall. Her cheeks flushed, not from drink this time, but from the chill in the hall. Tears fell softly across her smile. She marched towards them, shaking her head. Her balled hands flew down, her arms rigid.

'Don't destroy everything, Ali. Don't do what I did!' Janet's voice rose and probably carried to the back of the room. Around the hall it echoed. Heads in the few occupied seats turned to look at her. All open mouths and furrowed brows.

'Janet, it's okay. I'll go. I shouldn't have come.' Trevor pulled himself out of the embrace.

He started towards the double doors leading outside.

Ali's gaze flitted from Janet's face to Trevor's back.

Trevor walked away. And Ali saw what it wasn't. It wasn't his mum leaving his father. His abusive father who had ruined how Ali saw every relationship he'd had. How it fucked up his head, ruined how he saw friends, and how he felt unable to have anything for himself. How he never felt good enough. Because he had never let his mother leave. She'd stayed with his father for Ali.

If I blame him for everything bad in my life, then I have to blame him for what is good.

'Trevor.' The words sailed across the space to those ears he missed so much. Those ears that had listened when he cried. That might have doubted him. Fuck, he was a mess. Those ears had showed up today, despite Ali behaving just like his father. Tears streamed down Ali's face as he saw the same look of shock from the Christmas night when he first raised his hand to Trevor. He had ruined that night, but he wasn't going to ruin this one.

It was the same face. It was Trevor's face. It looked the same, but this time it was coming closer. Trevor licked his lower lip. They looked dry, probably chapped from the wind outside. But as they came closer… he smiled.

'Trevor. I'm sorry. Really fucking sorry.' Ali's breath caught in his throat.

'So, to conclude this extraordinary meeting of the PTA. Mr Morgan will be reinstated to his previous role. As a school, we express our deepest apologies and thank him for his patience during this difficult time.' Ladner clutched his hands together.

Ali snorted and glanced at Trevor.

'I appreciate your concern. But it's all come a bit late if I am honest.'

'Well, we can move on from that. Can't we?'

'I'm not sure I can.' Ali wanted to grab Trevor's hand and squeeze his fingers. Everything was moving so fast, but they had to have a proper talk, see what could be salvaged.

'With the next few weeks off. And no liability on our part. Just sign this contract and… it'll be like it never happened.'

'But it did. It did happen. So, no. Thank you.'

'We'll need an agreement signed, Mr Morgan. Before we can move for——'

'I quit.' Both words tasted bittersweet in Ali's mouth. 'It's not worth it anymore.'

Ladner's jaw dropped.

'You can't quit, Mr Morgan. You are an excellent teacher.'

'He *is* an excellent teacher.' Trevor gripped Ali's hand. He drew their hands out from under the table and placed them on the surface. His thumb played across the top of Ali's fingers. 'One of the best at your school. You even said so yourself with that little award you bestowed on him last year. *Teacher of the Year*, wasn't it?'

'Yes. And I stand by it.'

'Stand. By. It.' Ali enunciated each word with care, taking time to pronounce them clearly. 'And what about standing by other people like me? With all due respect, this school has let me down and severely let themselves down.'

Twenty-Six

A clutch of nerves gripped Trevor as Michael and Simon approached the circle of chairs Gina had set up. The lawyer had suggested a debrief between Ali and the students to "get things back on track." She'd insisted regardless of Ali's decision to leave; it would be good for them to know the impact of their actions. Trevor's heart raced. These were the kids who'd caused them so much damage, but also exposed so many things they had needed to deal with.

Mrs Addler had refused initially, but Gina had persisted. She smiled and led the two youths over. They retained their swagger and a cocky, arrogant air—but a scowl from Ladner settled them into chairs. Trevor brushed his hands against his trouser legs to dry them off.

'Anything you'd like to say?' Gina's tone remained gentle.

Michael grimaced. 'My mum says what you two do is wrong.' He sat back in his chair, once again the defiant teen they all feared.

'Is it wrong to love someone, Michael?' Trevor's

words felt sticky, and although his jaw tensed, he would see this through. 'Your mum loves you, right?'

Simon rolled his eyes and crossed his arms. This wasn't going as planned.

'Yeah,' Addler sneered. 'She's my mum.'

'She's your family. Would it be such a stretch for you to imagine that I saw Mr Morgan as my family?'

The puzzled look that crossed both their faces meant they were thinking at least. 'Because that's all I want to get across to you today. Get your minds out of the gutter for a moment and think about your family.' Something stirred in Trevor's stomach. Since he'd connected the dots on the plane, he wasn't going to take any more of their bullshit.

'I'm not going to apologise to you for loving someone. You love your brother, right, Simon?' Trevor gestured at the other lad who looked like he wanted to dissolve into his chair.

'Yeah.'

'What is family to you? Someone you trust? Someone who looks out for you?' Trevor caught Ali's gaze across the circle of chairs. The sadness caught Trevor's attention this time.

'But it's not the same. You don't choose to love your brother or your mum. That's, like, not the same at all. You and Mr Morgan, you chose—'

'Let me stop you for a minute.' Ali raised his hand. 'When you went to church, Michael, what did they teach you? To pick and choose who to love?'

Michael looked at Simon and shrugged.

'Treat others as you wish to be treated. If my memory serves me correctly.' Gina glanced up from her notepad.

'Something like that.' Michael looked over at Mrs Addler. Her back was to them as she talked to another parent.

'And it's not your job to be judge, jury, and executioner. Either of you.' Ali's measured tone seemed to be having an effect. Their bravado had visibly shrunk, and they looked like they wanted to flee by the way they squirmed in their seats.

'So I hope you can see. It's easy to make bold statements and think everything you've been told is true. I'm sorry, lads, but some of it is bullshit.' Ali held their gaze.

Trevor swallowed. They might just be fronting, but hopefully next time they'd think. Ideally, Michael wouldn't take everything Mrs Addler said as gospel.

'I guess… We messed up. Sorry, Mr Morgan.' Michael glanced up for a minute and nodded in Ali's direction. A tight smile played on Ali's lips. He'd clearly suffered throughout the past couple of weeks because it barely reached his eyes.

'Thank you. I appreciate that, Michael.'

Simon remained quiet. He kicked at the metal leg of the chair with his heel. He must have sensed the expectancy of the adults sitting in a circle facing him.

'Me too. I was pissed, man. Thought you'd turned George gay. Seeing those pictures made me really mad.'

He muttered and his foot bounced back and forth. 'And when I… when we saw you two at school. It hurt all over again.'

Nobody explained anything to him. Poor kid. He thought there was something wrong with his brother.

'Simon. It doesn't work like that. Your brother was born gay. Mr Morgan hasn't done anything wrong.' Trevor leaned forward because these boys needed to know how serious their actions had been. 'This could have ended up much worse. You get that, right?'

'We thought he was going after you...' Michael nodded towards Trevor. Simon's foot slowed and stopped.

Trevor laughed; he couldn't help it. An explosive laugh that vibrated his lips.

The adults cast him puzzled looks. He didn't fucking care at this point. He felt good, finally. After the longest fucking time, he didn't feel ashamed of himself. He was who he was, and if people didn't like it, they could get fucked.

'You've targeted an innocent man. It's not your job to jump into people's lives and save them. You're not Spider-Man.'

'Yeah.' Simon's energy appeared depleted. The two teenagers looked more lost than at the start of the meeting. The wind taken out of their sails.

Trevor continued, 'You have to accept nothing is going to change your brother. He is who he is. I talked to George this afternoon. And I told him what I thought had gone on. How you'd picked Mr Morgan to target him because he was gay.'

Simon's jaw jutted. Ali looked at him with wide eyes.

Trevor could stand on his own two feet when given the opportunity.

'He told me you've never been that close because of the age difference between you, right?'

'I haven't seen him in a while.' Simon's voice caught in his throat. 'He's always busy.'

'He told me your parents are no longer alive. Said he's always working to try and earn the money you'll need for the future.'

'Yeah.'

'But he's going to try and be there for you a bit more. Brothers share a bond. Like you and Michael have a bond. It's a friendship, but it can never go away.'

'I get that, but—'

'He's been there for you. He needs you as well, Simon. Just because you think he's the strong one. You see him that way.' Trevor caught Ali's gaze, then turned back to Simon. 'Sometimes you think one person has it all together. Outwardly, they seem okay. But you don't really know what's gone on in their past and how it's affecting their life now. They might have been to hell and back, and what they don't need is another person being a burden on them.'

Ali bit his lip and glanced away.

'Any relationship needs to be balanced for it to work. If one side is taking too much space, then it's not going to work. That's something I've learned myself in the past couple of days.'

Simon scratched at his forehead. Both lads looked as if they wanted to escape. They might not change overnight, however nice that would be, but they might think twice before going on a hate campaign again.

'That makes sense. He's my brother. My only family.'

'I have one more question. For Simon.' Trevor stood and brushed at his trousers, his hands dry this time. 'What was Mr Morgan shouting that night? In DV8.'

Simon glanced between Ali and Trevor. He let out a sigh and coughed into his hand.

'Mr Morgan was shouting, *I love him, I fucking love him*. He wouldn't shut up about it.' Ali's gaze remained rooted to the floor. For the first time in a long time, Trevor looked at Ali and smiled. A smile that started in his stomach, then ran through his cheeks and into his eyes.

Twenty-Seven

'You should have seen Mum's face.' Ali laughed and reached for Trevor's arm. He didn't yank it away but moved it slowly back into a folded position as Ali spoke.

Trevor glanced around the airport. He often did that when he was thinking.

'Mel was the first person I told. And she's pretended I never said it since.'

'That's messed up.'

'So that's it. It seems nuts to go back so soon. But I need to see her in the flesh.'

'Japan can wait.' It didn't matter to Ali where they were. To be close to Trevor once again, the familiar safety, the knowledge there was someone to lean on when he needed… it felt right, but he knew that without Mel's blessing Trevor wouldn't feel complete.

'You know I got you a ring? Seems dumb now. Imagine if I'd proposed to you. Fucking drunk.'

'I might have said yes.'

'You would have been right to laugh in my face.' Ali shook his head. Marriage wouldn't have fixed anything. They didn't need it for whatever they had going on.

'Drink?' A waiter clad all in black hovered with a pad. Ali didn't hesitate.

'Yes. A double vodka on the rocks. And he'll have a soda.'

Trevor cupped his chin with one hand and shifted in his seat. One final drink before they flew out. This would be the last one.

Glistening in the glass against an oversize chunk of ice, the vodka looked innocent enough. It would taste warm and fill Ali's mouth with a familiar comfort. He hadn't had a drink since seeing Osei three days ago.

Trevor had a right to know about his drinking. What he felt and why he did it. Ali hadn't been able to put it into words before.

'So much power in that glass.' Ali ran his finger over the cool rim. 'You know I can taste it on my tongue, even without taking a sip. Such a buzz. That sounds fucked up, doesn't it?'

Trevor held his gaze. He didn't look like the guy he'd first met. Where doubt had once kept his hands moving and brushing his hair away from his face, his fingers were steepled in front of his nose and he barely moved.

'The depression was the worst. Waking up in the morning, not knowing if I'd make it to the evening without crying. I never thought I had a problem, until I did.'

Trevor said, 'We both made excuses.'

'I'm sorry I pushed you and didn't listen to what you actually wanted. Fucking around didn't make either of us happy.'

'Yeah.' Trevor looked upset for a minute. His brow creased, his eyes rooted on the glass of vodka. Hopefully he wasn't thinking about last Christmas. But then Trevor grinned. That smile that had caught his attention the first time and kept him hooked.

'It wasn't all bad. That guy at the gym will be gutted he won't get any more of my dick.'

Ali snorted. This was what he wanted more than anything. They could joke around, they'd messed up, but they'd come through the other side.

'Do you think your auntie will be there?' Trying to understand Trevor's family was important.

This was why Ali had come—to be there for Trevor, who'd always put Ali first. Now it was about Trevor and what Trevor needed.

The rounded edge of the ice melted away, and Ali swirled it in the glass. He could smell it. He wanted more than anything to pick up the glass and throw back the liquid against his tongue. Something stopped him. Trevor's gaze returned to him, and he didn't look away. In those eyes he saw his past and his future, one blurry and the one coming clearer.

'You can't usually smell booze when you're drinking it. Did you notice that?'

'But on someone else, it stinks.' Trevor played with his straw. 'So you feel quitting school was the right choice?'

'Fuck. Yes. Scary, you know.' An idea had been brewing for a while in Ali's mind. 'I think I want to retrain and do counselling. For kids getting bullied and those having a shitty time.'

Trevor nodded. The dimple on his cheek was more pronounced when he considered an idea. 'Families are important. And maybe some families don't know how to handle their kids.'

'That's what I'm thinking. If Mrs Addler can screw up her kid like that, there must be a ton more out there.'

Trevor finished his Coke and pushed his glass away until it sat between the vodka and Ali. Like a chess master moving his piece across the board. He didn't need to say anything, but it was obvious what he was doing. He'd shown his hand, and the next move was Ali's to make.

'I can't believe Janet knew about us. Or she pretended not to. With fucking George between your legs, how could she not have known?' That grin again. Trevor didn't hold back now. He seemed carefree and had a lightness about his movements.

'Past tense. I'm trying to see how my actions played out and others got caught up in them. Like if I do something, it has a knock-on effect.'

'Soph said something similar.' Trevor's mention of his friend made Ali shiver. He'd been lucky Trevor had a friend to lean on. He'd have to make it up to her somehow.

'I'm glad you asked me to come,' Ali said.

'I'm glad you said yes.' Trevor smiled. Those hazel eyes, still and calm, drove Ali mad. He wouldn't push anything that wasn't meant to happen. They might well be better off as friends. Trevor needed time. He needed time.

Ali's heart lurched and the airport surroundings melted away. So close to everything he wanted and needed, so close—just one last person to fix.

Ali held the glass of vodka out in front of him.

'The thing now… it held so much power over me. You drink it.'

Trevor took the glass and sloshed the vodka around. The aroma rose in the air between them. Faint, a little sweet, sickly, easily masked.

He wrinkled his nose as he sniffed the liquid before placing it back on the table. He stood from his chair, shrugged on his jacket, and adjusted his bag strap over his shoulder.

'You want me to drink your sloppy seconds?' Trevor's gaze moved from the glass to Ali's. His smile widened and with a flick of his wrist he upturned the glass into the fake foliage of a palm tree stretching out of a black plant pot next to their table.

'No, thanks.' He winked and sauntered off towards their gate.

Twenty-Eight

Trevor hadn't imagined the three of them would be out in public like this. A year ago, Ali wouldn't have agreed to come. He would have been moody and refused, saying Trevor's family was his problem. The street around the hotel bustled with delivery guys and gossiping housewives on the way back from the market with plastic bags full of vegetables and fish. Ali's smile that morning had given him some hope. He wasn't sure where they were headed, but they had turned a corner.

'I don't see why I have to be dragged into this. It's not *my* problem.'

'Because you are the problem, Mel.' Trevor side-eyed his sister. He loved her, but she clearly got her stubbornness from their father. What she often underestimated was that Trevor could be just as stubborn; they were blood relations, after all. He hadn't taken no for an answer, and getting her to meet them at the main Zhongshan mountain road had been the first step. The steam from a bun shop wafted out into the street as they pushed past. Tea and a talk, he'd said.

Ali trailed behind them. He stopped at almost every

stall and shop to gawk at the dried fish or take pictures of the piles of fruit. *Such a tourist.* But it felt good to spend some time together away from Bristol. The sunshine helped, and they'd stripped off their UK winter clothes and replaced them with shorts and T-shirts.

'That's not likely, Trevor.' Mel glanced at herself and adjusted her hair in a shop window. 'Why are you hiding from Mum and Dad anyway?'

'We're not hiding.' They'd go to his parents in a couple of days, but he needed to get his head straight before making that leap. 'This one?' Trevor waved Ali over to a coffee shop tucked on the corner with a couple of wooden seats arranged outside.

The three of them settled down and Mel held the menu up like a barricade. Ali fiddled with his phone. He'd been taking pictures of them when they weren't looking. Ali grinned. It was sweet how Ali wanted to find a way to bond with both parents; not speaking the same language limited their interactions, but he'd said sharing the pictures would give their mum a laugh.

Ali put his hand on Trevor's arm. A simple gesture, but Mel glanced behind her, probably hoping nobody she knew was around. She sank down lower in her seat and pulled her jacket collar up higher around her ears.

'I don't know why you two can't just tell people you're friends,' Mel hissed. She'd been doing this for the past couple of hours, incredulous that they walked around so brazenly. They bothered her, and Trevor hoped to change her mind. If he could get through to his sister, then he could get through to anyone.

'Where did you learn this from? You weren't born a bigot. Someone put these ideas into your head, Mel.'

'Oh, it's National Attack Mel Day, is it? I'm fine, Trevor.'

'It's something important and I wanted to talk to you about it properly.'

'What?' Mel, ever suspicious, gritted her teeth.

'I wanted to talk to you about your church.'

Mel rolled her eyes. 'Again? Fine. The way my church sees it, you… and him'—Mel waved her hand towards Ali—'need to reconcile your queer lifestyle in the eyes of the church.'

'You know society has moved on, right? Many same-sex couples get married in church.'

Her forehead crinkled. 'The Catholic church still deems it a sin.'

Knowing his sister would be tricky, Trevor remained calm. It would take a while to get through to her. 'The queers just want the same things you do, Mel. Some churches accept gay people. They have lesbian priests and gay ministers.'

Mel looked taken aback by the bluntness. 'I don't think mine does.'

'Many churches do. You sound like Dee's mum.'

'It's not my idea. I don't see why you're attacking me.' Mel placed her hands on the chair arm rests to push herself up. 'Look, Trevor. This is a nice idea, but God judges those who—'

'God doesn't judge.' Trevor narrowed his eyes. 'People judge. People switch churches. Problem solved.'

Mel shrugged, then mumbled, 'Huh.' She lowered her arm, leaning forward on the table. A crack in her bluster, a glimmer of light. If he could see into her mind, Trevor would swear that sound meant she was thinking. But she wasn't an easy pushover.

'I just can't accept this. You're my little brother—' Tears came to her eyes. Often, she'd cry, then depending on how she put herself back together, if they could avoid her anger boiling over, there was hope.

Trevor placed a hand on her arm. 'I know, Mel. I've known my sexuality for a long time. And it's not going to change. I'm not going to change. Whether you like it or not.'

'I've tried. Tried, really hard, and every time I think I can accept it, something holds me back.'

'Mel.' Trevor pulled her into his arms as her sobs engulfed them both. Over her shoulder, Ali blinked and brushed at the edges of his eyes. He raised his phone, tilted his head to one side, and snapped a picture of them. Mel would kill him for that.

As the sobs subsided, Trevor held Mel out at arm's length. Their eyes met. 'You realise this is your problem, right? I haven't done anything, I'm just bumbling along. Living my life.' Trevor cracked a smile.

'I'm really worried about you. About everything.'

'And you don't think I'm worried? I need you, Mel. You're my sister.'

Mel sniffed and wiped her eyes with a tissue.

'I can try and accept you. God, I sound so grand. So full of myself. I mean, of course I can... but the church.

It's really important to me. I feel lost without it.'

'Just go to a different one.' Trevor had been reading up on the various churches that accepted members of the queer community. 'The Catholics are a bit, how to say this, over the top when it comes to gays. If they don't want me or my family, fine. I'd go get me some god somewhere else.'

Mel ran her tongue over her lip. 'Go somewhere else?' The words came slowly. 'But I worry about Mum and Dad. And what this secret will do to them. In the village. How people will react, what they will say?'

'There.' Trevor raised Mel's chin so their eyes met. 'That's the biggest obstacle you need to overcome. It is not a secret. It's who I am.'

'I get that. I think I can cope with you. But I am involved in my church. And they can't accept it.' She was spinning her wheels as he'd expected, so he'd researched.

On the flight back to China, in between naps and building his confidence to speak up, he'd researched churches that weren't bigoted, why some churches were bigoted, and how to save family members from turning against their own family in the name of god.

'Your current church leader sounds a bit like Pastor Bei Fang. A most hateful speaker.' An infamous sharer of hate on social media in China. Trevor grimaced at how one man had led to so much conflict and misunderstanding between families.

Ali shuffled his chair forward. 'Look, Mel. You *can* accept him. God already accepts him. You don't need to go and sing his gayness from the rooftops. Family first.

That's what the bible says.'

Who was this guy? Ali sounded like he'd swallowed a 'Coming out to God' manual, but fuck, he was right.

'Family first. Right?' Trevor nodded.

'Actually, no, it doesn't.' Ali shook his head, smiling. 'It says Mel first. Because Mel is the one to make the change. How other people think is not her problem. Unless Mel thinks she is all powerful and has to worry about everyone else's business?'

'But what about all the people I know there?' Mel spoke in the smallest voice yet. The tiny voice she used when she knew she was wrong.

'Fuck the church. Or just go to another one. This is your brother. Your one and only brother.' Ali cleared his throat. 'Sorry. Excuse my French.'

Mel put her hands to her face and pulled back the skin on her cheeks. She blew out, her cheeks puffed up and reddened. She glanced away as a waiter placed three cups, hot water, and dry tea in a dish down on the table. A tiny bell rang as the waiter returned inside.

Ali continued, 'Imagine, Mel. That waiter started telling Trevor to get out of here because he's gay. What would you do?'

Mel frowned. Her brow creased, but she turned to face Ali. 'I'd snap his neck. Nobody bullies my brother.'

'So don't do the same thing to him. You'll push him away.' Ali shrugged, leaving Mel to think over what he said. It appeared to be working because she played with the edge of the tea dish and chewed her lip.

'Do you remember Dee, Mel?' Trevor took her

hands. On the flight over, he'd talked with Ali about their early experiences with guys, something that had been a source of shame for them both.

'Imagine Trevor not being here, Mel,' Ali spoke gently. 'He's come back to sort this out with you. Dee didn't get that chance.'

Trevor let out the breath he was holding. Each mention of Dee caused another stab of hurt, yet knowing he couldn't do anything about it now made him certain that pushing his sister was the right thing to do. And judging by her expression, she understood too.

'Trevor. I'm so fucking sorry. I didn't think.'

'Don't do what his family did, Mel.' Tears glimmered in Trevor's eyes. 'What I did.' He would always blame himself for how he had acted. He'd let down his friend, someone who'd needed him, and he knew history couldn't be allowed to repeat itself.

'I didn't think. I should have seen—'

'Dee's mother and father have never gotten over how they treated him.' Trevor wiped the final tears from his sister's cheeks. 'And he's gone. He'll never come back. How we treated him is more of a sin than anything he ever did.'

Mel threw her arms around Trevor and pulled Ali into the embrace. Three heads pushed together, cheeks slick with new tears and kisses from Mel.

Through her choked sobs, she managed to say, 'I'll try.'

Twenty-Nine

Ali's head was clearer than it had been for weeks. Although, the last piece of his puzzle—Trevor—evaded him. They were together at least, sat on the stone steps at the foot of the hills overlooking the ocean.

China was miles away from Bristol, but they still felt worlds apart. Trevor held him at arm's length, and Ali could hardly blame him.

'I love you. But I don't know if I can forgive you. Or even if I should.' Trevor's gaze didn't leave the couple shuffling across the road in front of their hotel. The man helped his partner up and over the curb before they continued along the well-brushed pathway.

Trevor had his guard up. 'I need to protect myself. I can't just fall head over heels into you again, but I'm willing to try.' Trevor turned to face Ali, his hands on his knees.

'You are my family, Trevor. I'm going to spend some time at a clinic. Talk to some professionals.'

'I still need space, Ali. I went to England to escape what felt like a trap and walked straight into yours. I don't think you understand how much you made me suffer. And more than that, I let it happen. I didn't believe in myself, that I deserved any better.' Trevor's eyes gleamed around the edges. 'I did everything you wanted. That's how I always thought I could fix things. Maybe even that I could fix you. But I see now, it doesn't work like that.'

'You didn't need to fix me, Trevor. I needed to fix myself. And I want to make it last this time.'

Trevor pulled Ali closer. The distance between them was nothing compared to the distance between Trevor and his family. But Mel was coming round. She'd even taken a picture with them after they'd walked back from the coffee shop earlier. She'd demanded they delete it because her puffy red eyes looked awful, but they'd kept it.

'I'll go and see my parents. You take a walk up to the cliff top and back, and I think they'll be ready.'

'Okay.' Ali watched Trevor walk back towards the cluster of single-storey houses down by the road. He turned to face the cliff and the ocean.

Ali and Trevor had options. Their choices branched like the road twisting through the hills and mountains of rural Fujian. Ali walked the path up the cliff by himself with the ocean stretching out in front of him. A lonely place to be when he had everything he'd ever wanted within touching distance.

Ali wanted Trevor's hand on the small of his back, the warmth of his touch creating a connection, a guiding force across each bridge he might encounter. Structures in his past that had been unable to support the weight of his shame, that he'd caused to crumble.

Ali needed Trevor to swim alongside him as he battled life's moments alone. So alone, separated from each other, but like two streams, they were heading towards the same ocean. Rocks, boulders, and periods of drought stood between them and that rush, the collapsing and cascading bringing them back on course. The rains would fall again, and they would find their hands coming back together, and Trevor's hand would move across Ali's back. But after what he'd put Trevor through—he could wait. He owed him that much.

They'd both been shaken to their core. Nothing could rip them away from each other's gaze when they were together. Ali turned an image over in his mind: Trevor's smile that morning, cracked across his face. It disappeared, melted into the clouds hanging over the ocean. Close enough to touch, but it drifted for a moment and then was carried away.

Trevor's eyes had shone last time they were here as he pointed out a small fishing boat down by the rows of seaweed stacks, housing the catch for the year. Thick seaweed lay exposed across the dark wood. Trevor wasn't there with him this time. Ali stood alone on the cliff tops.

Ali let the wind rush across his face and cheeks. The tang of the salt air ruffled his jacket and filled his nostrils. He shivered, despite the warmth. For a long time, after Trevor moved out, he felt empty, broken, and without a sense of direction. But they might be able to lay paving stones and walk the path together.

With his eyes closed, a familiar warmth spread across the small of his back.

'Ali.' Trevor's voice awoke him from the colliding thoughts in his mind. Each one smoothing over the hurt and pain from the past few weeks.

'My parents are okay. They want to see you.'

'They do?'

Trevor grinned. 'Well, like I tried to tell you—I only told them the good things about you.' His eyebrow arched, and he laughed. A laugh that melted away the frigid bitterness settling across Ali's chest.

'Let's go.' Ali followed Trevor back along the path.

Trevor's mum fussed around the kitchen. It was small and dark with a fire roaring in the centre. The pork soup and celery bubbled together, filling the kitchen with a warm smell.

Trevor's father sat back on his chair and said something to his wife, who was rinsing off a board in a bucket of water. Trevor laughed out loud. Ali loved that laugh. He didn't remember Trevor being this relaxed last time they were here.

'My dad asked, how are we going to have children?' Trevor winked at Ali and replied to his father, who nodded and seemed to agree with the response.

Last time, years before, they had attempted to catch a fish for dinner outside. They'd shared a furtive kiss on the mountain before his sister and cousins rounded the corner. This time, Ali needed to fit into Trevor's world when he visited China. It wasn't about imposing his will on Trevor.

'I told Dad you want at least three.' Trevor wiped his hands on a dishtowel.

'You want kids?' Ali's puzzled expression brought a wider grin to Trevor's mouth.

'No. Do you?'

'You're going to keep mistranslating me, aren't you?' Ali grinned.

'Yup.' Trevor stepped closer and his fingers encircled Ali's ears. He played with each one, exploring the curves and swirls. Ali glanced around; this was the most intimate they had been in front of anyone, let alone Trevor's parents.

Trevor's father held a small bottle of beer in one hand, his head cocked to one side like he was working out a puzzle. A bemused expression lit up his face. This world, so different to how they grew up, must be shocking for them, Ali thought. They'd grown their own food and lived around close family in their immediate villages for generations. Now, their son who lived in England was standing in the kitchen playing with a strange man's ears.

'We have kids. Hundreds of them. We're teachers.' Ali grinned.

'You always say that.' Trevor didn't look disappointed. He shared the same quizzical look his father had. 'Do you? Still have kids? Didn't you quit your job?'

'Let's see,' Ali winked. 'I'll have some new charges hopefully soon. New Year, new Ali.'

A rush of air entered the kitchen, followed by the slamming of the front door.

Trevor dropped the towel to the table and crossed his arms.

Mel stood in the doorway. Her hands on her hips, a smile playing across her lips.

'Hi, boys.' She grinned at them both.

'Mel.' Trevor looked nervously at Ali.

She stepped into the kitchen. 'I've been thinking about you two—nonstop. It's sort of weird, actually.'

Their mother looked from one to the other and shook her head slowly, but she was smiling.

Mel continued, 'And I've been trying to convince myself that being gay was an act of God.'

'Uh-huh.' Trevor smiled.

'And you know what, I know you always doubt me. And you think I am brainwashed or whatever.'

'I'm listening, sis.' Trevor inched slowly between his sister and Ali.

'But this morning I read something, and I can't shake it off. 'God's Good Gift to All People.' Do you know what that *actually* means for people like you?'

Trevor glanced at his mother. His sister was talking a mile a minute and pacing the kitchen now.

'I hope it means what I think it means.'

'It means fuck that church. Trevor, it means I was wrong. It means you haven't done anything wrong. The church is wrong.'

'So, what are you saying?' Ali dangled his arm over Trevor's shoulder and grinned.

'It means they are the messed-up ones. They are the sinners. Do you not see? They've taken the good word of the Bible and twisted it for their own means and purposes. I can't believe I didn't see it.'

'Wow,' Trevor mouthed. A cool rush hit Ali's back.

'I know, right? I am a genius. I basically cracked their code. Okay, well, reading helped me. But now I get it. God loves freaking everyone. He made you. He made marriage and other churches. So, I just broke up with the Catholics.'

'Just like that, huh?' Their mother rolled her eyes to the heavens after Trevor translated into the local Minan dialect.

'Yes. I ditched them. And I'm going to try out this new church on Sunday.'

'Wow. I love you.' Trevor shook his head.

She bounced across the kitchen and pulled them both into a bear hug.

'I'm actually sorry, little bro. You know, that you felt bad or whatever.'

'Or whatever.' Trevor squeezed his sister.

Ali's heart warmed when the siblings bumped into each other's shoulders. Mel's gaze rooted to her younger brother's face. Trevor's eyes creased, his hands resting on Mel's shoulders. They would never normally throw their arms around each other and hug. It wasn't them, yet they expressed how they felt by being close and being kind when it mattered. They'd cry happy tears later; Ali knew this meant the world to Trevor. Ali had seen his fear of rejection and isolation tear Trevor apart, and he'd been too selfish to help. Wrapped up in his own head, he'd failed to notice that Trevor needed Mel as a sounding board—to have the support of his family.

'Come on, I wanna buy you both a beer.' Mel tapped the table with the corner of her phone.

Trevor's face fell. 'Ali doesn't drink now.'

'Well, fine. But I do. Come on, losers. I'm buying. Orange juice it seems. You always were so much fun to hang out with.'

Ali smiled. 'Okay. We'll meet you down there. I just want to jump in the shower.' Social situations could be awkward because alcohol was everyone's go-to, to relax, to feel calm and have a good time. He'd have to learn what it meant to have a good time without taking it too far. He'd get there. He knew what he needed to do.

They entered the darkened karaoke shop through a swinging door from the street. Yellowed stickers peeled off from the KTV door. Red and blue lights flashed above the entrance.

Mel was already in a booth screaming Adele into the microphone. They winced.

'Hey, boo.' A voice from behind startled Trevor.

'Auntie!' His mother's elder sister stood with a smile on her face. Her eyes flashed back and forth between Ali and Trevor.

'So, this must be him?'

'Him?' Ali felt the familiar rush of nervous shame. It was automatic after so many years of beating himself up about his sexuality. Although, each time, with Trevor rested up against his shoulder, their arms touching, he stood a fraction taller.

'I just talked to your mother. She said you guys were here.'

'Already? We just left home about twenty minutes ago.'

She laughed. Her whole body shook under her tight, peach T-shirt.

'Well. You know around here, news travels faster than a fangbian noodle man on his trike when the police show up.' She chuckled again but extended her hands and pulled them both in.

'You look well, Auntie.' Trevor's words felt loaded with what Ali knew about her past. Families weren't perfect, and people fucked up. He hoped she was in a safer place now anyway.

'I'm good,' she smiled. 'Now, that racket can only mean one thing. Your sister is singing some Adele. Let me try and smooth over some of her notes.' She winced and winked before turning away from them. 'Can you grab me a Qingdao, darling?' She wrenched open the booth door and shoved herself into the cramped space before doubling the volume of the song in an instant.

Trevor put his hand around Ali's waist and steered him towards the small bar at the back.

'You want something?' Trevor asked after ordering his aunt's beer. Ali's gaze flicked through the line of temptation behind the bar. Malibu, brandy, and vodka. Shiny bottles that once spelt out a good time: heated energy and intense conversations forgotten the next morning. Now they looked duller to Ali. The shining light and excitement he needed stood right next to him, and that man was all he wanted. That much was clear now. He'd fucked up, many times, but he wasn't going to make the same mistakes again.

Trevor shifted on his feet and turned away from the bar towards Ali. Those eyes, those brows, that face—he'd do anything to keep that glimmer of a smile shining in his eyes.

Ali planted a kiss on Trevor's cheek. He savoured the flavour, and something stirred in his stomach.

'Yeah. Tea, please. No sugar.'

Acknowledgements

Andrew Hodges (The Narrative Craft).
Brenna Bailey-Davies (Bookmarten Editorial).
Annie Percik.
Matthew Webster-Moore.
Jennifer Lawler.

* 9 7 8 1 9 1 5 0 7 3 4 6 4 *